Wilderness

Dennis Danvers

POCKET STAR BOOKS

New York   London   Toronto   Sydney   Tokyo   Singapore

A Pocket Star Book published by
POCKET BOOKS, a division of Simon & Schuster Inc.
1230 Avenue of the Americas, New York, NY 10020

ISBN: 0-671-72828-8

First Pocket Books printing June 1992

10 9 8 7 6 5 4 3 2 1

POCKET STAR BOOKS and colophon are registered
trademarks of Simon & Schuster Inc.

Cover art by Gerber Studio

Printed in the U.S.A.

For Really

Acknowledgments

For information on wolves, I am indebted to more books and articles than I can mention. Especially helpful were David Mech's *The Wolf*, Barry Lopez's *Of Wolves and Men*, and Roberta Hall and Henry Sharp's *Wolf and Man: Evolution in Parallel*. I would also like to thank Dr. John Mecom for allowing me to sit in on his class and for telling me about the penguins.

My wife, Retha Lee (Really), gave me the moral and emotional support necessary to finish this book. She has also helped create these pages, providing honest criticism as well as researching hypnosis and topiaries.

I would also like to thank those who believed in this book and guided it into print—Ellington White, Lee Smith, Liz Darhansoff, Lynn Pleshette, and Ann Patty.

PART
ONE

The wolf is of the wilderness, and inseparable from it. But it can get by elsewhere.

—Durward Allen
The Wolves of Minong

Chapter

1

The medical buildings in Richmond were packed in together like components on a circuit board. Though ugly, they had the comforting geometry of machinery. Sick people battled the worst traffic in the city to reach the place—except for the more serious who were brought by ambulance.

One large building was devoted to mental illness: the Mental Health Clinic. It had its own tiny parking lot with a sign reading "Mental Health Parking Only. All Others Will Be Towed."

Alice had found humor in this sign, but when she tried to share it with her psychiatrist, Dr. Adams, he didn't seem to get it.

"I can't explain," she'd said.

"Oh, give it a try." He smiled. He had a nice smile.

"Why should I?" she asked, really wanting to know.

He chuckled. "Now, now. I'm asking the questions here."

No, Alice thought, I am.

He always made the effort to understand—even when it was something she wanted to let go. She'd come to him, more than anything else, for understanding. But it was hard to be understood, and somehow his determination made it harder still.

In the waiting room today, a despondent-looking woman sat staring into the far corner where there was nothing to see but the arcs in the carpet where the vacuum had passed. Alice had stared there herself when she'd first come. Now this woman stared each week as she waited for her son, who had taken over the hour before Alice's when the Swedish man whose hour it had been committed suicide. Alice had liked the Swedish man, whose name, he said, was Benny. He had asked her to lunch, but she'd declined with an abrupt, "No, thank you." It was that or lie to him—make up a boyfriend or a job that claimed her day and night. But she didn't want to lie to him. "Sweden is much different from here," he said to her many times.

The woman staring into the corner had glanced up and saw Alice looking at her. Alice smiled and nodded.

"I'm at the end of my rope," the woman said.

Alice glanced above the door to check the clock, which was set ten minutes slow. The woman's son was running over. "I'm sorry," Alice said.

"He quit bringing his boyfriends home," the woman said. "I told him he was breaking his poor father's heart. But now he goes off nights—who knows where."

The woman looked back to the corner. She didn't seem to expect an answer. Alice didn't know who went off, the father or the son or both. It didn't matter. The woman still waited and had no idea why she was alone.

4

Alice returned to her magazine, a *New Yorker*. The sly, cynical cartoons depressed her. They seemed like inside jokes. But she couldn't read as she waited to talk to the doctor—Luther, he insisted she call him. She thought about what she might say to him. He was the only person she was honest with. She looked forward each week to the moments of bluntness she allowed herself here. Elsewhere she was quiet, almost invisible. She'd lied for so long, it felt good to talk to someone else as she did sometimes in the mirror when she got drunk or high. This mirror talked back, of course, though he didn't say much that helped. He was such an odd little man, each word thoughtful. Sometimes it made her tired just to listen to him, but he listened to her, that was the important thing, and eventually he might believe her.

In the middle of the magazine, a kelly green Colorado landscape shone from the page. She read the copy: "The most precious thing you can own. Land . . . what else can give you so much pleasure now and for years to come? . . . It's the perfect place to acquire a substantial part of the American dream."

The door to the office opened, and Dr. Adams came out. A tall, awkward boy slumped beside him. Adams, a short man, put a hand on the boy's shoulder and looked up into his puffy eyes. Adams wore the same smile Alice had seen when she cried in his office. He seemed to think crying was good medicine and must be greeted with grim good humor.

"Now remember what we talked about," he said. The boy imitated Adams's smile and nodded. Alice looked over at the mother, now standing as well, her purse held in front of her as if she feared a blow to the stomach. Does Luther think words can make any difference? Alice wondered. And is he right? The mother and son, returned to each other, looked caged and helpless. Alice stood as they passed and thought what she would say to them if she were the doctor and they paid her to listen. "It doesn't matter," she would say, "it just doesn't matter."

"Thank you, doctor," the woman said, as she did each week, and led her son away. Adams turned a fresh smile on Alice and gestured toward the open door.

Adams's office smelled of books and would have been cozy if it weren't for the overwhelming scent of perfumed tissue. Prints of French Impressionists and another slow clock occupied the wall to her left, books filled the walls behind and to the right, while Adams, his diplomas behind him, sat before her, his legs crossed. There were no windows, though Alice knew the door in the corner led to an office with windows she'd glimpsed one afternoon.

He glanced to his right. "Sorry I'm running late. Bit of a crisis a while ago."

"They always look so desperate."

Adams nodded. "Yes, but Simon made substantial progress today. It was something of a breakthrough for him."

Alice wore her long black hair in a single braid. She picked it up from her shoulder and brushed the end against her cheek. She suspected Luther of goading her for her lack of substantial progress. "Progress toward what?" she said. "Just what did he break through?"

Adams cocked his head with kindly disapproval. "Now we're not here to discuss Simon, but you. Simon can take care of himself."

"Luther, you know what I mean. What is the point of this?"

"I believe you wanted help."

The help she wanted wasn't his to give, or anyone's. But there was no point in saying that. She would just go on talking about herself, knowing it wouldn't change anything in herself or in the world but doing it anyway because she liked talking to him, even though

6

it made her angry. "Okay," she said. "I'll quit whining."

"So how's it going?"

"It's going."

"As I remember, we were talking about dating and men last time. Have you had a chance to think about what we said?"

She looked at one of the prints, a woman in a park sitting under some trees, reading. Adams always began in this direct way. Once he'd even said, "Let's get down to business, shall we?"

"There's not much to think about, is there? I mean, I do what I do for good reasons."

"But you're not happy with the way things are."

Alice sighed. She was weary of the circle they were headed toward. "Of course I'm not happy. Only an idiot would be happy in my situation. But you talk like it's just a matter of changing my mind, and— poof—everything will be okay."

"But didn't you come to see me to help you 'change your mind,' as you put it?"

"No, I came to see you because Dr. Dougherty thought I was crazy and referred me to you."

He uncrossed his legs and looked hurt. "This is really bothering you, isn't it, Alice? I know that it must be hard for you to see any progress, but believe me, I certainly can. You've really opened up these last six months and explored territory you wouldn't have set foot in when you first came here. Alice, I believe I can help you. I'd tell you if I didn't think I could."

She put her fingertips against her forehead and grimaced. "I know. I'm sorry. I just don't feel like we're getting anywhere."

"I understand. But dating is an area of serious concern for you, and one I believe we have not explored sufficiently. Now, have you seen any men recently?"

"Do you mean have I picked anyone up?"

Luther shook his head. "Why are you so hard on yourself if this is truly the only choice you have?"

"Because I don't like it. Because it's frustrating and depressing, and it pisses me off."

"Then why do you do it?"

"I get horny, doctor, like anyone else."

"Do you find your encounters with these men satisfying?"

"No, I don't even like them."

"Then why don't you find someone you like? You're personable, charming, and attractive. It shouldn't be too difficult for someone like you to meet men."

"You're right. It's easy. But I don't want to like them. I don't want to get involved with somebody and have to tell him the truth."

"Why not? Have you ever tried it? You're unhappy now. What have you got to lose?"

"Oh, come on, doctor, would you believe me?"

"That's not the point. The point is you did tell me, a complete stranger, and I haven't run away."

"It's not the same thing. I pay you not to run away. Besides, why isn't it the point? Do you believe me? I want to know." Alice had never had the opportunity to ask him this before or had been afraid to take it.

"I believe you are sincere."

"Come on, doctor, that's not what I mean, and you know it. Please don't evade me."

He smiled ironically behind a peaked roof of fingers, cornered with no graceful exit. "Very well," he said quietly. "No, I don't believe you actually are a werewolf, but, as I say, I do believe you sincerely believe you are, and I still like and respect you just the same."

Alice fell back in her chair. "Finally, after six months of dancing through the forest, you're straight with me. Thank you. I was beginning to give up hope."

"I'm glad you haven't completely lost faith in me. I

know it must be terribly frightening for you. And tonight's the night, isn't it?" He tried to sound sympathetic, but he might have been talking about a tooth extraction.

"It's not frightening to me. I've been changing into a wolf once a month since I was thirteen. It's only an inconvenience. Being a monster is actually rather boring."

"You're not a monster, Alice."

"How do you know? Why don't you come see for yourself?"

He shook his head and smiled. "I really couldn't do that."

"You sit there every week believing I only imagine what I know to be real. All I'm doing is asking you to see for yourself. It takes no time at all. There's a small window in the basement door I usually cover up, but you could look through it. You'd be perfectly safe in case my imagination tried to bite you."

His smile had faded. He was losing control of the situation. Alice knew she could only stray so far before he brought her back in line. "We've been through this before," he said. "What happens between us happens in this office. I don't lay down many rules, but I have my reasons for that one."

"Wouldn't you say I'm something of a special case?"

"To me, all my patients are special cases."

She crossed her arms and sat up straight, her eyes glistening. "Good for you, doctor."

"I tell you what I will do, though." He leaned forward, put his hand on the arm of her chair. "Why don't you come here this evening. We'll see this thing through together, here. What do you say?"

The tears flowed down her face, and she stabbed at them with the tissue he handed her. It smelled like a perfumed old woman. "It would be too dangerous for me to come here tonight."

"Suit yourself, but the offer stands." He busied himself with fixing a cup of coffee, as she blew her nose and sat back in her chair. It didn't suit herself. It suited him, so reasonable and above it all. Sometimes she hated him, but he was the only one she had to talk to, the only one who knew what she was, even if he didn't believe her.

"Coffee?"

She shook her head. "I have enough going on tonight without caffeine."

He sat back down with his coffee and smiled at her.

She held up the tightly wadded tissue in her hand. "You need to quit using this brand of tissue. It stinks."

He looked like a TV housewife who'd been told her laundry was dingy or her glassware spotted. "What's wrong with it?"

She held the box under his nose. "Smell."

He made a face. "My God, it does smell dreadful."

As she left Adams's office, Alice checked her watch. She still had plenty of time. She needed to go by the university and see her adviser. Today was the last day of preregistration for the fall semester. Unless she wanted to stand in line for hours, she needed to sign up now, in late March, for a class that wouldn't start until September. Most semesters she took a course. The books she read, the lectures she heard, told of other lives, other minds, that she could brush against without fear on either side. She liked the professors, too, the ones who had a passion for something. It didn't matter whether it was astronomy or aesthetics.

She herself didn't want a degree and a career, but the school seemed to have trouble grasping that fact. "You will have to declare a major sooner or later," she had been told by a squinty-eyed man in the registrar's office.

"Will I learn more then?" she'd asked. It was a smart-ass question, and later she'd regretted it. She wasn't here primarily to learn, though she certainly did. What she was curious about wasn't taught here. And besides, before she was out of high school she'd read everything she could find on abnormal psychology, shape shifting, wolves, shamans, and werewolves. For a week many years ago she'd plowed through stacks of books on Greek myth and religion researching an Arcadian cult whose initiation rites included the transformation of the initiate into a wolf for nine years. She identified with the initiate in spite of the distraction of the footnotes and the obvious fact that the author never once believed that humans actually turned into wolves. Why search for knowledge about herself in classes where she knew more about werewolves than the professors did?

It was when she wasn't looking that she learned something new, as when she took Shakespeare and was elated for the fifteen weeks and four moons of the semester. His language was gorgeous, but what impressed her was his tolerance, his refusal to judge even his villains. When she took genetics, she realized that in every cell of her body there was one gene or several that made her what she was. At first she thought she was the product of recessive genes—only expressed when mated with an identical gene. Generations could go by with the odds always slender. If she had ancestors who were werewolves, they could easily all be dead before she was born. More and more, though, she had come to believe she was a freak mutation, an anomaly that began with her and, when she died childless, would end with her.

This semester she hadn't taken a course and wished she had. In class she never spoke unless called upon. The grades didn't matter, they were always good. She liked sitting in the classroom, among the rows of students. She liked reading a book late at night that those same students were reading and liked listening to them talk about it the next day. She even liked the tests, especially the essays, where she let herself say what she'd thought to herself as others spoke.

The university, however, didn't seem to believe in taking courses for pleasure alone and wanted to make sure she had the proper guidance. She'd accumulated enough hours to become conspicuous, and the university insisted that this semester she must follow the rules, and according to the rules everyone must be advised. In her case, this task had fallen to Dr. Summers, whom Alice had never met. She sat on the bench in the hall outside his door and waited. Inside, she could hear a man and woman talking through the open door. "I don't understand why I have to take all these things I don't care about," the girl said.

"Exactly which things don't you care about?" The man's voice, apparently Dr. Summers's, was low and kind. Alice couldn't detect a trace of sarcasm in it.

"Like physics."

"Have you had some sort of bad experience with physics?"

"No."

"Do you know what physics is?"

"Sure. Matter and stuff, right?"

"Stephanie, trust me. Take Caravatti, section 003 or 004. If you don't like it, I'll buy your books for a semester."

"Oh, Dr. Summers!" The girl laughed. "You don't have to do that." Alice guessed from the sound of the laughter that Dr. Summers was good-looking.

"Okay," he said, "take the white sheet and the blue sheet to registration. The pink sheet is yours. But it's too dim to read, so be sure to copy down your schedule."

After the rustle of pages and a scrape of chairs, a tall girl in black hurried past, and Dr. Summers stood beside the bench at the door of his office. He was good-looking, though not in the tweedy way she'd expected. He was wearing blue jeans and a sweatshirt.

He looked as if he should be camping somewhere. Only the glasses made him look like a college professor. His beard and hair, both shaggy, were laced with gray and silver. His eyes were large and kind.

"Alice White?" he said.

She stood and nodded.

He towered beside her but bent toward her as he spoke. "Erik Summers. It's a pleasure. Sorry, I'm running late. Come on in."

As they went into the office, he gestured toward the chair where Stephanie had just sat. "Younger students sometimes take a little longer to advise. *I* know there are no boring subjects, only boring teachers. But try convincing a nineteen-year-old of that."

She offered him the registration form, but he seemed not to notice. He opened a folder and leafed through it. "Tell me about yourself."

She shrugged. "There's not much to tell. I'm just taking a few courses. I'm a special student."

"But if somebody held a gun to your head, you'd say you were a biology major, so they assigned you to me."

She laughed. "Something like that."

He was leafing through the pages as he spoke, occasionally lingering over one page or another. "What sorts of things are you interested in?"

"Animal studies, wildlife. And literature. I take a lot of literature courses."

"Good combination."

"I like it."

"Have you ever thought about getting a degree?"

"I don't want a degree."

He looked at her as if studying her, a finger to his lips, his brow furrowed into deep lines. "You sound positively opposed to the idea."

"No, it's not that. I just don't want one. It's not for me."

He raised his eyebrows and smiled. "They come in

13

all shapes and sizes, you know. Great things, degrees. But then I would think that. I've got three and wish I had a good reason to get another." He took the registration form from her hand. "So what do you want to take in the fall?"

"I want to take ecology."

He bent over her transcript, moving his finger up and down. She studied his profile. Who was he away from this office? she wondered. On the wall behind him was a poster of a pair of penguins, a chick at their feet. The jeans jacket draped over the back of his chair smelled of woodsmoke. She liked it and took a deep breath.

"Have you taken Intro?" he asked.

"No."

"I'm afraid it's a prerequisite for ecology."

"I know."

He looked at her as if she'd said something quite interesting. "So why not take the prerequisite?"

"I started it once before. We spent the first half of the course on the cell. I felt like I was in one. I dropped. I couldn't stand listening to him drone on about amino acids for another moment."

"Was 'him' Dr. Granger, by chance?"

Alice smiled and nodded.

Erik leaned forward and spoke in low, confidential tones. "You should hear him hold forth on lipids in the faculty dining room." He returned to the folder and flipped to a new page. "You have excellent grades."

"I work hard."

"How did you get into genetics? You don't have the prerequisites for that, either."

"I just went to registration and asked for it."

"Why didn't you do that this time?"

She laughed. "Somebody got wise to me."

"So I'm your punishment?"

"Only if you don't let me take ecology."

He smiled at her, and she could see he was taken with her. She could ask him to have coffee with her, and he would probably go. But he knew who she was. He held her file in his hands. What if she liked him as much as she thought she might? Then what? Adams told her she had nothing to lose, but maybe she should keep it that way.

"I teach a section of ecology," he said.

"Yes, I know." She didn't mention that she'd planned to take a different section.

"I'll make a deal with you."

"Do you make deals with all your advisees?"

"You heard that business with Stephanie?"

"Yes."

"We're a social species, we bargain. Here's the deal—you take Intro with someone besides Dr. Granger, let's say Dr. Phillips, at the same time you're in my ecology, and I'll waive the prerequisite."

"I work. I don't have time to take two classes in one semester."

"Okay, then take it after."

"I thought it was a prerequisite."

"Well, we'll pretend that ecology is a prerequisite for Intro. It really doesn't matter." He spread his hands. She liked their shape, slender and long. "I can understand your hesitation spending a semester with a textbook titled *The Cell,* but just give Dr. Phillips a chance. Meiosis will be a religious experience."

She laughed and held up her hands. "Okay, okay, I promise to take it, but I *really* want to take ecology first."

"Deal." He scribbled on the form and handed it back to her. "If they give you any crap, which they probably won't because they never bother to check these forms anyway, just have them call me."

She stood. "Thanks."

He followed her to the door. "Don't thank me. You haven't taken the course yet."

He watched her walk down the hall, knowing he was being unprofessional but not caring. Her long braid swung back and forth. He imagined his hands on her hips. When she disappeared around the corner, he turned away and went back to his desk.

He read the information from the top of her transcript. She was thirty-two, she was single, and she lived, he saw with a start, next door to the rented house he had moved into in January. He realized now he had seen her before once or twice, apparently coming and going from work, but always at a distance. He had never noticed how attractive she was. He turned to her application form. Her Xeroxed face smiled at him. She had large brown eyes, a high forehead, and a straight thin nose. Her mouth was large with full lips that she held pursed in the photograph as if thinking about something ironic. Her skin was smooth, pale in contrast with her dark hair. In the photo, her hair was also in a braid draped over her right shoulder. She was not conventionally beautiful, but she was the most striking woman Erik had ever seen. He looked at the photograph again. It wasn't just the way she looked; it was something else, her "presence" in the room. He didn't know what else to call it.

He'd never dated a student before. He didn't believe in it. But, he reasoned, she wasn't his student yet, or she could switch to Phillips's section. It came home to him that come September she would be sitting in his classroom for fifteen weeks. He stared at her photograph. Eventually, he thought, he would ask her out. He closed the file and returned it to the drawer. "Idiot," he said quietly, addressing himself.

Alice sat at the bar and watched the men in the mirror. She would choose one and stare into the glass until he saw her in the mirror and came over, offering himself. It always worked, it seemed, if she chose with care. She watched their eyes and could tell if they were

16

available. The place was nearly full, near the end of happy hour. She looked down into her drinks, two for one. She poured the remains of one into the other and took a deep swallow. She liked Dr. Summers. He watched me go, she thought. She was sure of it.

She'd stopped at the grocery store after leaving school. She should have gone straight home, she supposed, but she'd gone out of her way to come here, the motel bar where she came to pick up men or, as this evening, just to drink. She had a few hours before sunset, and she needed a drink.

She remembered two women talking once before class. "I met him at a party," one said. "From the moment I laid eyes on him I knew I wanted to sleep with him. So I was shameless. I called him up and asked him out."

"So how was it?" the other one asked.

"We got married two months later."

Alice remembered thinking nothing like that would ever happen to her.

"Alice. I was afraid I'd never see you again." A man was standing beside her, smiling. She couldn't remember his name. She'd slept with him three or four weeks ago.

She returned to her drink. "I'm waiting to meet someone," she said.

"Forget him. Come with me. I've been dying to see you again."

She looked him in the eye. She hoped her face was completely devoid of emotion. "I'm waiting to meet my fiancé," she said.

He nodded and disappeared into the crowd.

Kevin, the bartender, pointed to her empty glass. "Another?"

She nodded. As he mixed the drink, he kept his eyes on her. "I don't know why you won't go home with me. I'm a nice guy. I have a nice apartment. You won't have to tell me you've got a fiancé."

17

"You're my bartender, Kevin."

"Right. A bartender, hardly a priest."

"Okay, let's say I sleep with you. How are you going to feel when I won't sleep with you again? How are you going to feel when I come in here and pick up other men?"

"I don't feel so great now."

"You'd feel worse if I slept with you."

"Try me."

"No."

"Okay, have it your way." He set her drink before her and started filling a sink with hot water. Clouds of steam rose up before him. "Don't look now, but there's a guy by the cigarette machine who wants to be your love slave."

"The redhead?"

"The very same."

"He looks sleazy."

"Sometimes you like sleazy."

"Not tonight, okay?" She glared at him.

"Just joking, Alice." He began filling a second sink. "It's none of my business, but maybe a fiancé wouldn't be such a bad idea."

"You don't know what you're talking about."

"Maybe so, but here comes sleazy."

The redheaded man stepped up to the bar and leaned against it, gesturing at Kevin but staring at Alice.

"What do you want besides my girlfriend you're staring at," Kevin snapped, and the man turned toward the bar and asked for a glass of water.

When he'd gone, Alice said, "Thanks."

Kevin shrugged. "I figure you gotta be tired of lying all the time, so this one's on me. Besides, the guy's a prick."

Alice's mother, Ruth, sat at Alice's kitchen table as if she would soon be asked to leave: she kept her coat on, her purse by her feet. She always sat that way when she visited Alice, and usually Alice would prompt her to take off her coat and relax. But in less than an hour the full moon would rise, and Alice had much to do before then. She could already feel herself changing.

The actual physical transformation of her body into the body of a wolf was the last change to occur. But hours before, she was aware of her senses changing. She could smell that her mother had taken aspirin before she'd come, smell too the unmistakable odor of her mother's anxiety.

"You are not listening to me," her mother was saying.

"Yes, I am," said Alice.

"What am I going to tell your father?" her mother asked with a toss of her hands.

Alice continued to move around the kitchen putting up groceries. Her mother had been waiting for her when she came home. "Tell him I will see him Sunday—on his birthday—and that I will be delighted to spend all day with him."

Her mother sighed, but with restraint. "But he is expecting you for dinner tonight, Alice."

"That's not my fault. I told you I would have to check my calendar, but you went ahead and settled on tonight without even checking with me."

"I told you I was thinking about tonight, and you said fine."

"I said I would let you know."

"Well, you didn't let me know, did you?" Her mother looked around the kitchen, inspecting it from her chair. "What's so important that you can't have dinner with your father?"

"I have a date."

"If this date's so important, how come your father and I never meet any of the men you go out with?"

"It's not anything serious, okay? It's just a guy."

"Just serious enough to stand up your father."

"He will understand. I have other plans."

" 'He will understand' indeed. Maybe he won't say anything to you—mustn't upset Alice—but I'll certainly hear about it!"

"Good God, Mother, he's not a child! I have plans. And I'm sick to death of hearing about the arguments you and Daddy may or may not have because of something I do or do not do, understand?" She turned from her mother and began to stack canned goods into the cabinet. "If you will excuse me, I have to get ready."

Her mother stood up quickly, almost tottering back and forth from the effort. But when she closed the door behind her the only sound was the click of the door catching.

Alice waited until even her wolf-sensitive ears could no longer hear her mother's car, then went out to her own car to get the last of her groceries—a twenty-five-pound bag of dog food she had not wanted to explain to her mother. She closed the trunk and grasped the top of the bag in her hands. As she started to pull it up to her chest, she froze. She felt someone watching her. She looked up to see Dr. Summers sitting on the porch of the house next door, smoking a cigarette. The house had been empty for months, a small measure of privacy she had valued, but now it had been rented, apparently by Dr. Summers. He smiled at her.

"Good evening," he said. "I'm your new neighbor."

Startled, she heard the note of tenderness in his voice. It might have been a hand stretched forth slowly, palm open, to touch her. She sniffed the air and looked into his eyes. Her hands tightened round the top of the bag. For a moment she didn't move. He wanted her. She broke his gaze and looked down and away. "Good evening," she said, hoisted the bag to her chest, wrapped her arms around it, and hurried into the house, trying not to think about the look in her own eyes as she'd breathed him in.

The basement windows are boarded over, the heavy door at the top of the stairs securely locked. The basement is damp and musty. The floor slopes to a drain. Behind the hot-water heater, a faucet drips into a metal pan. The full moon rises, but she does not see it.

The wolf walks along the walls, smelling, rubbing up against them. First one way, then the other. She is not looking for a way out. She knows there is none. She marks the corners, the bottom of the stairs.

Her journey around the room takes a long time, but she is not bored. She must get the feel of the place again. She stops at the bottom of the stairs and shits.

She hears a dog howl—high and thin, barely audible. She moves in a circle, then sets her haunches upon the floor, her muzzle thrust toward the bare light bulb hanging over her. A chord rises through her and echoes in the small space. The dog offers a counterpoint, but a screen door slams, a voice screams, and the dog is silent. The wolf turns three times round (counterclockwise) and lies upon the floor with a heavy sigh.

At one time she ran in the country. She sees herself then, she sees herself now. When she comes to the woman now, it is always here in this small place. It is full of her scent and no one else's.

She raises herself up, hind legs first, and circles around the room again. At the food she pauses and lunges, pressing her paws against the paper, tearing at it with her jaws. Small brown cylinders fly in all directions. She chases after them, skittering across the floor, sliding into the wall, yelping excitedly. She settles down to eat the food pellets, all of them, stuffing herself. The crunching roars in her head. What she wants and cannot find is play, like the ravens who used to spring into the air at her charge, then flutter down slowly behind her.

She stretches, pushing her front paws against the wall. She howls long and deep, then listens. She lies down in the silence. As a wolf she doesn't think in words, but then she doesn't need words to feel lonely.

Chapter
2

After Alice left his office, Erik had gone to teach his last class before spring break.

"Dr. Summers, can we have class outside?" It was the one who doted on her hair, whose hair Erik had doted on himself—luxuriant, thick, different from the rest of her, a chromium frame round a detail from Gauguin. He continued to check the roll as if he had not heard, finding the empty seats of those who had begun their spring break a day early. He had learned to adjust to those who could not adjust to an assigned seat and found them where they'd strayed—into the corners or closer to someone who didn't know they were there. The last class before a holiday, he was surprised any of them were here.

He wanted to tell them about the penguins today.

Perhaps in the bright sun and the clipped grass, they would care. He wanted them to care even more than he wanted them to learn. Looking up, he said, "All right, sounds good to me." They had forgotten the question or assumed he had never heard it. They looked at him condescendingly. He had lost his place, poor old fart. "Let's have class outside," he said in his announcements voice, "out the back door, beneath the trees, on the hill." They laughed, stirred to their feet with more noise than was necessary. The one with the hair tossed it and arched her eyebrows at her friends. Some resented this forced migration and grumbled. "The rest of the year you can stay in this building," he told them. A colleague, interrupted in his recitation of the formulae for inertia, turned from his lectern and gave a professionally restrained grimace as Erik and his herd passed and echoed down the stairs.

They settled on the grass like a mixed flock of birds. Perched or sprawled or leaning against trees, they jutted from the landscape at diverse angles. The young man who always lingered after class to ask questions stood slightly apart with his notebook and pen ready as if he had come to interview them all. Erik looked admiringly at the carefully tanned legs of one of the young women who lay posed on the grass. He saw himself lying beside her, his hand upon her thigh, looking down into her eyes. The sweet pang of this imagined moment gave him the energy to begin:

"We were talking about migration as a means of adaptation. As you know, birds, especially, migrate with the seasons, often returning to a very precise location each year. One of the big questions about this behavior is how do these animals know where they are, where they are going—especially with such remarkable accuracy—even when the terrain, the weather, and every other thing that might affect their ability to navigate varies radically from year to year?

"One theory is that they navigate, just as sailors navigate, by using the stars. To test this idea out, one fellow got permission to use a planetarium and set loose a bunch of geese in it. I don't know who cleaned up the mess after it was over, but science is often messy." He paused in the small laughter to light a cigarette. At the bottom of the hill, across the street, children were playing in the playground behind the Catholic school. A basketball spurted through the breaks in the fence and bounced down the hill as an awkward and pudgy boy stumbled after it. His classmates, the more competent ones, stood erect and laughed, their arms folded in nine-year-old contempt. Erik's thoughts stumbled down the hill after the clumsy one, then turned abruptly back to the class.

"Anyway, what he did was arrange the stars in such a way as to fool the geese into thinking it was time to migrate. Sure enough, the geese started flying in the right direction. But the only problem with the star navigation theory is that birds in the wild seem unaffected by overcast skies, but when our planetarium experimenter blanked out the stars, the birds quit trying to migrate. He then reasoned, again using the analogy of sailors, that the birds could somehow sense the Earth's magnetic field, though he could not imagine how. He set up a huge electromagnet in the middle of the room and flipped it on. The birds then started flying in a circle around and around the magnet like moths around a flame. So he thought he had his answer." He paused a moment to let them see in their minds' eyes the wheeling birds.

"The only problem with this answer, however, is that the Earth's magnetic field varies a significant amount, so that navigation based on it would vary—does vary—along with it. Many birds, however, return not just to approximately the same place, but to a place more precisely located than we, with the most sophisticated equipment—the sort we've developed for guided missiles and so forth—could locate. In other words, we don't know how birds do it.

"Let me give you an example, a bird that doesn't even fly—the penguin. There is a variety of penguin who live around the Ascension Islands, and in the spring, when young penguins' fancy turns to love, they set out for Antarctica, a part of the world where it is a balmy forty below in springtime. When they reach Antarctica, they don't stop there but begin waddling inland several miles through the harshest terrain on the planet, where they build a nest from rocks—since there isn't anything else to build a nest from. They pair off there, choosing each other on the basis of criteria known only to penguins. The female deposits her eggs in the nest, and then one of them—they take turns—sits on the eggs while the other treks back to the sea to catch fish to bring back for both of them. They keep this up until the babies hatch and they're old enough to follow their parents back to the sea. Whereupon, the family heads north.

"Now all that is not the remarkable part. Penguins, you see, mate for life." He paused in the wake of that phrase, touched by it in spite of his scientific training. "The next spring the couple make the same journey again and manage to find each other among thousands of penguins. We used to think, with our usual lack of imagination, that they must just consider themselves lucky to find any old nest to use, but with the aid of radio transmitters and satellites, we've been able to track some of them to find out that each year they return to precisely the same nest. Think about this— the weather, by any standard, is horrible, the terrain is not only harsh but constantly changing as ice cliffs break off and shift. Imagine yourself heading for the mall, only to find that all the streets went in different directions and that some did not exist at all anymore. Still, they unerringly return to the same spot.

"Not content, experimenters decided to move a

nest, just to see what the couple returning home would do. When the rocks were moved three feet or less, the penguins did nothing, apparently accepting a certain amount of uncertainty, but once the nest was moved more than three feet the penguins would move it back to the precise spot where it had been before, rock by rock. If you went back to your dorms now, and the building had been moved four feet, you probably wouldn't even notice, and you certainly wouldn't do anything about it, figuring that the administration was just fiddling with your reality again. But how do the penguins know it has been moved at all? With our most sophisticated equipment, we could not detect in such a landscape such a minuscule shift on the surface of the globe. We don't have the faintest idea how they do it." He stopped. They were prepared for this by now, the brighter ones, anyway. The man was positively crazy about uncertainty. "He is always telling us what we don't know instead of what we do," was a typical comment on student evaluations. Only occasionally was this offered as praise.

The young man who had stood raised his hand, not letting the outdoors affect his sense of decorum, and Erik nodded at him. "Why do they do it?" he asked.

"If you mean, why do they travel such distances to lay their eggs, that's a little easier. They go where it's safe—for penguins, at least. There are very few predators to eat the eggs or the parents. Why they are so precise about the location of their nest, we don't know. I like to think it's because they like to know where they are. Most creatures do."

The girl with the beautiful legs was staring up into the sky, apparently bored, possibly asleep behind her sunglasses. His fantasy lost its charm. He could not lose himself in eyes that were closed. The rest of the class shifted uncomfortably in the grass, glancing at their watches. He did not want to talk about territoriality, the next item in the notes that lay at his feet. He wanted to migrate. The sun and warm breeze, the grass and trees and freedom of spring, the youth scattered all around him restless to move, seemed to him a harsher environment than the frozen waters through which the penguin and his mate unerringly swam toward home. The girl with the luxuriant hair said brightly into the silence, "Dr. Summers, can we leave early today? Lots of us have planes and things to catch." Erik dismissed the class with a wave of his hand. He did not bother to return to his office but took a long, circuitous route to his newly rented house.

His house was the middle of five one-story, peak-roofed boxes, quite different from the older row houses in this part of town. He liked to sit on the porch in the evenings. Inside the house everything was alien, furniture he wouldn't have chosen, every room a dead end, windows that wouldn't open. He'd explored it, marked it with his belongings, placed them with care like tiles in a mosaic, but now he ignored them as if they too were the source of strangeness.

When Debra, his soon to be ex-wife, had called on Wednesday to explain about the papers he should sign, she told him about her new bedroom curtains. "They are cheery," she said. "You would like them."

"Why are you telling me about your bedroom curtains?" he said. "You are divorcing me. Why don't you just take care of business and get off the phone?"

"You don't have to snap at me. I think you're making too much of this. I just told you about my curtains; I was making conversation."

"Making conversation. Last week you told me about the carburetor on your car. I know you, Debra. You don't talk about carburetors to make conversation. You don't talk about that kind of shit to anybody but me. We're getting divorced. Don't talk to me about your carburetor or your curtains or anything else you wouldn't chat about over lunch with some member of your board. Okay? Is that clear?"

There was a long silence on the other end. She might've been crying; he couldn't tell. "I just thought we could still be friends," she said quietly. "Even though our lives have taken different directions, I hoped we could still be friends." He saw them slicing through the ocean toward different poles.

Their separation had originally been his idea. He complained she had no time for him and didn't seem to care about their marriage. She said she did care, and he agreed to come back, but by then she resented the implications of what he'd been saying and wasn't so sure their marriage could work anymore.

They'd kept this up for months, back and forth, like two strong animals tethered with elastic bashing into each other, lurching away, and springing back. The pain became addictive. The last time it had been her turn to win him back, she'd called a lawyer instead. He couldn't really blame her. He'd started it. It seemed fitting she should end it.

From the porch, he watched his neighbors. He knew none of their names, but he tried to figure out who went with whom and what their lives were like and whether they were happy or not. Spring break had now begun, but he was not sure he wanted the freedom. Freedom to sit on this porch all day and watch total strangers go about their lives. Perhaps the familiar contours of classes and papers and the fragile energy of his students would be better. He liked to teach, liked at least the feeling that occasionally he could bring things to life for them. The other part of his job—the research—had become increasingly odious to him. In grad school he was taught to laugh at the idea that analysis kills. Now he wasn't so sure.

Most of his neighbors were now indoors, and rush-hour traffic hadn't begun, leaving only the cooing of mourning doves. He listened to them and smiled. Squirrels ran along the power lines and jumped from tree to tree. He followed the progress of a young male from the sycamore in his front yard to the tile roof of a house over a block away. He wondered how large an urban squirrel's territory might be.

An old Chevrolet pulled up next door, its tires rubbing against the curb. The woman, small inside the huge car, made a task of getting out and glared at the house as she came up the walk. She knocked on the door and sighed. When no one answered her knock, she turned to Erik, about twenty feet away. "She should be here," she said.

"Her car isn't here," Erik offered. He'd already noticed with regret that Alice wasn't home.

"I can see that. I'm Alice's mother. I told her I might be coming by this afternoon. You're new in that house, aren't you?" She looked at him with polite suspicion.

"Yes, I just moved in last week," Erik began, but they both turned toward the blue Toyota parking in front of his house.

Alice stepped out of the car, the low sun in her eyes. She was small, no more than five feet. She shielded her eyes with her hand and squinted at her mother. Erik turned all his attention on Alice as if she had come to visit him. He stood up, hoping the mother would include him in Alice's homecoming, but she had completely forgotten him, concentrating instead on complaining to her daughter that she had had to wait.

"I have been at the store, Mother." She pulled a bag of groceries from the trunk of the car and held them up as proof. She had not even noticed Erik was there.

Erik debated whether to step forward and announce himself, but the two women were already at Alice's porch with their groceries and argument well in hand. He sat back down and lit a cigarette, pondering the phenomenon of his neighbor.

Since he had separated from Debra, he had been noticing other women, almost all other women. His father had told him he needed to get back into circulation, but Erik conjured up images of a blood clot detaching itself from an arterial wall.

He was not sure what he needed. His reactions to women—lust, tenderness, curiosity—often seemed indistinguishable. "Go out and get laid," his father had advised on another occasion after several beers. Erik had said nothing. After a few moments of silence his father had muttered, "Debra is a bitch."

"She's just changing, Dad. Her career is more important to her right now than relationships."

"Jesus, Erik, listen to yourself. She dumped you, and you're defending her with her own party line."

"She did not 'dump me,' and just because she wants to be a success doesn't make her a bitch."

"I don't know why not. Every man I ever knew who 'wanted to be a success' was a bastard. She reminds me of one of those people who look out from magazine ads and condescend to tell me what Scotch they're drinking." He'd looked down into his beer and shaken his head.

Once when Erik had made the identical gesture in midargument, Debra had stopped short. "My God," she'd said. "I'm arguing with your goddamn father." Debra and his father had never gotten along.

His father ran a tree service, in all ways modest. "Leave it alone," he often advised his potential customers. "Trees can take care of themselves better than most people can." But many who wanted to spend money on tree health were not in the habit of leaving things alone and found someone else eager to whip their trees into shape. He'd once told a precise woman whose oaks provided a dramatic setting for her roses that whoever butchered those trees for her had screwed her royally, a mixed metaphor too opinionated for the hired help. Word got around that Mr. Summers was crude and unstable. Now he mostly got calls to cut down dead trees before they fell down. Since Erik had quit working for him, he'd found it hard to find anyone who gave a damn about the trees. "It's all just firewood to them," he said, and shook his head.

Sometimes his father would call Erik to help out with difficult jobs. When Erik returned home, he and Debra would argue about it, Debra insisting he was being taken advantage of and Erik insisting he was not. Erik was grateful he would not have to live through that argument again. He knew his father had his flaws, but it wasn't possible for him to take advantage of Erik by asking for his help.

When Erik's parents divorced when he was ten, he could see his father needed his help more than his mother did, so he'd elected to live with him. They'd stayed on in the suburban house, now too big for them. When Erik had gone off to college, his father had rented a tiny place by the river, where he still lived. Erik's mother had moved to California, where she lived with his stepfather. As he was growing up, no one would talk to Erik about why his parents were getting a divorce. His mother had once sat with him for over an hour when he was eight talking to him about death and God because his cat had died. But about divorcing his father, she'd said nothing. His father would only say his mother had good reason. Only recently, as they'd sat on the bank of the river by his father's house, his father had confessed that he'd cheated on his wife many times. "She put up with it till she just couldn't take any more."

"Why did you do it?" Erik asked. He wasn't angry. He was glad finally to know his mother's good reason.

"I liked being a young rascal. I liked the intrigue." He looked out over the water and laughed. "I'm an old rascal now. Don't like that quite as much, but it's safer."

The next evening Erik talked to his mother on the phone. "Dad told me why you left him," he said.

His mother sounded amused. Many things amused his mother that he thought should make her cry. "And what did he say?"

"He said he cheated on you, and you got sick of it."

"Well, son, he did cheat on me, every chance he got, which you can imagine with your father was quite a number of chances. But I wouldn't have left him if I hadn't met Jeff. I left your father for Jeff, not because he'd been a bad little boy."

Jeff was Erik's stepfather, a man so like his mother, it unnerved him. They narrated jokes with the same rhythm and humor, doted on the same arias and country-and-western songs. Erik's first memory of Jeff was at a party at his parents' when Erik was nine. Jeff and his mother put Hank Williams on the stereo and danced while everyone watched because they were so good. Jeff had also been Debra's favorite in-law. At family gatherings the two of them sat in a corner talking and smiling until the last guests were drifting away.

Alice's mother now emerged alone. Erik watched her silently. Her shoes clicked on the rough pavement as she tried to move quickly, her head tilted to one side, but she stumbled on rocks and cracks in the pavement, muttering angrily to herself.

Too bad they had argued, Erik thought. Alice might have come out to say good-bye to her mother, and he would have stepped out of the shadows and invited her in for a drink. They could have talked, and he might have placed his hands on her hips as he'd imagined only a few hours ago.

Perhaps now he could rise from his porch and stroll casually to Alice's front door for, maybe, dinner? He lit another cigarette and tried to figure out what he could say if he were brave enough to knock on her door, when Alice came out to her car. He stared at her, watching her movements as she opened the trunk and hoisted a bag out of the trunk. As she turned to leave, he stumbled to his feet, said something he could not remember later, and apparently startled her so badly, she almost dropped the bag of dog food she was carrying.

She disappeared into her house, and he sat back down on the porch. "Idiot," he said to himself.

Chapter

3

She awoke gradually, the concrete floor drawing the warmth from her body. The light from the single bulb was harsh and annoying. Even though the windows were boarded over, she knew it was morning because she was a woman again. The change always came in her sleep, and she woke shortly after dawn. She had no memories of the actual change, only dreamlike impressions. She'd stood in the surf once when she was six. A series of breakers struck her, then swept her up, pummeling her body like huge beating wings. The change felt something like that, only it didn't just happen to her; it was something she did as well. Every muscle ached. Her skin felt stretched like a taut drumskin.

She rolled over to a sitting position, pulling her legs

up against her breasts, brushing the grit from her face and body. The concrete was cold and hard under her butt. She stood, her legs wobbly as if she had been running all night. She straightened up, then crouched again involuntarily. It felt as if an invisible hand had seized her right ovary, squeezed hard, and let it go. She always ovulated after the change. She sometimes wondered if she would quit changing with menopause. She didn't think she would, any more than she would cease feeling desire.

The spasm subsided, and she stood up straight and took a series of deep breaths. The damp air smelled of shit. She cleaned up after herself, or her other self— she never knew how to think of it. The wolf seemed like someone else, who was also her at the same time.

"My, but we were hungry last night," she muttered as she swept up dog food from the corners and under the stairs.

As she opened the door at the top of the stairs, bright spring sunlight pushed her back like a crowd of boisterous people. She shielded her eyes with her forearm and shuffled into the kitchen. Her head throbbed, and it was an effort to lift her chin from her chest. Leaning on the counter, she listened to the last few gurgles of the coffeepot. It was one of her most valued possessions: it had a timer. When she saw it in the store, she thought of these mornings, how desperately she wanted coffee and how hard it was to go through the endless steps to make it, only to sit at the table and fall asleep in her chair before it was done.

She poured her coffee, cradled the cup in her palms—face in the rising steam—and breathed deeply. She took an ice tray from the freezer, dumped the cubes in the sink, and dropped one in her coffee. It cracked and popped, then melted to a sliver. She drank off the coffee and poured another cup.

She shuffled to the bathroom. When she was in the mental hospital when she was fourteen, she'd seen patients on Thorazine walk this way. Once she had a bath she would be all right. She put her coffee on the edge of the tub and put the plug in the drain. She opened the hot water all the way, the cold a quarter turn, then splashed some of the still-cold water in her face.

As the bathtub filled, she went to the stereo in the living room and put on an old Dylan record, leaving the arm up so that it would play over and over. His moaning surrealism appealed to her on these mornings. "Like a rolling stone . . ." whined loudly through the room. The room was nothing like Dylan's voice—the wood floor neatly swept, the furniture spare and precise, the plants shining in prettily glazed pots. She thought, I live in the cover of a magazine. Naked and grimy, she struck a pose—one hand upon the back of the beige sofa, the other in her snarled, matted hair.

She didn't have to work today because it was Saturday. She usually had to call in sick the day after she changed. The headache might not go away until sundown. Her body would be sore for several days. She'd developed the fiction of severe menstrual cramps to account for her regular absenteeism. Her boss, a woman, understood and suggested gynecologists, herbal teas, acupuncture, drugs. When Alice actually did suffer from cramps, she dutifully went to work and did not complain. This was her penance for deceit.

She worked as a travel agent. She arranged for people to go to Jamaica or Australia and smiled prettily: "No, I have never been, but I understand that it is lovely." Actually she understood no such thing. She felt safer staying put, not wanting to upset the balance she had established. In this house, in her mother's house, in the bar she sometimes visited, she felt, if not at home, at least less alien, with some measure or illusion of control. High over the ocean in a pressurized cabin, she could see herself changing, exposed, surrounded by terrified tourists.

When she was not working or taking classes, she spent most of her time reading old novels and biographies. On Sunday afternoons she liked to go to a play, spoiling herself with an expensive ticket. During intermission she sipped wine and eavesdropped on the couples discussing the play or their plans for later. She had no friends. It was easier that way. She liked her job at the travel agency because she had few co-workers. When customers became too friendly, she transformed, with a dismissive smile, into the clerk whose private life was her own as she handed them their itinerary and receipt.

When she wanted sex, she went to the bar. Most of the men there were staying at the motel. It was easy to sleep with them but to keep them out of her life. She didn't like going there, often swore she'd never go back. She'd made the mistake of telling this to Adams, and now he wanted to talk of nothing else. Her being a werewolf didn't seem to interest him much as a subject of conversation.

And she supposed it wasn't very interesting. After almost twenty years, being a werewolf had a chilling dailiness about it. Learning about werewolves, wolves, science, and magic hadn't made any difference in the pattern of her life, had made nothing less painful. She had expected to grow more resigned as she grew older, but that hadn't happened. Adams was the last slender vein of hope left. Maybe she could stop changing or learn resignation. At least she got to talk about it. Even though he thought she was crazy, talking to him made her feel more sane. Even if he didn't believe her, at least someone else knew the truth, increasing the population of her real world to two.

She'd gone to a regular physician to begin with, hoping what she was might show up as a stain in her blood or a shadow on her X rays. He said, "There's nothing wrong with you."

"I'm a werewolf," she said. "I change into a wolf every full moon, and I want to stop."

He was young. He looked like a blond balloon with glasses. He left her on the tissue-covered table and returned in fifteen minutes in high spirits. "I have already spoken with him," he said as he handed her a slip with Adams's phone number. "He'll be expecting your call. He's a specialist."

"A psychiatrist."

"Yes."

She called Adams anyway. She reasoned he was a doctor, whatever else he was. He would know medicine, and once she persuaded him she was sane, he might help her. But she hadn't anticipated the impossibility of persuading a psychiatrist that you were sane and a werewolf at the same time.

She let herself go limp in the tub, listened to the water seep out through the overflow. She left the hot water running at a trickle to keep the water hot for hours. Her head bobbed, her neck relaxed, the shampoo made a sizzling sound in the water. She could go to the bar tonight without having to worry—the wolf wouldn't be back for another month—but knew she probably wouldn't. She would be horny, she always was the night after, but she would also be most desperate to be someone who didn't go to bars, who went out on dates with nice men who wanted to get to know her. She sat up and scrubbed herself with a washcloth until her skin was red. She decided to call her mother this afternoon and apologize for practically throwing her out of the house yesterday, maybe take her out to lunch.

She lay back in the water to rinse herself, then lay floating. She closed her eyes and imagined herself with Dr. Summers. She had to think to remember his first name, Erik. She said his name to him. He was walking beside her, holding her hand. He turned to her. His look was the one he'd worn last night when he saw her. He took her in his arms and kissed her.

She opened her eyes and stared up at the ceiling. "Shit," she said. "He lives *next door,* Alice." She propped herself up and drank some coffee, now grown too cold. It would be different, she thought, if he lived across town and didn't know where I lived. If I'm really going to try going out with somebody, I should at least have someplace to hide.

Or maybe not. Don't I lock myself up enough as it is?

She slid down into the water, propped her feet on the spigots, and twiddled her toes. She would have to think about it. She could discuss it with Luther. He'd love it, she thought, if I were the one to bring up sex.

She closed her eyes and summoned up the image of Erik holding her, touching her. She spread her legs, bracing her feet upon the wall, and began to masturbate, holding the image in her mind. She came with a shudder, sloshing water onto the floor. She smiled to herself. She would clean it up later. For now she would enjoy being numb. She placed a folded washcloth behind her head. In a few minutes she was asleep.

Something woke her. She wasn't sure what. Amid the peaceful sloshing of water and the sound of her own breathing, she could hear only Dylan's wailing. She sat up, water sloshing noisily, then she heard it again, a knock at the door.

She was certain it would be her mother, come to extract her apology before Alice had a chance to offer it. Dylan was now singing, "Mama's in the factory, she ain't got no shoes," an image her mother would not appreciate but could certainly hear from the front porch. Why don't I bathe in silence, Alice asked herself, like civilized people do?

She rinsed, stood, called out, "Coming!" as she

wound her hair in a towel. She fumbled with the stereo, and Dylan's harmonica stopped in midsqueal. She yanked the door open, tying her robe as she squinted into the sun. Dr. Summers smiled at her through the haze of screen wire. She closed her eyes and winced. "I thought you were my mother," she said.

"I'm sorry. I've gotten you out of the shower."

"Tub."

"Tub," he repeated, seeming to think about this. "Look, I'm sorry. I'll just come back later."

"Can I help you?" she asked as if he were a selling a product or a religion she had no use for.

"Actually, I was going to invite you to lunch. I'm Erik Summers—I live next door. We talked yesterday, at school." He gestured with his left hand as if she might not know who he was or where next door was. She'd seen this look on the faces of other men she'd liked and sent away. "I hope I'm not too early. I wanted to catch you before you made other plans. I knew you were up—I saw you in the kitchen earlier." He gestured toward his house. "Our windows face."

How much would he have seen? she wondered. No more than neck and shoulders. She remembered him sitting on his porch, smoking a cigarette, looking at her.

She pulled her robe tighter and looked up at him. The towel on top of her head unwound and fell. "Damn," she said, and pushed the wet hair from her face. "Why don't you come in?"

He stepped inside, and she felt a surge of panic. She gripped her arms so her hands wouldn't shake. "Could I bum a cigarette?" she asked.

He gave her a cigarette and lit it for her. She inhaled deeply, blowing the smoke out in a huge cloud. "I've quit," she said. "This is a treat."

He stood at the door. He hadn't taken his eyes off her.

She looked around the room, wondering what to do with him now that she'd invited him in. "Would you like some coffee?" she said.

"Yes, that would be nice."

He followed her into the kitchen, watched as she set out cup and spoon and sugar and milk. She found this task comforting. When her parents had company it had been her job to serve the coffee.

"Cream and sugar?" she asked.

"Just black."

She laughed. "Me too. My mother told me when I was little that it was rude not to set out milk and sugar because people might not want to put you out by asking for it. She used to conjure up this dreadful soul of a guest who choked down black coffee in the name of politeness, all the while longing for milk and sugar." All this came spilling out of her as she poured the coffee. She handed him his cup, glancing up at him to see if he cared that she'd once been a child, that her life was more than this moment.

He took the cup from her hands and smiled. "My father just sends people into the kitchen with instructions to find whatever they want."

They stood for a moment holding their coffee cups. "Let's go into the living room," she said.

They sat on the sofa. She draped her hair over her shoulder and worked on the ends with a comb. She felt safer doing something. "I'm sorry," she said. "If I let it dry like this, it will be impossible."

"That's quite all right." He had been looking around the room, taking in all he could from the sofa. "I love your house," he said, "especially that photograph."

He had chosen her favorite thing—a photograph of a moonlit stand of birches after a snow. The details were crisp and vivid. The odd lighting and the low angle—about waist height—made the trees seem like giants. "Isn't that wonderful? My great-aunt did that. She's very good."

"It's marvelous. Do you have anything else of hers?"

"There's one in the bedroom." She worked at a particularly stubborn tangle. "How long have you lived next door?" she asked.

"Just a few weeks."

"How do you like it?"

"It's a lot better than where I was living. They called it an efficiency for some reason."

She laughed and placed the comb on the table. She turned toward him, drawing her legs up onto the sofa, wrapping the bottom of her robe around them. Her right arm lay along the back of the sofa. Her left hand held her wet hair like a rope.

"Have you just moved to town?" she asked.

"No, I've lived here most of my life. I'm going through a divorce. In fact, it will be final on Monday."

"I'm sorry. How long were you married?"

"Almost eight years."

"That's a long time."

"Yeah, I guess it is." He looked down, and his voice lost its cheery, social edge.

"I'm sorry. I'm being too nosy. I get it from my mother."

"I met her yesterday. She seemed to think I would know you."

"That's her way of finding out whether you do. She likes me to meet men so she will have someone to disapprove of."

"And is there someone she particularly disapproves of at the moment?"

She laughed. "You're not what I would have expected a college professor to be like."

He feigned offense. "And just what did you expect?"

"Someone more cerebral and intellectual and less . . . assertive."

He laughed. " 'Assertive.' Is that a euphemism for nosy?"

"No. You just want to know whether you're wasting your time coming over here today. I don't see anything wrong with that. So no, I don't have anyone for my mother to disapprove of, but I should warn you that that's because I want it that way."

"Does that mean you don't want to have lunch with me?"

"Why don't we just talk right now." She took up the comb, held a small elastic band between her teeth, and began braiding her hair. Her hands shook as she went through the familiar motions. She was proud of herself for not lying to him, but frightened. Now she wanted to find safer ground. "Do you have a particular specialty in biology?"

"Penguins."

"Really?"

"Go ahead and laugh. It sounds funny to me, too. Emperors, kings, jackasses—I am a bona fide penguin expert."

"How did you get into that?"

He watched her hands as she braided her hair. "One of my professors in grad school was a penguin man. He needed an assistant, and here I am, though I'm not a big name like he was."

"Why not?" She plucked the small elastic band from her mouth and bound the end of her braid.

"I don't do any field research. To make it in the wildlife business, you have to spend a lot of time in the wilderness."

"Don't you like the wilderness?"

"It's not that. It's what you have to leave behind to head into the wilderness."

"Like a wife?"

"That's one thing." He lit a cigarette. "What do you do?"

"I'm a travel agent."

"So you must travel a lot."

"No. I never go anywhere."

"Not even to lunch?"

44

She smiled back. "Do you always ask your advisees out to lunch?"

"No, this is my first time. In fact, I never do. I have a policy against it."

"So why are you breaking it?"

She had thought he might say something flip, laugh off the obvious, but he remained serious, his voice soft and low. "I decided I wanted to see you again more than I wanted to keep my policy."

"I'm flattered," she said. "I guess I should give you an answer, then, instead of keeping you in suspense."

"Take all the time you want. I'm enjoying this." He held up his cup. "I figure I can make this last at least another ten minutes."

"I'll even give you a refill." She took a deep breath. "I think I can even risk lunch. Did you have someplace in mind?"

"I thought we could eat at the restaurant at the museum." He nodded at her aunt's photograph. "There's a photography exhibit there you might like to see."

"Sounds good," she said, noting how he had expanded their lunch into a stroll through galleries. She kneaded a sore muscle on the inside of her thigh. Walking around will do me good, she thought. Even though her nerves were racing, her headache was all but gone. "Could we leave now? I'm really starving. I haven't had anything but coffee all day."

"Fine."

"I'll go change," she said. "Just make yourself at home."

As she pulled on jeans and a sweatshirt, she heard him moving around in the living room. "You have a lot of books on wolves," he called out.

"Yes," she said as she slipped on her boots. "They're very interesting."

"You have some pretty technical stuff here."

She looked at herself in the mirror. She'd put on what she would have worn to go to the museum by herself. Except for a bra. She unhooked it, slipped it off, and tossed it onto the dresser. As she stepped into the living room, he looked up from the books and broke into a smile. "You look wonderful."

"In jeans and a sweatshirt?"

He laughed and shrugged. "I can't explain it, either."

The exhibit was built around an idea, lashed to the mast of a theory. Photographs by dozens of different photographers were placed in pairs. Text, covering more wall space than the photographs, lectured on the basically sound reasons, the vibrant and spectral resonances, the conceptual and perceptual interpenetration of contexture and line, that had formed the courtship and eventual arranged marriages of the hapless pairs. The photographs kept up their quiet dignity as best they could.

The large crowd moved clumsily through the galleries. A few chose to read the walls, looking from photograph to text like spectators at a tennis match, while those who only wanted to see the photos moved awkwardly around them, hanging back or trying to move ahead. In one of the smaller rooms, a ripple in the crowd pressed Alice against Erik.

"Maybe this wasn't such a good idea," he said. "I didn't know it would be so crowded."

"I'm having a wonderful time," she said, and squeezed his arm.

Over lunch she'd asked him, as she often did the men she slept with, what he read.

He looked down and shook his head. "I used to read all the time. These days I just read articles about how deep emperor Penguins can dive written by some poor sod who sat on a boat for days logging in data." He looked up and smiled. "I go to a lot of movies."

"What kind?"

"Any kind. Something I can get all wrapped up in one way or another." His hands made a wrapping movement in the air. "I'm the guy nobody likes to sit behind who laughs too loud and cries at the drop of a hat."

"Is that what your wife says—that you laugh too loud and cry too much?"

"Is it that obvious?" He seemed pleased to have been found out.

"Just a lucky guess. Did you go to a lot of movies together?"

"We used to, but we fought too much about them, so I started going by myself."

"You fought about *movies?*"

He looked down and shook his head. "It seems pretty ludicrous to me, too."

He smiled, but his face was sad, his brow furrowed into deep crevices. She wanted to reach out and smooth those lines with her fingertips, to take the pain away, but she gripped her fork and did not move. She could see he still wanted to laugh too loud and cry over nothing. She wanted to do those things as well.

A break in the gallery crowd deposited them before a photograph that made them both stare. In what looked like the 1930s, a couple sat in the corner booth of a restaurant. Mirrors on either wall showed their faces, his behind her and hers behind him, as they stared into each other's eyes, riveted with love.

"When I saw you sitting on the bench yesterday, it startled me," he said.

"Why is that?" She didn't turn from the photograph. She now noticed that the couple held hands beneath the table.

"I find you very interesting."

She turned from the picture and smiled up at him. "Interesting? No one's ever told me I'm 'interesting' before. 'Beautiful,' 'sexy,' 'irresistible'—I've heard all those. This is my first 'interesting.'"

He laughed. "You are all those, but I didn't want to say any of them because they make it sound as if you just look good, and there's something more than that. I'm drawn to you. You're, you're . . ." He waved his hand in the air.

" 'Interesting.' "

He shrugged his shoulders. "How about fascinating? I could go with fascinating, definitely."

She laughed. "And you're silly."

"That's what my mother always said."

He put his arm around her, and they moved on to the next pair of images without even looking at what had been paired with the couple. She felt his hand upon her waist. It felt nice. "I think you're dangerous," she said.

She tried to read the placard of text beside her as they waited in the crowd to reach the next pair of photographs.

"What in the hell is this saying?" she asked.

He leaned forward and read it through, his face a mask of seriousness, his nose only inches from the Plexiglas.

"As best I can make out, it's saying that this picture of a duck and that one of a freight train don't have a damn thing in common, and that's why they're put here together."

"That's what I thought it said, but I was hoping I was wrong."

They had been facing one another, smiling. They held each other's eyes for a moment.

"It's too bad about the duck," she said, stepping in front of the photographs. "I rather like him."

"Seen one duck, you seen 'em all. But a train picture, that's something else."

"No taste," she said.

"Now that you mention it, the more I look at this train, the more it looks like a duck."

She studied the photo, hunting for duck. "I'm still looking for 'the intersection of motion and stasis.' "

"It's over there under the duck," he said.

"Could you let us by, please?" A small man with a

sleeping girl slumped at his shoulder stood before them, trying to get by.

They stepped back, pressing into the crowd behind them, and watched the man make his way along the wall toward the bathroom. One of the little girl's arms bounced as he walked, as if she were waving.

"Cute little girl," he said.

"Do you have any kids?"

"No, Debra, my wife, didn't want children."

"What about you?"

He smiled. "Well, I tried not to think about it too much. I couldn't very well manage it on my own. But I'd like to be a daddy someday, help a child discover the world. What about you?"

She shook her head abruptly. "I can't have children." She lied automatically, saying "can't" for "shouldn't."

"I'm sorry."

"Me too."

They escaped from the crowded room into one of the broader hallways and strolled arm in arm down its center. When they caught a glimpse of a photograph that interested them, they would wait for a break in the crowd and take a closer look.

"I love this one," she said. The scene was an old-fashioned library, an antique writing desk in the center. By virtue of a double exposure, the ceiling gave way to open sky. A man above the desk was walking away into the clouds.

Alice stared. Something in it reminded her of the first time she had changed. She lay in her room reading, waiting for sleep. The usually muffled sounds of her parents' arguing had, as the dusk approached, grown sharper and more distinct, until she could hear each word, her mother's persistent muttered accusations, her father's slurred but strident defense. She went to the window and opened it. The smell of the approaching summer night filled the room. She pried the screen loose with a rattail comb and climbed through, dropping barefoot to the dirt. She walked down to the woods, slipped her gown over her head, and let it drop. She lay on the ground, and the wolf came to her, suddenly, like a car wreck, a jolt that changed everything. She felt calm and still, not really frightened, waiting to see if she would survive. The senses were slow and subtle. Flesh and bone were quick and brutal, as her body reshaped itself around her. Before she could think about what was happening to her, she was the wolf. At dawn she awoke in the woods. Each cell of her body ached with fatigue, but she was alive with the excitement of what had come to her. She returned to her room and left the screen undone, for she was sure the wolf would come again. Only then was she frightened, knowing she must keep it hidden from everyone.

"Alice?" It was Erik, still beside her, his arm still around her waist.

She looked up at him, his face full of concern, and she could imagine that somehow, some time, she could tell him what she was and he would understand —that such concern would not be wasted or withered by the truth. She squeezed his waist in gratitude for this fantasy. "I think I'm ready to go home now," she said.

As they drove back to her house, Alice thought, I will not go to bed with him, I will not go to bed with him, I will not go to bed with him. He was telling her about penguins. She pictured them in the ocean, in the desolate wasteland of ice and rock, returning year after year, together, and she winced that she had never found the same nest twice.

"You must be a good teacher," she said, watching his profile as he drove. The light shone on the downy hair round his eye, glinted from the brown of his iris.

"I don't know about that," he said, "but I do love my subject."

"When we studied animals in school, they were

presented as things—like atomic particles. In fact, my teachers made the atomic particles sound more interesting than the animals."

"I know exactly what you mean," he said, an outspread hand in the air. "Somehow we've gotten the idea that to be scientific means we think everything's a machine." A truck cut in front of him, and he hit the brakes. His hand came to rest on the wheel, and his voice was quieter. "I love animals. They're so mysterious. That's why I do what I do." He looked over at her, a sad smile on his face. "But I know people who don't even like the animals they study. They just study them, as if the world were their stamp collection and all the animals were stamps."

She looked away from him to the billboards and apartment complexes that lined the freeway, but she was keenly aware of him beside her as they hurtled through the bleak landscape. Something inside her gave way like an ice cliff sheering off. She closed her eyes and put her forehead against the glass.

"Are you all right?" he asked, putting his hand on her shoulder.

She pressed his hand with her own. "I'm fine," she said. She opened her eyes and turned back to face him. "I was just thinking about animals."

They stood in the sunlight as she unlocked the door. He stood behind her, holding the screen, looking down the street at a group of children playing freeze tag. She'd never invited a man into her house before. Even her father had only been here once, when she'd first moved in and he and her mother had brought her a plant. She liked Erik. She wanted him to sit on her sofa and talk with her or eat dinner at her table. She wanted just once to be with a man the way she imagined other women were.

She pushed open the door, and he followed her in. Her house felt cool and safe like dense woods after the unseasonably warm spring day. "I'll put on some music," she said. He sat on the sofa in the same spot he'd occupied before and watched her.

As she sat down beside him, he said, "I'm glad I came over."

"Me too," she said. "Would you like something to drink?"

He was looking at her in a way that was unmistakable. All day they had been trading such looks. That's why he had lingered at her doorway until she'd invited him in. That's why, she admitted to herself, she had, too. She knew she should look away, rise and fetch iced tea, talk about penguins, photographs, God, or anything. But she didn't want to look away. He reached out and touched her cheek, kissed her softly on her cheekbone. She closed her eyes and observed quietly, "We don't know each other," but this was not an objection. Compared with the other men she'd slept with, it wasn't even true.

She laid her hand on his and pressed his palm against her cheek as he continued to kiss her on her eyes and cheeks and mouth. He trembled slightly. She moved her hands to the back of his head and pulled him to her. He slipped his hand under her sweatshirt and began to caress her breasts.

The sofa was too short for lovemaking, and she feared such gentleness might be too delicate to be moved. But she mumbled that they should go to the bedroom, and they walked easily down the hall.

The sheets were cold and clean against her skin. The sunlight through the ivy that hung in strands outside her window cast shadows of leaves and vines twining across his chest and arms. He put his mouth to her breast, and she traced her fingers through the hair at his temples and closed her eyes. He kissed her body, slowly and deliberately, as if each kiss mattered. They made love the same way. She curled up against him and fell asleep.

* * *

Alice awoke slowly at first, relishing her senses as they came to her in the deep shadows of the room, smiling to herself. She looked over at Erik. It was dusk, and murky bands of light lay across his naked body. She started to touch him but wondered what she would say now. She couldn't tell him the truth. He was a scientist, for God's sake, and wouldn't believe her anyway. It was stupid and selfish. She sat up in bed, her fists clenched, as if she wished to strike him. He smiled as his eyes came open, not seeing her clenched fists, looking instead into her eyes.

"Come here," he said quietly.

She lay down beside him, her hands now open and caressing.

"Tell me about yourself," he said.

Her hands, caressing his back, stopped for a moment. She did not want to lie to him, but she wanted somehow to be believed. She thought, I'm certainly the most mysterious animal he's ever encountered. She decided to proceed for now as if he might believe her. Perhaps Luther was right. "I grew up on a farm," she began, leading him to the hidden territory where eventually she might reveal herself completely, though for now, even part of the truth was frightening enough.

Chapter

4

Alice's father, named Robert because his parents were apparently unaware of the inevitability of nicknames, was called Bob White throughout his life. He had been a salesman—sporting goods, insurance, furniture, and, most consistently, real estate. But somewhere along the way he had lost the knack. He still possessed the earnestness that made customers trust him, but he'd lost track of his purpose. The sales pitch degenerated into well-intentioned conversation, and customers found him pleasant but not persuasive.

When Alice was twelve and her father forty-eight, he lost the last in a series of jobs that had required him to sell shoddier and shoddier homes to people who could not afford any better. After years of attempting to persuade unhappy people that buying property would make them happy, Bob White invested all his

54

savings in a farm in southwest Virginia, where he could start a new life free of all the troubles he could no longer face.

He knew nothing about farming but was easily persuaded by a better salesman than himself that because the farm came fully equipped, as if it were a home appliance, he could support his family quite easily from the bounty of its rich soil. He hired a series of "hands" from the neighboring town, young men who knew only a little more about farming than he did, who belonged to Future Farmers because they liked the jackets. Bob White and his hands planted a variety of crops so that they might wither and die from drought or insects or neglect. Some malevolent deity beyond the reach of sincere persuasion seemed to curse each crop in a different way.

But Bob White's affability would not die, though it often required the help of drink. He sat on the porch of the farmhouse and looked out from his hilltop at the fields and the woods beyond and explained to his family how the new seed or equipment or spray would bring success soon enough, as if Mother Nature were a customer who was almost sold. "I love the idea of making my living from the land," he had said when they bought the farm. But it was only the idea that ever visited him. The land lived its own life, quite indifferent to Bob White. His wife and children tended a vegetable garden that kept the family in food. The cash crops succeeded just often enough to drag out Bob White's career as a farmer into a sentence of some seven years ending in bankruptcy. Alice moved back to Richmond when she was eighteen and did not have to witness this final humiliation. Her parents moved back the following year, to be close to her.

After the first year on the farm, Alice's brother, Ted, five years older than Alice, was drafted into the army. He returned home after basic training in high spirits. Alice understood his elation—he had escaped their father's dreams. One month later, while crawling through another farmer's fields, he was blown apart by a land mine. Alice grieved for the loss of her brother. He had been her only companion, exploring the woods around the farm with her as he told her his plans for escape. With Ted gone, she was consigned to this hopeless stretch of land, her mother's bitterness, and her father's boozy optimism.

It was at this time, beneath the first full moon of summer, that she first became a wolf. It was the most joyous event of her young life. On those nights the burden of her life became surprisingly light. Without questioning, as if questioning might steal the gift, she reveled in the monthly freedom of a night in the deep woods that lay beyond the fields, lay beyond the helpless tedium of her life on her father's farm.

The following summer, when Alice was fourteen, the newest hand was hired, a young man home from his first year at the university, full of arrogance for being one of the few college men in his desolate little town. He was quick to assert his authority over Bob White. Whatever task he might be given, he always found something less strenuous closer to the house where he had seen his boss's pretty daughter watching him from the windows as he posed at working.

"You've been watching me," he said to her as she leaned against one of the empty stock pens in the bright morning sun.

She hadn't expected this. She'd hoped to be pursued once she found the courage to venture out into his territory, had already written about it in her diary as if it had actually happened. "I have not," she said, watching as he pried nails from a short, rotten board and spiders scurried away from the claw of his hammer.

He shrugged without looking at her. "I've seen you at the windows." He wrenched a nail free with a screech. "How old are you?"

"Sixteen," she lied. It was the oldest she thought she

could get away with and, according to the conventional wisdom, the youngest a college man would pursue.

He stood with the board in one hand, the hammer
in the other, his arms crooked so that his biceps might
show. He looked down at her. "Your name's Alice,
right?"

"Yes, and you're Dale."

He flashed his teeth, looked over at her window.
"So, you got a boyfriend?"

"No, I don't have a particular boyfriend."

"You just kind of play the field, then, huh?"

She gave the tiniest of nods. "I guess you could say
that." She was having trouble swallowing. She looked
down at his scuffed boots as he stepped to the fence
and rested the board on top of it, tossing the hammer
back into the tool box with a clatter.

"You're real pretty, you know that?"

She stared into his chest. "Thanks," she said quietly.

"Why don't you meet me tonight after supper?"

"What for?" she said.

He laughed, and she looked up at him. "What's so
funny?"

Still laughing, he tapped the board on top of the
fence. "Nothing," he said, "nothing at all." He leaned
toward her, spoke quietly. "We can go for a walk."

She looked bravely into his eyes. "I'll try to get
away."

He straightened up, smiled, pointed the board at
her. "Don't keep me waiting." He rested the board on
his shoulder and walked away. When he was almost to
the barn he spun around and walked backward,
pointing a thumb into the darkness. "On the other
side of the barn," he called, and disappeared into the
shadows.

She lay on her bed in the hot afternoon, tracing her
fingers nub by nub across the chenille bedspread. The

window was open, but the curtains barely stirred. An oscillating fan on the dresser brushed back and forth across her legs.

She wondered what he would say to her tonight behind the barn. In her fantasies he hadn't had a voice, only words, like a character in a novel.

Her mother was talking to her father in the kitchen. The squash was being eaten up, did he have any Sevin dust? He couldn't quite remember, maybe in the barn. Alice sniffed the hot air drifting in through the window.

She sat up in bed and looked at her calendar. Over June, a unicorn in a blue landscape gazed at its reflection in a pool. She looked back to May and found a tiny x in the corner of one of the days and began to count. But she already knew the answer. She could hear the fan roaring like an airplane. She walked over, turned it off, and leaned on the windowsill, looking out into the baked yard. She would change tonight. She couldn't meet him.

She turned her back on the yard and walked to her dresser, staring at herself in the mirror. How could she be so stupid? She should have kept better track. Now he would think she didn't like him or was scared like some little girl who couldn't go out after dark. That would be it. He wouldn't have any more to do with her.

The top of the dresser was covered with her unicorn collection—all shapes and sizes and colors in glass and fabric and plastic and wood. She glared at them with loathing. Uncle Ed's wife, Jan, the one with the voice like Glinda the Good, had given her a unicorn for her sixth birthday, then another the next Christmas. She'd had to keep them out. They were gifts. Before she knew it and with no encouragement from her, it had become her unicorn collection. Now cousins she'd never met sent them for birthdays and Christmas. "Oh, she has a unicorn collection," they said to one another, "she'll love this." They had no idea who she was or what she loved.

She opened the top drawer and raked the unicorns into it, shoving them to the back behind the baggy underwear she never wore, and slammed the drawer shut.

She looked back to her reflection, demanding more than helplessness. It would still be light after supper. She wouldn't change until after dark. Usually she just locked her door and opened her window. Her parents never cared. They were too busy fighting anyway. She could just meet him and tell him she had chores but would come tomorrow night for sure.

She saw her father crossing the yard, headed toward the barn, apparently looking for the Sevin dust. It was there all right. She could smell it.

Supper was eaten from trays around the snowy ghosts on the TV screen. The only other light in the room was a ceramic panther on top of the TV with a light bulb in its hollow side. "I thought you liked this show," her mother said when Alice rose to leave them. On the screen, three men pretended to be the same man while indistinguishable minor celebrities wittily interrogated them to find out the truth. "It's stupid," Alice said.

Her mother pursed her lips. "You seem to think everything is stupid these days."

Alice's father laughed. "It's supposed to be stupid, Alice. That's why people get a kick out it. Do you think I care which one of these guys is a big-game hunter?"

"No, Daddy." She leaned against the back of her father's chair and put her hands on his chest. "Can I please go now?"

"Suit yourself." He patted her hands. "But I won't tell you which one it was."

"It's the creep with the skinny mustache," she said

as she took the remains of her TV dinner to the kitchen. On her way out the back door, she could hear her mother complaining that he spoiled her rotten. What a laugh, she thought, stuck on this stupid farm.

Outside, the sky was just beginning to turn with the setting sun. She calculated she had at least an hour before dark. The barn was east of the house; the woods, east of the barn at the bottom of the hill. She stood by the dark coolness of the barn and looked into the woods, already deep in shadow. In the heavy, hot air lightning bugs flashed in the twilight.

What if he doesn't come? she thought. What does he want with me, anyway? She looked down at her body, skinny and flat. He couldn't possibly believe I'm sixteen. He was just having fun with me, teasing the boss's kid.

She kicked a stone and watched it arc into the shadows. She looked through the cool dark tunnel of the barn at the setting sun. A blaze of deep red and purple rested on the horizon. It would be dark sooner than she'd thought.

A light breeze gusted through the barn, and she caught his smell. She searched the shadows and found him at the other end of the barn, standing in the corner. She walked the length of the barn in long, angry strides. She stopped a couple of yards in front of him, her arms wrapped around her chest.

"Jesus, you got eyes like a fuckin' cat," he said.

"So what are you doing here? You said to meet you over there. Were you just going to stand here and see how long I would wait?"

He stepped into the pale light, his hands up. "Hey, don't get all bent out of shape, okay? I was just waiting until it got a little darker. Your old man might not exactly approve of this little rendezvous."

"I can't stay," she said.

He took another step forward, smiled at her. "Come on, don't be mad."

"I'm not mad, really. I've got chores to do. I'll meet you tomorrow night for sure."

He didn't speak for a while. He looked at the house where the gray light of the television glowed in the living room window. "What kind of chores you got to do at night?"

"I've got to wash dishes."

He laughed softly. "You washing up those little aluminum pans these days? At my house, we just throw them away."

He took a pack of cigarettes from his pants pocket, lit one, and held them out to her. "You got time for a cigarette, don't you?"

"I guess so." As he lit her cigarette, she bent forward, holding her hair in one hand as she'd seen Lauren Bacall do in the movies. She blew out the smoke in a cloud over her head. She looked at the house and saw a faint star just above the roof. "I've really got to go," she said.

He flipped his cigarette into the yard. It landed in a shower of sparks. "If you don't like me, why don't you just fuckin' say so."

"It's not that, really. I do like you. I like you a lot. I just can't stay."

He stepped up to her and plucked the cigarette from her hand. He dropped it to the ground and crushed it under his heel, smiling at her.

"Nobody's asking you to stay all night," he said, and cupped his hands behind her head. He pulled, and she stumbled into him. She returned his kiss and clung to him. She thought she would cry. She had dreamed about kissing him. It wasn't fair that it should happen tonight.

He led her to the corner of the barn and lay down on some hay, pulling her down on top of him. "Please," she said, "I have to go. I promise I'll come back tomorrow."

"Tomorrow sounds good, too, but let's take care of tonight first."

His arms were locked around her. She pushed at his chest, and he rolled over on top of her. "Please let me go," she said. He smiled down at her, holding her with one arm as he unzipped her jeans. She got a hand free and struck at his face. "Stop it!" she screamed.

A dark shape swept down at her, and she felt the back of his fist thud against her cheekbone.

"Shut the fuck up," he hissed.

She became perfectly still. The pain in her cheek dissolved and flowed into her limbs. She could feel the wolf coming. She'd never tried to stop it before, wasn't sure if she could. He held her pinned as he struggled with his own jeans. His eyes were faint glints of light above her. She closed her eyes, shuddered, and changed.

The wolf opens her eyes and fixes them on his. His eyes are wide with fear, but he does not look away. She bares her teeth in warning. He does not back away. With a quick lunge she fastens her jaws around his throat and tears it open with a single wrenching movement.

In the morning, she lay on her bed and confessed first to her parents, then to the sheriff, to her doctor, and finally to the psychiatrist brought in from the city. She told them everything. To her parents, to whom she had lied for over a year, she described her life as a werewolf in precise detail. "Look at the calendar," she told them. "Every time you see a little x, that's when I've changed."

Her father paced up and down the room, checking his watch, as her mother sat on the edge of the bed and told her all of this could wait for the doctor, and for now she should rest.

After he took her temperature, the doctor spent little time with her but said he had a psychiatrist friend nearby who might be persuaded to come. Her parents looked terrified. She did not know what to say.

Alice could never quite remember what she said to

the psychiatrist. All she could remember was that he remained so calm and reasonable, nodding his head in the most reassuring way, until finally she realized he would never believe her, that he thought she was crazy. It was even his job to think she was crazy.

She let her voice trail off in the middle of describing how her transformation made her feel. "Could I please see my mom and dad?" she asked.

He let them into the room, and they sat on the bed, her father at the end and her mother beside her.

"She's had a terrible shock," the psychiatrist said. "Add to that the feelings of guilt such an attack often precipitates, and a delusion of the sort she is experiencing is not at all unheard of."

"Will it go away?" her father asked. Her mother squeezed her hand but did not look at her.

The psychiatrist smiled, tolerant of foolish questions. "That's difficult to say, but I should think, after a few weeks' treatment, she should be fine. They're very resilient at this age."

All three of them turned to Alice and smiled at her as if she had just entered the room.

The official report gave the cause of the boy's death as a fatal wound from the attack of some animal, possibly a large dog, as the victim was apparently attempting to rape Alice White. The dog was not located. No charges were filed.

In the weeks that followed, Alice responded to treatment so that she was released from the mental hospital less than a month later by a trio of psychiatrists whose condescending smiles, Alice noticed, bore a remarkable resemblance to those of the boy she had killed.

It was this story that Alice told Erik, leaving out the impossibility that she was a werewolf and the aftermath in the mental hospital, inventing a knife with which she'd slit the boy's throat in the struggle.

They lay in the dim twilight. Outside, mourning

doves called to one another. He'd listened quietly, propped up on one arm as she'd stared straight ahead and told her story as honestly as she could. But it wasn't enough. She couldn't tell him enough. She began to cry, and he took her in his arms and rocked her back and forth. "I killed him," she said over and over.

"He tried to rape you," he said.

"I am a monster," she said.

But he continued to soothe her, kissing her on top of the head. "Don't be silly," he told her.

She could not tell him how the boy looked in the morning, covered with congealed blood, his throat torn away, flies thick upon the wound. She wanted to, but she could not bring herself to tell him.

Chapter

5

Alice heard the clank of a plate from the kitchen and smelled coffee. She opened her eyes and rolled her head on the pillow. Erik wasn't in bed. He must be in the kitchen. She pulled herself to the edge of the bed and peered over. Her clothes were scattered out of reach. The dishes were gone, and the wine bottles. The clock said ten o'clock.

She pulled herself upright using the bars of her brass bed. Her palms smelled of brass. She remembered her hands wrapped hard around the bars last night and smiled to herself. She pulled her hair up off her neck and rested her forehead on her knees. How many bottles of wine had they drunk? Three. She'd had two, and he'd gotten one from next door, plus a joint, plus some ice cream for dessert. They'd eaten dinner sitting in bed.

They'd talked, made love, made dinner, talked, made love. Somewhere in there had been ice cream. She winced, remembering she'd told him about Adams. She'd made it sound as though she were only seeing him because of—what was Adams's phrase?— "the fear of intimacy in her relationships."

"Are you afraid of me?" he'd asked.

She'd told him no, but now wondered if that was the truth. She was afraid, but not *of* him. She was afraid that now he might go away, the way she always did, even with the men she'd liked and who wanted her to stay.

She'd asked him a little about his marriage, his divorce. He didn't seem to mind talking about it as much as she minded hearing about it. She'd had other men talk about wives and ex-wives before, and sometimes it was boring and sometimes it was interesting, depending on the man; and as long as they were talking about someone else, they didn't ask too many questions about her. But she didn't like to think about Erik belonging to someone else who still had the power to make him hurt so. According to the magazines in doctors' offices and Laundromats, recently divorced men were a bad risk, but, she thought, he'd have to be pretty dreadful to be a worse risk than me.

She swung her legs over the side of the bed and stood. The sheets were a rumpled mess. She never knew making love could be so loving. She always thought the phrase itself a sad euphemism for people too delicate to say "fuck." Not that she and Erik hadn't fucked. She smiled to herself. They'd done that all right.

And now he was in her kitchen. He hadn't fled; she hadn't driven him away. She went into the bathroom, scrubbed her face with cold water, and brushed at the tangles in her hair. She looked at herself in the mirror. Her hair hung down in waves where it had been twisted into a braid. She wanted him. She didn't care if it was impossible. She was impossible herself. She wanted him anyway. She just didn't want to think about it. She was tired of thinking so much.

He called to her from the bedroom in a phony French accent, "Where are you, my darling? Where have you fled, my little desert flower?" She laughed. He was imitating Pepe le Pew again. Last night they'd wrestled in bed, pretending to be animals from a cartoon.

She stepped into the bedroom, and he grinned. "You are a vision of loveliness," he said. "I have made for us, how you say? Le breakfast in bed. I see you have dressed for the occasion, no?" He held a tray of food in each hand. He nodded toward the bed. "Allow me to serve you."

She slipped into bed. He placed a tray in her lap and kissed her. He'd made Spanish omelets, coffee, and toast. He propped himself up beside her.

"Eat," he said.

"You forgot the cream and sugar for the coffee."

"Suffer."

They ate quietly for a while, the tines of the forks clicking on the plates. She didn't know what to say to him. She'd never done this before. She knew how to chase him away, how to make him feel there'd been some drunken misunderstanding and now it was over. But she didn't know how to just wait to see what would happen next. Nothing was ever supposed to happen next before.

"This is delicious," she said. "How did you make this sauce?"

"I got it next door. I made jars and jars of it last summer just before Debra and I broke up, so I took it with me when I moved out."

"And she got the television?"

"Something like that."

Alice took another bite, savoring the spicy sauce as tears came to her eyes.

"Is it too hot?" he asked.

"No, I like it." She picked up a piece of toast and

looked at it. "You shouldn't have gone to all this trouble," she said.

"No trouble. I always get up early. I love to cook. When Debra and I were together, I did nearly all the cooking."

Alice imagined them seated at a small table, talking and laughing. She pictured Debra as slim and long-legged, running her foot up and down the back of Erik's calf. "Did you make her breakfast in bed?" she asked.

He didn't notice that she'd stopped eating. He was cheerful and animated, only slightly nervous. Unlike me, he's done this before, she thought.

"I used to make her breakfast in bed," he was saying, "until she started working weekends all the time."

"You told me last night she worked all the time. Just what is it she does?"

He shifted slightly, leaning his head back against the wall. "She's a museum director, at the Grier Museum. She's quite good at it. She knows how to run things. No matter what shit goes wrong, she's calm while everyone else is freaking out, then one by one she tells them what to do, and they do it, and everything's okay again. It's incredible. Only I know that underneath all that efficiency she's a seething mass of insecurity."

Alice preferred the Debra she'd constructed in her mind the night before—a cold, unreachable workaholic. This new one was more complicated and frightened her.

"Is she attractive?" she said.

"Very."

"So what you're saying is that you two split up because you're both such wonderful, attractive people?"

He laughed and looked at her. "Thanks. I'm glad you think I'm wonderful and attractive."

She turned and looked into his eyes. "I would've

thought that was obvious." They leaned toward each other and kissed, awkwardly balancing their food in front of them. "Let's get these out of the way," he said, and put their trays on the floor.

He held her in his arms and kissed her. He smiled at her. "I think you're wonderful and attractive, too."

"Do you really?" she asked.

He looked into her eyes. "Really."

She looked away. "It's just that you just split up with your wife. I thought this might be kind of sudden for you. I mean, you still talk about her all the time. Everything's 'before Debra' and 'after Debra.' It's like the fucking birth of Christ or something."

She was afraid he would be angry, but he turned her face toward him with his fingertips. His face was kind. He spoke softly. "Tomorrow morning Debra and I will be divorced, and frankly, I'll be relieved. I don't want to be married to Debra anymore. It was good once, and then it went bad. We caused each other a whole lot of pain, and now I think it's time to end it and move on. And there is no place in the world I'd rather be than with you right now. Okay?"

She smiled and nodded. "Okay. I'm sorry if I was a bitch."

"You weren't a bitch. I shouldn't have brought up Debra every five minutes."

"I've never gotten jealous before. I didn't like the way it felt. I thought I was going to jump out of my skin."

He cocked his head to one side. "You've never gotten jealous before? Not just a little?"

"Oh, I've been jealous, I guess. But that was different. I've been jealous because other women have boyfriends and husbands and children and a life I've never had. But that's all general. I've never been jealous of one woman because of one man. I've never done this before."

"You mean you've never been involved with anyone ever?"

She shook her head. "I've never had a boyfriend. I've never dated. I've never spent more than one night with a man in my life. Never."

"Why not?"

She hadn't expected to have to deal with this so soon. She had decided to take a chance with Erik, to jump in with both feet, as her father would say. Now she had the sensation of falling. She lay back and closed her eyes. "I can't tell you," she said. "Not yet."

"Is it because of that boy who tried to rape you?"

"That's part of it, but it's more than that. It's something about who I am. It's kind of complicated." She opened her eyes and looked into his. "It's not that I don't trust you. It's something real hard for me to talk about. I promise I'll tell you when I'm ready, okay?"

He said nothing for a moment. He seemed to be studying her face. "Okay," he said. "I don't need to know everything about you today or next week. I'm willing to take my time."

She pulled him to her and kissed him tenderly, then passionately. They made love. Afterward they lay quietly, his head on her chest. She liked his weight upon her. The rise and fall of his breathing was the only sound. She made figure-eights on his back with her fingertips.

"Is there anything you'd like to know about me?" he said.

"Everything," she said.

He laughed and propped himself up on one arm. "Okay. You want me to start with conception or skip right to birth?"

"Tell me about your dad."

"He's great. He's the one who taught me to cook. When I was a kid, he got up early and fixed breakfast, and I'd stroll in wearing a hat and six guns—I was a cowboy most of the time in those days. He played the saloon keeper, gave me milk in a shot glass, hammered

70

it up with lots of podnuhs and yups and nopes. Then he set me up on a step stool and showed me how to fry the bacon or make pancakes. I loved it."

"You must've been cute."

"So I'm told. What about you? What kind of kid were you?"

"Up to about ten I was a fairy princess. Then I started reading science fiction and became an astronaut. I used to sit in my father's car. He was a ham operator, and we had a shortwave in the car. I'd tune it in to the weirdest foreign-language transmission I could find and pretend I was going to Alpha Centauri." She held an imaginary microphone in front of her mouth and spoke in a deep voice. "This is Astronaut Alice White requesting permission to land on your planet." She hung up the microphone. "One time my dad caught me. I was lost in my own little world, screaming and hollering about asteroids and aliens, when I look up and there he is, looking in the window at me. I was afraid he'd be mad. Instead he just said, 'With all these asteroids in the neighborhood, you'd better put on your seat belt,' and walked out of the garage."

"Your dad sounds a lot like mine." He put his arms around her and pulled her on top of him. "You are the sexiest astronaut I've ever seen."

She kissed his chest and laid her head down. "I'm glad you think so." She ran her fingers through the hair on his chest. "I think *you* are very sexy."

They lay quietly. His hand caressed her thigh, her hips, the small of her back. She felt weightless, contented. Her mind wandered into a future filled with such moments. She wanted that future, wished to reach out and seize it. She opened her eyes and watched his hand moving across her skin. "Erik?"

"Hmm?"

"Can I ask you something?"

"Sure."

"Why did you and Debra break up?"

His hand stopped. He gestured with it as he spoke. "Well, we both changed a lot. She became more conventional. More and more she wanted, I don't know, the usual things that people want, a good job, stability, the creature comforts, I think they're called."

"And you didn't?"

"Well, I'm not saying that. She just wanted them more."

She put her hands on his chest and propped her chin upon them. She smiled at him. "So what was the problem?"

He grinned. "Are you always like this?"

"I'm sorry, I just thought there must be more to it, you know? It's none of my business, really."

"Sure it's your business. And there is more to it, though I usually don't admit it. To be honest, I didn't mind her wanting those things or status or career or whatever else she wanted. I just wanted her to want me a little more. That's why I left her to begin with, to get her attention." He shrugged. "Then I wasn't sure what I wanted to do with it when I got it."

"And what about her? What did she want?"

"For the last seven months, at least, a divorce. Before that, I don't know. I don't know if she knows."

"I like you, Erik," she said. "I like you a lot." She ran the back of her hand along his beard. "I know I want you."

"I like you a lot, too," he said. "I've really enjoyed yesterday and last night and this morning."

"Not me. I always scream like that."

"Me too."

He smiled and touched her cheek. "Can I ask you something?"

She nodded.

"Why me? Did I just sort of come along at the right time?"

She thought about this. "Sort of. I mean, if I'd met you a year ago, I wouldn't have been ready for this. But it's more than that. I trust you in a way I've never trusted anyone else."

"You mean, when you met me?"

"I liked you then, but it was when I saw you that night. You were sitting on your porch, and I was getting something out of the car."

"You're kidding. I thought I hadn't made any impression at all."

"That just shows you how wrong you can be." She rolled off him and looked at the clock on the bedside table. "Jesus, Erik, I have to be at my parents' in an hour."

"Does that mean I should go home?"

"Would you like to go with me?"

"To meet your parents? Sure."

"You don't have to."

He smiled at her. "I want to. What's more, I want you to meet my dad on Wednesday. I'm going over there for dinner."

"Are you sure it will be all right?"

"The only women I've ever known my dad not to like are Margaret Thatcher and Debra. He will be delighted."

"Will he like me?"

"My dad, are you kidding? He'll go crazy over you. What about your folks, won't this be kind of sudden for them?"

She laughed. "Erik, my parents have been waiting for this all their life, some sign that their daughter is normal. They'll have to live with sudden."

"Will they like me?"

"My dad will. I don't know about my mom. You might be another anxiety for her collection."

"You're forgetting: we've already met. I like your mom. She's just worried about her little girl."

"Maybe." She sat up in bed, looking down at her

sweaty body. "Right now her little girl needs to take a bath. I can't go to my parents smelling like this."

He nuzzled his cheek against her stomach. "I like the way you smell."

"I guess so, since I smell like you."

"You smell like you, too. I like it."

"What does he do for a living, Alice?" Alice's mother asked her as they stood in her mother's kitchen preparing coffee for "the men," Erik and her father, who were struggling with their own conversation in the living room. It was Alice's father's sixty-eighth birthday, and they'd already made it through dinner and birthday cake with her mother uncharacteristically silent, stealing nervous glances at Erik whenever she could.

"He teaches biology at the university, Mother."

"He told your father he was interested in penguins. That seems like an odd interest for a grown man. Alice, don't use those; use the good china. He couldn't be making much money just studying penguins."

Alice took down the "good china," layered with dust. She loathed it. It had belonged to her grandmother. She supposed that as a young woman her mother had loathed this china as well. Now it was a family tradition, an uninspired wedding present of seventy years ago lingering on to haunt them with its murky pink flowers and gilt edges. If I were finally to throw this stuff to the floor, Alice thought, maybe we could be just two women in a kitchen, talking. "He makes quite enough money, Mother. He teaches several different courses."

"I wouldn't think there'd be much interest in penguins," Alice's mother said as she walked across the kitchen to get the milk from the refrigerator, setting it beside the creamer for Alice to pour. She leaned her back against the counter where Alice worked so that she might look her in the face. "Practical things aren't

74

as interesting, I suppose, but we can't always do what we want in this world, you know. Look at your poor father."

Alice stared down into the tray, now ready for presentation to the men in the living room. "I don't want to fight with you today, Mother. Erik is a wonderful man. I thought you would be happy—you are always trying to fix me up, always telling me to get out more. Now I have a 'fellow,' okay? So you're supposed to be happy."

"It's just that we don't know anything about him, dear."

"I'll have him send you a résumé."

"There is no need to be sassy." She looked at the refrigerator as if for understanding.

"I'm sorry, Mother. I just wanted you to be happy for me instead of cross-examining me."

"'Cross-examining' you? I don't know where you get these ideas. I'm just concerned about you." She put her hand on Alice's and looked concerned. "Are you pregnant, dear?"

Alice looked from the hand to the face and smiled at it. "No, Mother, I use birth control." She picked up the tray and made for the living room, her mother trailing behind her awkwardly. It was the closest Alice had ever come to throwing the good china to the floor.

Erik and her father seemed to have been talking about the farm. Her father was quite cheery. "I was just telling Rick about the time the raccoon got into the house and you were so frightened."

"Bob, Alice wasn't even living at the farm anymore when that happened, and Alice's friend's name is Erik, not Rick," said Alice's mother. She turned to Erik. "You'll have to forgive Mr. White—he doesn't remember things too well." She spoke as if Mr. White were not present.

While Mr. White looked down into his lap for a

moment, Erik spoke to Mrs. White. "I get called 'Rick' often; it's a common mistake. It doesn't bother me."

"Is it a family name?" Mrs. White asked, making conversation, searching for clues.

"No, I'm named after Erik the Red. My father likes old sagas and legends."

Mr. White leaned forward on his chair. "He discovered Iceland, didn't he?"

"Yes, he did."

Mr. White smiled at his wife, proud of himself. "I read about that when I was a boy."

"When did you and Alice actually meet?" Mrs. White asked. "Erik lives next door to Alice," she explained to Mr. White, who had already been told this.

"Just a few days ago," Erik said cheerfully, sensing the direction the conversation was to take, preparing his defense.

"Well, you certainly seem to have gotten to know one another in a hurry," said Mrs. White. "Bob and I have known each other since we were children."

Alice started to intervene to save Erik, but he had already spoken. "How did you and Mr. White meet?" he asked.

Mrs. White laughed and smoothed her skirt, looking down at it as if the secrets of her past could be found in its pattern of trim flowers and strangely docile wild beasts. "You don't want to hear about that."

"Oh, but I do," said Erik. He leaned forward on his chair, his elbows resting on his thighs.

She became girlish, cocking her head to one side and smoothing back her hair. "Alice has heard this before, of course, but she can stand to hear it again." Alice only smiled, enjoying this conspiracy between her lover and her mother. Besides, she liked the story and the effect it always had on her parents. She settled back onto her chair as her mother began, watching Erik hear the story she already knew.

"Well, we were just kids. We lived in Denver then. My sister and I had a little playhouse in the backyard. It was just an old storage shed, actually, that my father let us fix up. We put up curtains—silly things, really, that my mother had thrown away. She was always throwing things away. They had huge roses on them, I remember. And we had a little miniature tea set we'd play with for hours. We even had pictures from magazines on the walls we said were paintings." She paused, smiling at her own silliness. She put her hand to her mouth and gave a little shrug.

"Well, one day we were in the playhouse, and a group of boys started throwing rocks from the alley. Bob was one of those boys." She smiled at him, and he looked quite pleased with himself. "There must have been at least five or six of them because the rocks made a terrible racket. We, my sister and I, kicked up a terrible fuss, of course, but really we thought it was great fun. I think we were probably getting a little too old for playing tea anyway. My sister, she was always a bit of a tomboy, wanted to throw rocks back, but I told her not to because that would only encourage them. Just then one of the rocks came through the window and landed right in the middle of the tea set. It was a lump of coal, I remember, and it made a terrible mess. Well, we started yelling for our father then, and the boys ran off. All of them, that is, except Bob. He was so sweet. He came up to the playhouse, afraid he'd hurt one of us, I think, and apologized for what they'd done and even helped clean up. Of course, I was a bit huffy at first, but he was so sweet I couldn't stay mad at him. When we'd cleaned up the mess, we went to the park. My mother made us take my sister."

"We always had to take her sister," Mr. White said. "She even sat between us at the movies."

Mrs. White smiled. "Now, Bob, that isn't entirely

true. We did manage to be alone sometimes." Bob smiled back, his eyes gleaming.

Erik said, "That's a wonderful story, Mrs. White."

"Oh, call me Ruth."

"How long have you been married now?" Erik asked.

Bob answered proudly, "Forty-five happy years."

"It's forty-six, dear," said Ruth, but added, "Forty-six happy years."

"I wish I had met Alice when she was young," said Erik.

Ruth was pleased. "You still have plenty of time," she said. "You might not have liked her so well when she was little."

"He doesn't need to hear any childhood stories, Mother," Alice said.

"Sure he does, don't you, Erik?"

Erik held up his hands. "I remain neutral."

"Well, sometime when Alice isn't around, I'll tell you all about her."

Bob leaned forward. "She was quite a tomboy."

"Dad," said Alice.

"I understand you know all about penguins," Ruth said. "I'd love to hear about them."

Erik told them about penguins. Bob was particularly intrigued by the jackass penguin, whose call sounds like the bray of a donkey. "Isn't that interesting," he said, and was saddened to hear that their habitats were threatened.

On the way home, Alice imagined her parents as if in a shimmering sphere, like the glass balls full of falling snow, with a gentle snowlike shower of rocks falling harmlessly around them forever. "You are amazing," she said to Erik.

"What do you mean?"

"The way you won over my parents like that."

"They're nice, I like them."

"They're not always so nice."

"No one is."

"They used to fight all the time when we lived on the farm."

"They seem to get along okay now—they've stayed together all these years."

"I know. It amazes me." She laughed. "You sure had them going with your penguins."

He sighed. "I have a confession to make. Sometimes I wish I'd never heard of penguins. Not to study, anyway. Every month I read everything that's been done on penguins and shuffle around a few ideas and try to find something to say." He looked over at her. "And I've never even seen one in the wild." He braked for a stoplight and kept his eyes on it. "I use blood samples from Sea World—God, what a depressing place that is, a palace of cuteness—then I turn them into charts and tables and equations. My articles bore *me*. They must be death to anyone else."

"Is that why you haven't done any field research, because you didn't want to leave Debra?"

"After Debra and I split up—A.D., I guess I should say—I thought at first I'd go out there. Then some friends of mine in Florida—a man-and-wife penguin team—called me up after they heard about my separation and asked me to go with them to Antarctica for the spring. They'd already lined up the money. They were sure I'd jump at it since I always made it sound like it was just my marriage that kept me here." He smiled sadly. "I told them no."

"Why?"

"I was scared," he said. "I didn't know if I could handle being an Antarctic hermit. The penguins might know exactly where they were, but I was afraid I wouldn't know where in hell I was."

"Do you know where you are now?"

"Robinson and Grove."

"Come on, you know what I mean."

The light changed, and they started moving again.

He looked over at her. "I'm here with you, and I'd like to spend the night with you again. Unless you need some time alone."

She almost laughed. "I've had enough time alone to last me for a long, long time. I was hoping you would stay with me tonight. I have to go to work tomorrow."

After dinner and lovemaking they lay in bed in the darkness. Alice stared at the ceiling, happy and frightened. "Are you awake?" she whispered.

"Yes."

"When is your divorce final tomorrow?"

"Debra goes to court at ten."

"Do you feel sad?"

"A little, but mostly I feel relieved." He pulled her to him. "When do you get home from work? I'll fix you dinner at my place."

She squeezed him in her arms as hard as she could. "I'd love to," she said. "I'll be home by six."

They lay entwined as she thought of seeing him day after day. Then she thought to ask him if he needed to spend some time alone and whispered the question into the darkness. But he had already fallen asleep.

Chapter

6

At two o'clock, Alice was still awake. Erik lay like a shadowy ridge beside her. Most of his face was in shadow, though the silver in his beard shone with moonlight. She wanted to reach out, take his shoulder, rock him awake. She wanted to tell him she'd never felt this way before, but she knew he wouldn't believe her. Her life was unbelievable, even to herself. She'd never acted on her strongest feelings, ran from those she most desired. She'd changed jobs twice because of men. Once because of a boss who didn't ask her to work late, didn't make a show of her birthday, didn't treat her different in any way, except that his eyes lingered on her and his smiles were sad and affectionate. She left another job because of the man who brought the food cart each morning and at lunch, then sat on the edge of her desk and flirted, as she flirted back.

So what am I doing now? she thought. She looked over at Erik. This is the man I woke up with this morning and will wake up with tomorrow, if I ever get to sleep. She found his shirt on the floor and took one of his cigarettes. She walked into the living room and brought back the ashtray and set it on the bedside table. She watched him a moment in the match glow, the light flickering along his back. She untangled the sheets and covered him. It had grown chilly, but for now she liked the cold against her skin. She propped herself up in bed, watching herself smoke in the dresser mirror.

She often had trouble sleeping during the early waning of the moon. She lay awake thinking and remembering. Just before she started seeing Luther, she'd thought for a week about killing herself—different ways, like drowning or feeding poisoned meat to the wolf—studying the ache that made her want to die, never quite sure where it came from, sure it would never go away. She had decided to get a book on poisons from the library, but when she'd reached for the phone book in the morning to call the library about its hours, she'd called a doctor from the Yellow Pages instead. She'd chosen him because his name, Kevin Dougherty, had somehow appealed to her, though almost immediately he'd passed her on to Luther.

She'd sworn she'd never go to another shrink after the ones in the hospital. But then she'd made lots of plans and sworn to many things that now seemed stupid and impossible. At fourteen, during the two weeks at the mental hospital, she'd planned out the rest of her life.

When she first arrived there, she forced herself to be calm and made a point of appearing to sleep nights. In the day room, watching the other patients shuffling or being led through their drugged days, she made her plans: she would move back to Richmond when she turned eighteen and get a house with a basement. Her brother had had a life insurance policy for $100,000, and she'd been the beneficiary. It was hers when she turned eighteen. Her parents intended her for college, but she knew if she dug in her heels, she would get her way. She could buy a house, and get a job, and never kill anyone again.

Sometimes she imagined what the doctors would do to her if she stayed in the hospital until the next moon, and the wolf skittered up and down those tile halls before their very eyes. Kill her, most likely, or try to, and then she would kill them. She was reasonably sure they would dissect her, eventually. They would have to. They would have to figure her out. Even when one of them sat down beside her in the dayroom or came to her room and made small talk, it was as if they listened to her words with a stethoscope, looking for signs. She imagined them debating her diagnosis over coffee in the staff lounge, where often their voices spilled out into the halls as if the patients walking past couldn't hear them or wouldn't care if they did.

In the city, no one would notice if she kept to herself. Her mother used to tell her when they lived on the farm: "In the city no one knows you; here, everyone does." She vowed to stay alone. She couldn't tell anyone what she was, what she'd done. No one would believe her, anyway. She supposed that she might want men, but in the city, unless all the books and movies lied, she could find them, and lose them just as easily, and never have to see them again.

But she couldn't go to the city at fourteen. She couldn't go anywhere. What was she to do with the wolf for four years—she calculated in her head— fifty-two moons? When everything else was worked out, there was still that. She stayed in her room and worried over it.

Her room was six by eight feet. It had a bed, a sink, a toilet. On the wall above the sink where a mirror should have been was a landscape print of a high meadow with a stream. The greens were too green, the blues were too blue, and the whole thing gleamed like Naugahyde.

She would have to imprison the wolf somehow.

She lay in her bed and traveled in a widening circle around the farm, looking for a place. On the second day of her search, she found it. She spent another going through it in her mind to make sure it would work, or at least be safe. The next day she smiled at the young, shy doctor and asked if she might see her father and mother. By the end of the week her father came for her. As they filled out the forms, everyone smiled: it had just been shock, she was over it now.

Two weeks later, the first full moon, she told her parents she was going to a slumber party at a friend's in town who would pick her up down by the road. She walked out of sight of the house and doubled back into the woods. Two fences beyond was an old brick building, hunched under ivy.

The roof, the windows, the doors, were gone. Only the walls, two feet thick, and a huge incinerator still stood. She opened the heavy metal door of the incinerator and crawled inside. It still smelled of ashes. Broken beer bottles glinted in the deep soot. She shone her flashlight up the chimney and climbed the iron rungs set into the brick. They were cold and rough, and her hands came away black, but they didn't budge as she climbed to the top of the broken chimney and onto the top of the wall beside it.

From here she could just see over the trees to her house on the top of the next hill. She walked along the top of the wall to a maple at the corner of the building. She stepped into the crown of the tree and walked along a broad limb to the trunk where the boards her brother had nailed two years before were still there and creaked only slightly beneath her weight. She climbed down, went inside the building, and fastened the heavy padlock on the hasp of the iron door. She put the key in her pocket, climbed up the tree, across the wall, and down the chimney.

She took off her clothes and lay on her back in the soft soot, watching the sky turn dark. When the first star appeared, she saw it through a blur of tears. She wondered just before she changed whether the wolf would feel saved or betrayed. They seemed to meet for a moment, Alice and the wolf, and each knew the other was frightened and alone.

When she went back to school in the fall, at first everyone kept their distance, except for Willoughby. Willoughby was actually Alexis Willoughby, but everyone called her Willoughby. She was tall and had enormous hands she kept in her pockets. Her large, frank eyes startled most everyone. Her hair frizzed round her head like a cloud of red smoke. Her forehead was high and freckled, and her cheekbones would have been the envy of all the cheerleaders if one of them had looked close enough to notice.

She came up beside Alice in the bathroom between classes and talked to her in the mirror as she brushed her wiry red hair. "I knew Dale," she said. "He was friends with my big brother." She put a brass barrette between her teeth and pulled back her hair. She caught Alice's eye. "He took me to the lake once in his car." She took the barrette from her mouth and clamped it around her hair, looking now into her own eyes. "He raped me," she said. She looked back to Alice. "I'm glad you killed him, Alice, I'm glad he's dead."

"I didn't kill him," Alice said.

Willoughby shrugged. "I'm still glad he's dead."

After that, in spite of the resolves she'd made in the hospital, Willoughby became her friend.

Now, she put out her cigarette and curled up against Erik, inhaling the smell of his skin, listening to the sound of his breathing like the ocean at a great distance. She'd never been able to tell Willoughby the truth. Alice waited for her friend to accept her oddness, so she would feel safe enough to confess what she was. But Willoughby could never leave it alone. By the time they were juniors in high school and had been friends for two years, Alice's isolation from everyone but Willoughby and the necessary adults had become a cause for Willoughby, especially where boys were concerned:

"Dammit, Alice. Go out with anybody. You don't have to like them. You don't have to fuck them. You don't even have to talk with them, if you don't want to." They were sitting in the loft of the barn the August before their senior year. Only a few months before, Willoughby had fixed her up with a date for the junior prom. At first Alice had agreed, but then she'd canceled out at the last minute. When peevish, Willoughby still reminded her of the jilted boy's rented tux.

Alice's voice was low and soft. "Do you?"

"Do I what?"

"Do you fuck them?"

Willoughby looked back to the house where the geese were strutting through the yard in single file. "Yes," she said.

"Do you like it?"

"Sometimes." She turned back to Alice. "I like it with Evan."

"He's very good?"

Willoughby arched her brows and smiled. "Yes, he's *very* good."

Alice's father had come out into the yard and was casting food to the geese. He was smiling, almost dreamy, as he waved his arm in a lazy arc and the geese pecked frantically at his feet. He never killed them, could only manage to sell the birds so ornery even he couldn't like them. Her mother wondered why he kept any of them. Alice knew. Only her father could love geese.

"Derrick wants to go out with you," Willoughby said casually. Derrick was the boy whose rented tux was on Alice's conscience. He had also been Willoughby's sophomore boyfriend. Alice suspected that fixing her up with Derrick for the prom had been part of the process Willoughby and Derrick called "being just friends."

Alice turned to Willoughby, who was lying back on the straw, staring up at the ceiling. "Is Derrick good?" she asked.

Willoughby sat upright, a gleam in her eye. She was so excited, Alice thought she might cry. "Alice?" she said. "This is Alice White asking me this? Oh, God. Well, he's good. He's very good." She brushed that away with the back of her hand. "No. He's sweet, you know? But not *too* sweet. Do you know what I mean?"

Alice shrugged. "I think so. In books it's that way."

Willoughby laughed. "He's definitely better than books."

"Maybe you've been reading the wrong books." Alice laughed.

Willoughby arched an eyebrow. "No, I've just been dating the right guys." She took Alice's hands. "Come on. Let me fix you up. Please say yes."

Alice squeezed her hands. "No, don't do that," she said. "I'll do it."

The next weekend she found Derrick in his car on the shopping mall parking lot where everyone hung out. She got into the car and said she was sorry about standing him up and wanted to apologize. He was nice about it, gave her a beer, and talked with her. She didn't remember what about. College, more than likely. After she finished her beer she asked him to take her to the lake.

They made love on a blanket spread out over clover. At first he couldn't seem to decide whether he wanted to rape or caress her, and she wasn't sure what she wanted from him, either. But then he *was* sweet, but not too sweet, and she clung to him under the sky as if she might fall into the earth if she let him go. They lay on the blanket for another hour, then he drove her back to her car, where they talked until just before dawn.

On Sunday he called, but she wouldn't talk to him. She wouldn't talk to Willoughby, either, when her calls started Sunday evening. On Monday school started, but she managed to stay clear of him. But on Tuesday he was waiting for her at her locker. Willoughby must've told him which one was hers.

She tried to be nice, make excuses, but after a week he called her a bitch loud enough for Mr. Swope, the shop teacher, to hear him and write him up for detention.

"What's your fucking problem?" Willoughby asked her. "Do you think you're too good for anybody? Derrick's crazy about you, and you just fuck him and drop him."

Alice said, "Leave me alone." And Willoughby did. Alice knew that at any time she could have broken the silence, but she didn't. It made it easier to go when she left for the city. Three years later she got an invitation to Willoughby's wedding. She went and cried and drank too much champagne. They talked for a few minutes while Evan's brother snapped their picture and Willoughby's aunt burst upon them to hug the bride. For years after that she got Christmas cards inviting her to come visit Willoughby and Evan and their daughter. Alice never went, and eventually the cards quit coming. Alice's mother heard that Willoughby had a son now too and had been divorced and moved away, but she didn't know where.

Willoughby had covered for her many times when she'd had to be away from the house on the full moon. Hardly with no questions asked, but with none answered. Alice had often thought of finding out where Willoughby lived and writing her, telling her everything, but she never did. She told Luther Adams instead. But it wasn't the same. It hadn't even been hard. Luther was southern and genteel. Seemingly nothing could ruffle his polite smile, his hospitable concern. Willoughby had been a friend.

Alice rose and shifted the blinds to let in more of the moon and sat down on the chair beside the bed. Erik is sweet, she thought as she watched him sleep, but not too sweet. More than that, he is so loving. Was that only because she hadn't picked him up? Was it only the frantic indifference of her usual sexual partners that made Erik seem special? She didn't think so.

When she allowed herself to fantasize about marriage, of actually being with someone for a long, long time, she didn't think of her parents, but of her great-aunt and -uncle, Ann and Howard. They'd come to visit when she was a child, and the bond between them had been so different from her parents' deliberate, though sentimental, understanding, that they'd become a source of fascination for Alice. Alice knew a pair of twins at school; Ann and Howard were much like that, but the twins seemed two of the same thing, while Ann and Howard were different halves of one thing. Once when Alice stayed up to hear the grownups talk, she remembered, Ann's deep laugh had rung out and she'd said, "Howard and I are mates, bookends for the same book." Then Alice's mother spotted Alice and sent her to bed with hugs and kisses from them all. Alice lay in bed and wondered what it meant to be mates, wondered whether her parents were mates.

The same summer she lost Willoughby was the last time she saw Ann, though she still wrote to her often. "You're unhappy, aren't you, dear?" Ann said to her. "You can always come stay with me and Howard if you're unhappy here." They walked out to feed apples to Gypsy, the pony her father had gotten to cheer her up, even though he couldn't afford it. Ann held the apple firm in her long, thin fingers as Gypsy's huge teeth bit into it.

"Watch out," Alice said. "He'll take your fingers along with the apple."

Ann laughed, never taking her eyes from Gypsy's mouth. "I'm old, but I'm fast," she said. "He won't get me." She surrendered the apple to Gypsy and turned to Alice. "Your father tells me you don't ride anymore. Is that right? You used to love to ride."

Gypsy thrust his head through the fence toward Alice, who held an apple at her side. Alice let him take it from her palm. "I just lost interest," she said, not looking into Ann's large, penetrating eyes. She had begun to wonder whether it was right to ride a horse. It wasn't as if she knew it was wrong, she just didn't know. She was a favorite of other people's pets. Willoughby's black chow Fay (for Fay Wray) used to lean against her and lay her bearlike head in her lap, and Alice would run her fingers through Fay's thick fur. But she fought with Willoughby about Fay's tricks—rolling over, playing dead, begging. Willoughby took this as further evidence that Alice needed to lighten up.

"Perhaps he misses you, Alice," Ann said, rubbing Gypsy's nose.

"I come to see him once in a while."

As they walked back to the house, Ann said, "Remember what I told you. You can always come stay with me and Howard for however long you want."

Then, and many times later, she thought of going to Ann's. But the very thing that drew her there kept her away. She couldn't invade the lives of the two happiest people she knew. Ann, she'd often thought, might even believe her, might even take care of her. Alice looked back at Gypsy, now standing, his head slightly drooped, switching and stamping at flies. She didn't want to be alone, but she didn't want to be taken care of, either, especially by two people who had each other so completely. Her presence might come between them; their bond might make her feel more alone.

She stood by the bed and looked down at Erik. He lay on his side, his back to her, his body in a lazy curve. She remembered on her porch two nights before when the approaching wolf had shown her his desire, shown her her own desire as well. It had felt sweet even then. She smiled. But not too sweet.

She pulled the sheet from Erik's back and crawled into the bed. She smelled his skin, rubbed her cheek against his shoulder. We are mates, she thought. We feel the same. She kissed his shoulders and neck, rubbed the inside of his thigh with her palm. "I want you," she whispered in his ear. He made small noises in his throat as if trying to speak. She took his penis in her hand and felt it grow hard in her grasp as she continued whispering in his ear. His eyes fluttered open, he turned to her and smiled. "I thought I was dreaming," he said.

"You are."

He closed his eyes. "Then please don't wake me."

"Don't worry," she said. "I wouldn't dream of it." She curled her body tight around him. "But you might have better dreams if we traded places."

He laughed. "I like the way you think."

"Thought has nothing to do with it." She rolled over him to her side of the bed, resting on her elbows and knees. He knelt behind her, pushing into her gently, caressing her back with open palms, until he was deep inside her. She gasped, biting her pillow to keep from screaming. As he moved harder, each thrust seemed to loosen something deep inside her until the scream wailed up, shaking her whole body— loud, inarticulate, shameless.

Listening to the echo in her mind, she lay in Erik's embrace, letting her tears flow like welcome rain. It had only lasted a moment, but she knew the sound, even though she'd never given voice to it before. It was freedom. She closed her eyes and fell into a deep, dreamless sleep.

Chapter

7

The first thing Erik did after returning home from Alice's Monday morning was defrost the refrigerator and scrub it clean as if performing some joyous task. He then sat in bed and made a grocery list. The room had always depressed him, but this morning the heavily painted white woodwork, as amorphous in its contours as ice cream, made a comfortable boundary around the room. The sun shone on the clothes in his doorless closet, and the rock brown stain on the ceiling above his bed looked like a woman in floor-length skirts, a mysterious hat towering above her head.

The list was extravagant. He began with dinner, but then moved on to flour and spices, onions and fresh garlic, broccoli and eggplant, fruit juice, grape leaves, tortillas, olive oil, rice. Lately he'd been eating fruit, sardines out of the tin, cheese he sliced with his pocketknife and lay on stale crackers, bland little "entrées" in plastic trays with names like Budget Gourmet and Lean Cuisine. He set the trays on the porch and watched a neighbor's cat lick them clean.

The supermarket was almost deserted. The stock boys talked across stacks of boxes about the cashiers and basketball. He bought a bouquet of flowers from the green bucket at the checkout stand, and the cashier smiled at him. "Girlfriend?" she said, and Erik bobbed his head and grinned.

He stood in front of his open refrigerator with half a dozen bags of groceries at his feet. He knew he should be rattled. He'd met a new advisee on Friday, slept with her Saturday, and fallen in love with her by Monday—and, he glanced at his watch, for the last hour or so, he'd been divorced. Change, he knew, was supposed to be traumatic, and, in contrast with his friends the penguins, his home had been moved a hell of a lot more than three feet.

Now the phone rang on the other side of the kitchen, and he climbed over the bags to answer it. He figured it would be his dad. He'd called him earlier to tell him about Alice and left a message on his machine.

"Hi, where have you been? I tried to reach you all weekend." It was Debra. She was bright and energetic. She often sounded that way over the telephone.

Erik looked back at his open refrigerator. The light blinked as the compressor kicked on. Frosty air leaked into the sunlight. "I went camping," he said. He didn't mention Alice because he didn't want Debra's friendly questions, her ironic advice, and her feigned indifference.

"Oh, where did you go?"

"Loft Mountain."

"That's awfully civilized for you, isn't it?" She was

teasing him about old conflicts. He supposed she thought this a gesture of goodwill. Under different circumstances, he might have agreed.

"What's up?" He looked at his grocery bags as if they were embarrassed guests loitering in the kitchen.

Debra's tone became matter-of-fact. "I was cleaning out some closets and found some things you might want. I thought you could come over tonight and get them."

"I can't tonight."

"We could have dinner," she said.

He knew this meant her reasons for wanting him to come over had nothing to do with anything in her closets. "No, really, I can't tonight."

"I thought we could just get together for old times' sake. I'll even cook. I could get away early—how about this afternoon?"

"I can't."

She gave a nervous laugh. "What about if I don't cook? I have a chicken in the fridge that's been pining for your attention."

"How was court?" he said.

He could hear her lighting a cigarette. "There wasn't much to it. The judge asked me a couple of questions and that was it. The whole thing didn't take five minutes."

"What were the two questions?"

"What difference does it make?"

"I'm curious."

"Whether we'd cohabitated for the last six months and whether I thought our marital problems could be resolved."

"And how did you answer?"

She sighed. "Erik, I answered the way I had to answer."

"So why are you calling me now with this bullshit about some junk you found in your closet?"

"Please don't," she said. Her voice was small and

far away. He knew exactly where she was, sitting on the side of the bed, her elbows on her knees. He reached out with his foot and kicked the refrigerator door closed.

"Okay," he said. "I can see you in an hour and a half. I've got stuff to do later on."

"I have to run up to the museum, but I'll meet you here in an hour and a half. We can talk, okay?" She spoke in a childlike voice he was sure no one had ever heard but him.

"Okay."

After he hung up, he leaned against the counter and tried to steady himself. He went to the bedroom and brought back half a joint. He smoked it as he finished putting away the groceries.

He put a small skillet on the stove and turned on the flame. He watched it absentmindedly as he passed a knife back and forth along a steel, then wiped the blade with a towel. He sliced a thin slab of eggplant and onion and added a little olive oil to the hot skillet. When the oil was hot, he added the onion and eggplant, separating the onion into rings. He crushed two cloves of garlic with the side of the blade, peeled and minced them. When the eggplant and onion were almost done, he slid the garlic from the blade into the pan and tossed it as it sizzled.

He and Deb had had these rendezvous before, though sometimes it had been he who'd found something in his closet. He shouldn't go. She would invite him into her bed. Even as he thought he wouldn't go, he felt the desire tugging at him.

When the garlic turned yellow, he added wine vinegar, oregano, and basil and tossed it until the vinegar evaporated. He removed the skillet from the flame and sliced a sub roll in half. He put the open roll on a platter, covered one half with the eggplant and onion, and sprinkled it with Romano cheese. On the other half he laid strips of provolone. He put the platter under the broiler, sat on the floor, his back propped against the washing machine, and watched it cook. The light dimmed abruptly as the sun went behind a cloud. The flames from the broiler cast a glow upon the floor.

I'll tell her about Alice, he thought, and then we'll fight, or what we call a fight. And then what? And what am I supposed to tell her? I met this girl three days ago, so just leave me alone? The cheese began to bubble.

He took his sandwich to the porch, sat on a folding chair, and put his feet on the railing. Deb will want to know all about Alice, he thought, and I don't really know her at all, at least not in any way that Debra would accept as real.

He looked over at Alice's house. She was at work now, at a travel agency. He tried to picture her, Alice in a suit tapping reservations into a computer terminal, dispensing envelopes of tickets. He'd lain in bed and watched her dress for work. "Put on those hose again," he'd said. "I enjoyed that."

"Later," she'd said, spritzing her neck with perfume. "You can take them off when I get home."

He looked at his watch: that was about six hours away. What is this big secret she can't tell me about? he wondered. She made it sound as if she'd spent her whole life cooped up until now. He knew reclusive people, colleagues who only emerged from isolation to present their findings on fungi or the aerodynamics of bats. She wasn't like them. She acted like someone who'd been locked out, not someone who locked herself in.

It began to rain, a heavy, perpendicular downpour. A light mist drifted onto the porch, collecting on his face and arms, on the sandwich in his hands. The rain was so loud, he could not hear himself chew, but he could just hear the faint rumble of distant thunder.

Most of the houses were deserted and dark on a

Monday, but lights shone from a few. The old woman across the street, whose cat sometimes visited him, stood behind her storm door and looked up and down the street. Erik could see a Victorian sofa perched behind her, a white glass lamp glowing beside it. He waved, but she didn't see him. Her eyes scanned the ground.

The wind began to pick up, and the rain leaned to the right as trash cans turned over and the streetlight flickered, then came on. The woman frowned and closed her door. A drop of water had collected on Erik's nose and fell to his lap. He set the platter on the porch and took off his shoes and socks, placing them beside the door. He stepped to the porch railing and vaulted over, landing in the grass with a splash, his feet almost completely submerged in the water. He arched his back and faced the rain, his arms and head flung back, his eyes shut. His clothes were instantly sodden and heavy, clinging to his thighs and chest. He gasped with the cold, turned twice around, then stopped, his arms wrapped around him. He looked up and down the street at the rapids forming along the curbs, the neatly trimmed yards submerged like tiny marshes. A car crept by, the beams from its headlights drenched in rain. The water parted in furrows before the tires and lapped over the curb, obliterating the sidewalk. He walked back to the porch with a bouncing step, his arms still wrapped around him. He continued to watch the rain as he stripped off his shirt and wrung it out over the railing and squeezed some of the water from his cuffs.

By the time he went in the house and dried himself and put on fresh clothes, the rain had stopped. Standing in his living room, his skin still pimpled with cold, he heard a faint clatter on the porch and saw the neighbor's cat, dry except for his paws, scavenging the last few bites of his sandwich.

* * *

"I just got home," Debra said. "Let me change. There's beer in the refrigerator."

As he got his beer and she changed her clothes, they talked to each other from separate rooms.

"Things must be slowing down at the museum for you to get away in the middle of the day." The beer was imported, and he searched for the bottle opener he could never find.

"Actually it's been hectic. We're packing up an exhibit today. If I'd stayed, I just would've hovered." She laughed at herself. "They practically jumped for joy when I said I was leaving."

She came into the kitchen, opened a drawer, and held up the bottle opener. "It's hidden in the same place it always is," she said. "You're looking good," she added, smiling at him like an old friend.

"So are you." She had changed from her suit into a loose-fitting gauze blouse and drawstring pants. Her feet were bare. She was a beautiful woman with large eyes and high cheekbones. When complimented on her beauty, she would smile with a slight grimace and touch her brow, then quickly move on to other things.

"I've lost weight," she said. "I've missed your cooking."

"I have, too."

He followed her into the living room. All the furniture was new to Erik except for the sofa they sat on. It had been a castoff from Debra's mother, who'd given it to them to reupholster when they were first married. "It's one hundred inches long," her mother had said several times to impress upon them its value, and Debra and Erik used to joke about it.

They both lit cigarettes. "I'm surprised you kept the sofa," he said.

"And where else would I get a hundred-inch sofa?"

He perched on the edge, holding his beer in both hands.

"It's too bad you can't stay for dinner," she said.

He laughed. "No, really. I have things I have to do."

"Maybe after a few beers I can persuade you." She curled up on the sofa, facing him. "You can spend some time this afternoon, can't you?"

"This is hard for me," he said. "I don't know what you want."

"I just want to see you. I've missed you. Just because we can't live together doesn't mean we can't be friends."

He looked at her. "Surely it doesn't help."

She laid her cheek against the back of the sofa and smiled ironically. "I suppose not."

He looked around the room, cataloging the strange and the familiar. "I've missed you, too," he said.

She reached out and turned his face to her with the tips of her fingers.

"You're a very sweet man, Erik." She held his eyes, uncurled herself, and leaned forward, kissing him. He held her close, his eyes clamped shut. She turned so that he held her cradled in his arms, looking up at him. He kissed her. If he were not holding her, he would be shaking. She laid her head against his chest. He rested his chin on top of her head, breathing the familiar smell of her hair, and waited. She whispered into the silence, "Would you like to make love?"

"I can't," he said.

"Do you want to?"

"Of course."

She drew back and searched his eyes. "Girlfriend, Erik?"

He nodded.

Her mouth tightened, and she sat up, retrieving her cigarette from the ashtray. "Anyone I know?"

"No."

She laughed. "Well, I can be thankful for that, at least."

"Debra."

"You're right, it's none of my business." When she was hurt she retreated to anger, protected herself with

it like a moat. Erik had never found a way across.
"Have you known her long?"

"Not very."

"But long enough, I take it."

"Debra." He reached for her hand, but she pulled away.

"Sorry. Forget I said that. Well, I guess this was a pretty stupid idea."

"No, it wasn't." He saw that soon she would cry.

She leaned back, clamping her eyes shut, but still the tears flowed. "Shit," she said, wiping the tears away. "Well, don't rush into anything," she said, now cheerful again, willing away the tears.

"I won't," he said, though he thought to himself, I already have.

She plucked a Kleenex from a box on the coffee table and dabbed at her eyes. "We're hanging a new photographic exhibit this week you'd probably like. It's full of images of noble poor people." She smiled at him as if he had just arrived. Only he would notice that one corner of her mouth gave her away.

"Maybe I'll come by and see it," he said.

Dr. Luther Adams sat in the white-tiled neatness of his solarium. A fountain gurgled in the corner, and the room smelled of greenery. The light poured in through skylights. It was like the aviary at the zoo, but no birds sang. Several times at the aviary he'd seen the same man. He wore a mechanic's shirt with his name, Ted, stitched above the pocket. When Luther came upon him, he looked serene sitting on the wooden bench, for who knows how long. Although Luther liked the idea of this room— the light, the plants, the running water—he was never so much at ease here with the glass-top table and the white metal furniture and the plump flowered cushions as Ted appeared to be, in the aviary.

Through the French doors were other rooms, a dozen or more. He forgot all the names his wife had given them—the sitting room, the sewing room, the guest room, the foyer. Luther only visited a handful. Sometimes in the hallway upstairs he didn't know what he would find if he were to open one of the doors he usually only counted on the way to the master bedroom or his study. Once he'd found Eleanor, his wife, in—what was it?—the reading room, reclining on a Victorian chaise longue, reading. She'd made nothing of his entrance. She'd just told him about the book in her hands, as if they'd met in that place each day for that very purpose.

This room was Eleanor's favorite. Here, they would have a cocktail before dinner and discuss their days. Even though she wasn't home now, he'd brought his drink here anyway and felt she was here somehow, reminding him to be careful of the glass he set on the table. He imagined her speaking, then listened to the peaceful hiss of the fountain.

When the sound ceased to soothe him, he saw her turn to him on her empty chair. "What's wrong, Luther? Something is bothering you."

He turned away and looked into the fountain, watched the water stream down over the carefully piled rocks to the pump below, concealed by a huge stone frog.

He took up his drink and cradled it in his hands. He thought about Alice. He saw her sitting in his office twining her braid around her hand like a snake, then tossing it behind her. Sometimes she held the end like a soft brush, stroked her cheek, and looked at the paintings on his walls. He wondered what her hair looked like when she took out the braid and let it fall in black waves. He wondered what she would look like naked, standing on the thick carpet before him. He was in love with her. It was an awful thing to admit to himself, but it was true, and he couldn't do a thing about it.

He was a faithful man. Not that he hadn't been in

love with other women during more than twenty years of marriage. But he'd never been unfaithful. He'd flirted, given gifts, even indulged in long glances and expensive wine over lunch. But he'd never been unfaithful. He wasn't sure why. The feelings seemed strong enough, real enough. But somehow he always managed to hold back. After a time, his infatuations —that's what he came to call such feelings—seemed like narrow escapes from danger. This time seemed different. He couldn't remember whether the other times had seemed different, too. Once he thought of keeping a journal, so that if he fell in love again, he would know if it were the same. But Eleanor might discover it, though she never entered his study, much less looked in his desk.

The condensation from his glass dripped on his chest, and he pushed himself upright. An iron curlicue dug into his spine, and the cushion beneath him began to inch forward again. Alice is a patient, he reminded himself. A patient with an acute sexual dysfunction. It would not only be unethical, it would be inhuman.

And now she'd called the office, desperate to see him. He usually didn't see patients on Monday, but Sarah, his secretary, had called a little while ago to say that Alice wanted to talk with him as soon as possible. Luther wondered about Sarah's calling him at home. Usually Sarah would have just left him a message on his desk. How did she know he would want to see her? Sarah did transcribe the sessions. Was there something in the tapes that gave him away even to Sarah? Perhaps Alice knows, he thought. Perhaps she has sensed my feelings. He shook his head. No, I have been careful. She couldn't know. She's just afraid to go anywhere. She's stuck on this business of whether I believe her or not. What a ridiculous little dance *that* was on Friday. What does she want to see me about today? What am I going to do with her?

He should have passed her on. This whole werewolf

business was out of his league. Most of his patients were depressed. They just needed simple therapy and wouldn't hurt a soul but themselves. Lord knows what Alice needed, and if a werewolf delusion wasn't potentially violent, he didn't know what was.

But he could just see himself calling up Charlie, his friend who dealt in hard-core cases: "I've been treating this woman for six months, and I'd like you to take over." Charlie would take one look at her and know exactly why the referral had taken so long. No, he would have to stick it out.

A sparrow landed on the skylight, pecked at itself in the glass, and flew away. We're not getting anywhere, he thought. If she doesn't see any progress soon, she's just going to quit coming. Her frustration dominated every session, accusing him of failure. He had trouble in the first place persuading her that he might help. "Whatever the reason," he'd told her, "you want to be happier with your life. Perhaps I can help you with that."

He rested his glass on his stomach and watched the bubbles break at the surface. He could hear the sparrow tapping again but didn't look up. He listened to the quick rhythm. Four beats, pause, four beats, pause.

She wasn't opening up to him. They were like two wrestlers circling for position. If only she would stay still. There must be some way to get her to talk about what's really going on with these hallucinatory episodes each month. She'd told him once that he couldn't possibly understand. But he hadn't been given the chance.

Perhaps hypnosis, he thought. He'd never gone in for that sort of thing. He wasn't sure why. He remembered during his residency one of the other residents hypnotizing a customer in a bar and suggesting he recite the Pledge of Allegiance whenever a woman came out of the bathroom.

104

He tried to picture hypnotizing Alice. She was so tense. She probably wouldn't lie down on the couch. She'd made fun of the damn thing the first time she'd come. Besides, the traffic made her nervous. She complained about him being buried downtown. Perhaps at night. No traffic. No one around to make her feel self-conscious. He had to do something.

He called her work number. The phone on the glass table was some American's idea of French. He felt as if he were talking through a plastic pipe.

"May I speak with Alice White, please?" He recognized her voice, but this was a professional call.

"This is Alice White," she said.

From her voice he had already conjured her up, hovering in the mists of the fountain.

"Hi, this is Luther Adams. Sarah said you wanted to see me this evening."

"If it's not too much trouble," she said.

Her voice had a beseeching tone he'd never heard before. He felt a surge of longing. "No trouble at all. As a matter of fact, I was just thinking about your case, and there's something I would like to discuss with you, a possible therapy. I can see you any time."

"I get off work at five-thirty," she said. "Is six okay?"

"I'll see you then."

He hung up the phone. I handled that well, he thought. There was something in her tone. She certainly wanted to see him. He suspected the beginnings of transference. That could prove useful in her treatment—handled properly, he reminded himself.

He heard Eleanor's key sliding into the door and sat upright on the chair.

As Eleanor joined him with a drink and settled comfortably onto her chair, he said, "How was shopping?"

She kicked off her shoes and rubbed her feet. "I didn't go shopping. I went to Maymont Park."

"You went to the park by yourself?"

"I wanted to get out of the house. I wrote letters."

He nodded. He suddenly remembered it had poured down rain an hour or so ago. "Did you get caught in the rain?" He made this sound like a moral lapse.

She laughed. "Oh, Luther, I won't melt. I was in one of the gazebos. It was thrilling, actually."

He didn't know what to say to that. "I have to go out this evening," he said. "I'm meeting a patient at six."

"On Monday? What's the emergency?"

"Not anything, really. She just wanted to talk to me as soon as possible."

"Is this the one who thinks she's a vampire?"

"Werewolf."

"Whatever. The nymphomaniac."

Luther bristled. "I'm sure you never heard that diagnosis from me. Alice avoids forming bonds with men, with anyone, actually. That hardly makes her a nymphomaniac."

Eleanor shrugged one shoulder and pointed at the fountain. "Has the pump been humming again?"

"No, it's been quiet the whole time I've been out here."

"Hmm," she said. "It hummed all yesterday afternoon. Maybe we should have somebody look at it."

Luther waited patiently through a discussion of the humming pump, then told her, "I'm thinking about using hypnosis with one of my patients, but I haven't done it in years."

"Is this Alice again?"

"No," he lied. "It's a new patient, a man. Ralph is his name." He paused. "I was wondering if I might practice on you—just getting you under."

She tilted her head back in surprise and smiled up at the skylight. "Sounds fun," she said, her eyes twinkling.

106

"I'm serious, Eleanor."

"Well, so am I."

"Europe, of course, is out of the question," the man said, adding in case Alice were uninformed, "These days."

He and his wife were shopping for a graduation gift for their daughter. "She wants to travel," the mother had said as if this were surprising.

"Above all," the father added, tapping on the counter, "it must be someplace safe."

It was closing time. Alice wasn't in the mood for yet another traveler looking for adventure someplace safe. "Will she be traveling alone?" she asked.

The mother looked to the tangle of tropical plants by the window and looked sad. The father chuckled. "Yes, quite alone—she won't want us tagging along."

The girl has other options, Alice thought. Surely she doesn't want to strike out from these two just to photograph ruins or admire the dead at Westminster Abbey. "There is a group trip to Russia that's quite nice—and exceptionally safe. Trained tour guides are with you every step of the way." Alice smiled. She felt mean, but their bewildered expressions were worth it.

"I don't think so," said the mother.

"Maybe the Caribbean. Does she like the beach? There are several cruises that are very reasonable."

The parents' eyes moved to the Jamaica poster on the wall. A deeply tanned blonde lay on the sand. A grass hut stood behind her. The black people were tucked away beyond the white border.

The mother laughed and touched her hair. "Are those cruises really as wild as they say?"

Alice smiled. "They're really quite fun."

The father stood up straighter. "I hear there's a nasty drug problem down there."

Probably not as bad as your daughter's high school, Alice thought, but she suggested that maybe they needed more time to think. She loaded them down with brochures. The one on top showed a reassuring bald eagle and a cracked bell. She followed them to the door and locked it behind them.

"You should've suggested Mexico," said Lisa after they left.

"They have earthquakes down there, my dear, and it's not entirely healthy for a young girl, is it?"

"I liked it," Lisa said, and added thoughtfully, "I got a great tan."

Lisa was young, a college student with blond hair as thick as an ermine's. She was earning college credit by sitting at the agency talking to her friends on the phone and reading fashion magazines. She couldn't understand why someone Alice's age didn't already have her degree—"since you're so smart and everything." Lisa had started school as an accounting major but soon switched to merchandising. "I'm going to be a model," she'd told Alice.

"I'm sure you'll do well. You're very photogenic."

"I'll try real hard."

Alice thought of the Little Engine That Could.

Now Lisa was standing, purse in hand. "Can you close up? I've got a big exam tomorrow." She wore a plunging black knit dress and precipitous heels. She'd spent the last fifteen minutes fixing her makeup.

Alice was bent over the day's deposit, recording checks. She swiveled on her chair and looked Lisa up and down. "You certainly look stunning tonight, Lisa. Go out and have a good time."

Lisa smiled over the cover of *Glamour*. "Thanks, Alice, you're so sweet."

Alice winced, but Lisa didn't seem to notice. Her heels rang down the back hall, then grew muffled and distant as the back door clicked behind her and she walked across the parking lot to her car, a tiny little thing impossible to enter in that dress without showing a good deal of thigh. Alice looked out through the side window and saw a man in a BMW looking back over his shoulder toward the parking lot as he headed blindly down the street.

As Alice added up the checks, she imagined turning into a wolf before Lisa's eyes: Lisa, a terror-stricken poster for a horror movie—the dress torn in front, a touch of blood on the breast, an abrasion like rouge on her cheek. Alice felt foolish and sad. She entered the totals, slid the deposit into the bag, and zipped it shut. Lisa's done nothing to me, she thought. No one has.

She just wished she could be one or the other, the woman or the wolf. But if that choice didn't exist, she had to learn to live with it, right? But could Erik live with it? She shook her head and leaned back on her chair. Why was she even worrying about that now? They hardly knew each other.

This morning they'd made plans to go to his father's on Wednesday. They had no plans for tomorrow, but she knew they would make some. She was afraid of pushing it, but she wasn't the only one pushing. He seemed to want her as much as she wanted him. She knew this sort of thing happened to other people. Ann and Howard had only known each other a month when they were married.

She put the deposit in the safe and turned out the lights. The Jamaica blonde was a tan blur in the darkness. She set the alarm and slid her key into the glass door. She looked at her reflection as the lock clunked into place. This morning Erik had told her she was beautiful. He was making her dinner tonight. They would make love. She smiled to herself—they might make love before they had dinner. Sometime, though, he would want her to talk about herself. A well-dressed couple passed her on their way to the restaurant next door, arm in arm, lost in each other. "I'm a werewolf," Alice imagined saying to them. "Who are you?"

She was glad she could talk to Luther before seeing Erik again. When she'd called to tell Erik she wouldn't be home until seven-thirty, she'd been relieved to get his answering machine. She had to catch her breath, figure out what she was going to do. She'd thought she would "keep her options open," as Lisa would say. But they had dissolved all around her. It was already too late simply to break things off. Even the thought felt like something breaking inside of her. She didn't even think she could slow things down. She thought of Guenevere in the William Morris poem, describing her falling in love with Lancelot as sliding down a steep, wet path into the sea. If she waited until Friday to talk to Luther, surely she would already have drowned.

She wound through a residential neighborhood to reach the freeway. She didn't like driving, and she hated having to think too much about it. She wished she could walk to work, but the houses close to the agency were too expensive for her.

In front of the middle school, a group of six or eight girls in drill team outfits huddled around a girl shorter than all the rest. Like me, Alice thought. The short one was trying to do something with her right hand. The others seemed to be coaching her. Alice hesitated at the stop sign, watching. A smile broke on the girl's face, and the rest cheered as the short girl held her hand high in the air, the middle finger extended. Alice watched them in her rearview mirror as she pulled away. They bounced up and down in delight, all laughing, all now brandishing their middle fingers.

Alice remembered having friends like that before she'd changed. Now she had no friends. She occasionally had lunch with co-workers, talked with people in her classes at school. She smiled to herself—and I've got a psychiatrist and a bartender.

Nothing like Erik had ever happened to her before. She didn't care if it was foolish or sudden or plain dumb luck. She didn't want to lose it. She didn't want to hide anymore.

*   *   *

110

When she found herself seated in Luther's office, she didn't know where to begin. She said, "I appreciate your seeing me on such short notice, doctor." She often found herself becoming formal when she needed someone. She wondered if everyone felt that way or only those like her, who had so much to conceal.

"Luther," he prompted her. "Think nothing of it. I was delighted to get your call."

And he seemed delighted. Leaning forward on his chair, his palms spread on its arms, he smiled and cocked his head. A boy about to hear secrets, Alice thought. "I spent two nights with the same man," she said. "Two whole days, in fact."

Luther leaned back, made a tent of his fingers, and propped them against his nose. "Is this someone you've mentioned previously?"

"Do you mean slept with?"

"Now, now. You often speak of men you haven't slept with. You're too hard on yourself, Alice."

"Am I? Then how did I get myself into this awful mess? Listen to me. He is a wonderful man. I told him I killed Dale. I told him he was my first date, and God knows he knows I'm no virgin. And so far he doesn't think I'm a crazy slut, but you tell me—how am I going to tell him I'm a werewolf?" Alice lit a cigarette.

"I thought you quit smoking." Luther now sat upright, his hands folded in his lap.

Alice smiled. "He smokes."

"Tell me about him."

"He's a teacher. A biologist. He studies penguins. I don't think he likes that part of it much. It's too"— she gestured with her hand to find words—"too abstract, too distant from what he is." She smiled. "He's a good teacher, though. I can tell that."

"And what else can you tell about him?"

Alice took a drag from her cigarette and put it out. "That he's too nice to deceive, and I don't want to leave him." Her voice broke. She bent over and sobbed.

Luther was startled. She had cried before, but never like this. He knelt beside her murmuring, "There, there," and offered her Kleenex. He thought he might cry himself.

Alice cried herself out and looked up at Luther, whose concern-wrought face touched her and almost made her laugh. "I'm okay, Luther," she said softly, and smiled at him. He put down the box of Kleenex and sat back on his chair. She looked him in the eye. "I just have to tell him is all. I have no other choice. And you can help me do that because you don't believe any of it." Her voice was still soft.

"I'm not sure I follow you."

"I want him to believe me. I've told you everything, and you don't believe me. Why should he? What could I have said or done to persuade you? What might persuade him?"

Luther shifted on his chair. "I don't see why you have to tell him anything just yet. Take your time."

"That's not the point. If I tell him tonight or next month, what's the difference? How do you gradually lead up to 'I'm a werewolf'?"

"I don't know, Alice, but I think you should prepare yourself for the possibility that he won't believe you. He's a man of science, after all."

Alice laughed. "If he were a plumber, it would be easier?"

Luther faked a good-humored smile. "I suppose not. All I'm saying is he'll want proof. Are you planning to make him the same offer you've made to me—to witness your transformation?"

Alice looked down into her lap. "I've thought of that. I'm afraid. I'm afraid he might be revolted by me, see me as a monster and run away."

Luther let the silence hang heavy for a moment, then said quietly, "Is that why you run away from men, Alice? Because you're afraid they will see you as a monster?"

She kept her head lowered. Her voice was barely audible. "Yes."

"Do you believe yourself to be a monster?"

For a long time she didn't answer. Luther toyed with repeating the question but didn't want to push too hard. She looked up at him and shook her head. Her face was covered with tears. "No," she said. "No, I don't. I've tried to believe it. I thought I should, that it would be—I don't know—safer if I did. But it's too lonely. I don't want to be alone anymore. I'd rather die."

Luther put a reassuring hand on her arm and started to say, "You're not going to die," but realized he couldn't say such a thing. He could only squeeze her arm and wonder when he should take his hand away.

He began to tell her about hypnosis, about how he might be able to understand her better, help her come to terms with herself better. She nodded and listened. "A more peaceful setting would be better for the first session," he said. "Could you come a little later this Friday, say, seven?"

She nodded again, smiling faintly.

He gave her arm one last squeeze and let her go. "I am very confident that hypnosis will facilitate your treatment immensely."

"Can we still talk?" she asked.

"Of course," Luther said. "Of course."

Alice hurried home. She felt numb. She didn't want to think about anything. She just wanted to see Erik. When she pulled up to the curb, Erik stepped down from his porch and met her at her car. He hugged her and whirled her around. "I didn't think you were ever going to get here," he said.

"Me either."

"You need help with those hose?"

"Definitely."

113

As they walked to her door arm in arm, he asked her if she'd seen the rain. "Wasn't it wonderful?" he said.

Suddenly, without thinking, she squeezed him hard around the waist and said, "I love you."

He grinned down at her. No one had ever looked at her with such joy before. "I love you, too," he said.

PART

TWO

To celebrate wilderness was to celebrate the wolf;
to want an end to wilderness and all it stood for
was to want the wolf's head.

—Barry Lopez
Of Wolves and Men

Chapter

8

Debra cried over lunch on Wednesday, but no one saw her. She ate in her office with work spread before her and the door closed. But now, on Friday, she was standing in the small exhibit hall with all her employees around her. It wouldn't do to cry now. Black-and-white photographs in shiny chromium frames leaned against the walls, waiting to be hung. The exhibit documented—or in harsher moments Debra might have said "romanticized"—the vitality of rural Appalachia.

She had been looking at the photographs, waiting for the stragglers before she gave her instructions, when the images touched her, but not delicately. She imagined Erik beside her, loving these pictures, exclaiming, "We are a wonderful species."

A portrait of an old couple hand in hand was

directly in front of her. The woman smiled; the man seemed solemn until she noticed he was toothless. His joy shone in his crinkled eyes. In the next photograph, women in limp dresses stood with children clinging to them as if they were trees. The men too seemed like trees, shaped by wind and weather to a drooping elegance or whittled to a sharpness. In almost every image, an animal—a dog, a cat, a horse—watched with interest (and, it seemed, affection) the lives of the humans. Amid the tumbling houses and rusty tractors, the people and the animals seemed equals.

"Is the height okay?" asked Sandy, a tall, lanky young woman whose main interests were anthropology and sex. She didn't shave her armpits, which Debra didn't mind, and often wore sleeveless tops, which Debra did.

Debra looked at the string snaking through the hall, marking the center line, and saw it was too high, as it always was when Sandy hung it. "It's fine," she said. The others looked disappointed. Debra knew they called her the Dragon Lady behind her back: they'd hoped to see her usual fire. They stood around her in a circle, wearing thin white cotton gloves for handling the photographs. They looked like cartoon animals. Gloveless, Debra was a human out of place. "Go ahead and hang it," she said as if calling for an execution. "I'll be in my office."

In her office was a telephone. She picked up the receiver and held down the button, imagining several different conversations with Erik, all of them disastrous. Words alone would accomplish nothing. They'd already accomplished too much. She remembered Monday, shrinking away from him and sulking because he had some new girlfriend. How stupid and childish. Of course he was going to try to find someone new. She'd divorced him, for Christ's sake. But if he knew how she really felt, if she showed him how she really felt, he would want her back. She had to see him. She stuffed the grant proposal she needed to finish into her satchel and went into the outer office.

Sue, her secretary, whose own life was a series of soap opera crises, nodded solemnly as Debra told her what half-truth to tell each person who might call. Debra winced as Sue called after her, "Don't worry, I'll cover for you." She recalled Sue's last crisis—her stepson by a former marriage had stolen a horse and put it in her backyard, where it managed to injure itself. Sue was first interrogated as an accomplice, then sued for the vet bills. Debra had loaned her money at some point in this mess but couldn't remember what for. Her co-workers couldn't figure out why Sue hadn't been fired long ago, but Debra kept her around for her intense loyalty and to remind herself of the chaos she avoided in her own life by keeping things under control.

I'm out of control now, she thought as she drove to Erik's house. That, at least, will please him. She had extracted the address on the pretext of forwarding the occasional mail that still came to him. She'd driven by twice during the week but couldn't bring herself to stop. What if the girlfriend's there, or he won't talk to me? she asked herself, but thought, He will admire my daring.

He met her at the door with a book in his hand. "What's wrong?" he said.

"I need to talk to you," she said.

He nodded and held open the door, gesturing toward a worn, boxy sofa he must have picked up at a yard sale. "You want something to drink?"

She sat down and tried a laugh. "Definitely. Scotch, if you've got it."

He arched one eyebrow and went into the kitchen.

She looked around the living room. It was a shabby place, like the one they'd lived in when they were first married. The ashtray by his chair was filled with butts, and stacks of books lay on the floor. His penguins again. She smiled to herself. She could see no evidence of the girlfriend.

He returned with Scotch for both of them. She took this as a good sign. He sat on his chair across from her.

"You seem to be all settled in," she said.

He looked around, shrugged his shoulders. "It's okay. I've been pretty busy. I haven't had time to fix it up."

"School stuff?"

"No. This is spring break. Other things. Is this a social call?"

"I need to talk to you."

He waited silently for her to go on.

"I feel stupid," she told him, but stopped—it might be dangerous if they compared feelings. "I've made a terrible mistake," she said.

He sipped his drink, looking over the glass at her. Usually he talks and I listen, she thought. He had complained about that.

After a long silence he spoke quietly. "What sort of mistake?"

"I shouldn't have divorced you. I miss you. I need . . . your influence in my life."

"My 'influence in your life'? What does that mean? I don't want to be your conscience, Debra."

"I love you, Erik," she said, her head down, contrite, as if confessing a sin.

"You divorced me, Debra. Isn't it a little late for this declaration? Besides, I thought that love wasn't enough for you, or so you said."

"It doesn't have to be that way. I've realized so many things these last few days."

He stood slowly, rummaged around on the coffee table for a cigarette, and paced back and forth, shaking his head. "Not too long ago you told me you realized some things—that you were you and I was me, and that was that. If things 'don't have to be that way,' why in hell did we go through all this shit?"

She picked up the battered blue throw pillow beside

her and clutched it to her stomach. She remembered it from his bachelor apartment when they were dating. She hadn't known he still had it. The seam was mended with rough, pink stitches. "I was wrong," she said. "I didn't realize how much I needed you."

He sat back down, still shaking his head. "This is too weird for me, Debra. It's too late. Remember how many times I told you I needed you? 'That will pass,' you said. Jesus. I'm still the same man, maybe more so. You're still the same woman. You want me to be one thing. I want you to be another. Fine. Irreconcilable differences. I have the goddamn papers to prove it. Your signature's on it, I believe."

She'd expected him to be frightened but not angry. He only ended sentences with "I believe" when he was furious.

"I was wrong," she said.

"And now you're right?"

"Yes."

"What if you change your mind again?"

"I won't."

He leaned back and closed his eyes. She could see he was gathering his thoughts against her, could hear him turning aside whatever she might say. "It's too late," he repeated without opening his eyes, his voice low and hollow.

She began to cry, her shoulders shaking as she closed in upon herself, her face buried in the pillow, her hands splayed across the top of her head. Each spasm of tears seemed to weaken her. She felt she would soon slump to the floor, helpless.

She heard the creak of the wood floor, felt his hand upon her back. She looked up, and he handed her a box of Kleenex. "Thanks," she said, and tried to smile.

"What am I going to do with you?" he said. His voice was quiet and gentle.

She blew her nose. "Take me back?" She smiled at him, hoping he would smile back, but he didn't.

"You know it's not that simple."

She lowered her head and tugged at his sleeve. He sat down cautiously beside her. "Please hold me," she said. He put his arms around her shoulders and rocked her back and forth. "I love you," she said.

He kissed the top of her head but didn't speak.

She pulled away to look at him. "Do you still love me?"

"Debra, why are you doing this?"

"I just want to know, Erik."

"It's more complicated than whether I love you or not."

"But do you?" She put her hand on his cheek and looked into his eyes. He looked sad and defeated, the line between his brows pinched into a crevice.

"I suppose I do."

"Only suppose?" She curled up against him, sought his mouth, and kissed him. She could feel his trembling all around her, taste her own tears. Suddenly he crushed her against him and kissed her hard. His breathing was heavy and ragged. He pushed her back onto the sofa, and she clung to him, arching up against him. She found his belt and struggled to unfasten it. He raised himself up on his arms, then stood, looking down at her. "I can't do this," he said.

His hands were spread open in front of him as if to push her away. She could see the fear in his eyes. He still loves me, she thought. She sat up and leaned toward him.

"I know you still want me."

"Yes, I still want you. But what the hell does that mean anymore?" He looked away from her and paced again. "I fuck you, and then what? Does that make everything all better? Like nothing ever happened?" He took his cigarette from the ashtray and lit a fresh one from it. He sat down on his chair with a sigh and picked up his glass. "Look, I'm sorry. I should never have let things go that far."

"I wanted them to," she said.

"Well, I didn't." His tone softened. "This has all been pretty hard on me, okay? I finally feel like I'm getting on with my life—as you told me many times I should do—then you show up and say, Sorry, it's all been a mistake. I love you, you love me, game's over, mistake rectified. Jesus, Debra, what do you expect me to do?"

"It's the girlfriend, isn't it, Erik?" She took a cigarette from his pack and lit it, inwardly cursing her trembling hands. "How long have you known her, a few weeks?" She knew it was the wrong thing to say as she said it, just the sort of pose that infuriated him. But it was too late now. She kept her face set in an icy smile.

He shook his head and grimaced. "Sometimes you are a real bitch, Debra." He moved to the edge of his chair and glared at her. "I've known her exactly one week. I love her, and what's more, I trust her."

"You're going to throw away eight years of marriage for someone you hardly know?"

"Seems to me we've already thrown that away, Debra. And I may not have known Alice for very long, but I've known her long enough to know I like her, and she likes me. Which is a hell of a lot more than I can say for us."

Soon she would cry again. So stupid, so pointless. She couldn't bear it again. She ran her palms down the tops of her thighs and stood. "Well, if that's the way you feel, I guess I should be going."

He said nothing. He opened the door and let her out without looking at her.

Through the window, he watched her get into her car. She sat, head bent, looking for her keys. She started the car and pulled away without a glance at the house. He leaned his forehead against the window and closed his eyes. After a moment the tears came. The crossed mullions pressed hard into his forehead, the sun burned red in his eyes.

Fifteen minutes later he was busily cleaning the

kitchen when the phone rang. He held a dripping sponge over the sink as he listened to Debra apologize. Her voice was small and fragile, full of tears. She said she wanted to see him again. After a long silence he promised her he would think about it. After he hung up he hurled the sponge against the wall and let it lie.

Half an hour later Alice called. "I've had a lousy day," he told her.

"I need to talk to you when I get home," she said.

"Is anything wrong?"

"No, I just need to tell you about something."

"I need to talk to you, too."

"I'll be home about four-fifteen."

"I'll be here."

"I'd rather talk at my house, if that's okay with you."

"Sure. Are you sure nothing's wrong?"

"I'm fine, really. I just need to tell you something about myself."

He knelt on the floor and cleaned up his mess but couldn't shake the feeling that something was terribly wrong with Alice.

Alice sat in the travel agency, waiting for four o'clock when she could go home. It was Friday, a week since she'd met Erik. She got off early every Friday for her appointment with Luther. Even though her appointment tonight wasn't until seven, she hadn't said anything. She had resolved to tell Erik the truth when she got home. She had called him to say she needed to talk, so that she couldn't back out.

There was a pile of reservations that needed to be entered in for a Holy Land tour, but she couldn't do even such mindless work today. She put Lisa to work instead.

"I'm not really sure how to do all that stuff on the computer yet," Lisa told her. Lisa had been working there since January.

"I guess it's time you learned, then, isn't it?" Alice said. "That is what you're here for, isn't it, to learn something?"

Now, as Lisa hissed curses, hunting keys on a machine oblivious of her charms, Alice thought about what she would say to Erik. She had rehearsed it, assembled evidence. Sometimes she imagined him persuaded, taking her in his arms. More often she imagined him thinking her crazy and pulling away.

What would it be like to be told, "I am a werewolf"? She herself couldn't be skeptical about anything. She laughed at *Enquirer* headlines in the grocery store—ALIEN FATHERS TWO-HEADED BOY—but then thought, It just might be true. Who would believe me if I were the headline? She looked at the people in other lines buying food or beer or a box of Pampers and wondered who they were, which one might be an alien or a vampire.

Or a werewolf. She felt like the only one. But that couldn't be true, could it? Which face might turn in recognition if she were to throw back her head and howl, while everyone else feared or, worse, pitied her?

She thought about waiting three weeks when Erik could see for himself, but she couldn't wait that long. He teased her now about "her secret" whenever she became vague or evasive. She never realized how much of her life turned on the single mystery. You've had no friends? You can't have children? What do you mean you got this house for the basement? What do you mean you can't tell me why?

It was absurd. It was just something that happened to her every month, something that would happen again. But it was more than that. It was always there: the wolf howling in the basement, shitting on the floor, inhaling the world like a vision. Turn me loose, she thought, and I'll crush a rabbit in my jaws or tear a boy's throat out. Erik's passion isn't for me. It's for this fiction I've created—the perfectly normal Alice

White who's had a few problems with men but is okay now. Not the real one, not the wild werewolf.

She had evolved this theory about herself. Wolves were social animals. By hunting in packs, they brought down prey much larger than themselves. Only one pair in a pack mated, and they most always for life. The other members of the pack helped raise the pups, bringing food to the mother when she still lay with the pups. Alice had never been in a litter, lying in the darkness, squirming, pressed in on all sides by wolf, siblings and mother. She'd never been taught to hunt, to play, to gesture, to mind her manners. Lone wolves had a rough, usually short, life. But at least they knew how to be wolves—knew they *were* wolves. What would her wolf know? She'd never seen another wolf, would have to travel hundreds of miles to see one outside of a zoo. Her wolf was born (as far as she could possibly know) the *only* wolf and, therefore, the last wolf that would ever be. A lone wolf had once been in a pack, could listen at the borders of a pack's territory and wait, perhaps, to be joined by another outcast. Her wolf was more than an outsider. She had no world to be outside of.

It was as a human that Alice felt most like a lone wolf. She had become adept at surviving apart, sitting on the outside, waiting. It was the great irony of her life: because she was two social animals, she was none.

"We've made up our minds." A voice startled her from above. It was the father of the graduate, standing at the counter. She hadn't heard him come in. He was alone this time, holding an Amtrak brochure in his hand. He looked the same—the same suit, the same tie, the same shirt. He handed Alice the brochure with his daughter's future itinerary boxed in bold black lines. He laid his palms on the counter in the identical pose.

As Alice worked at her computer, he was jovial and friendly. "My wife thought we should let her go to Europe like she wanted to, but I said she hasn't even seen any of this country yet. She needs to experience her own heritage."

Alice remembered that line from the brochure. She wondered what her own heritage was.

"What do you think?" the man asked her.

She looked up from the computer screen and held his eyes for a moment. "It doesn't matter much one way or the other," she said. "She wants to travel." She tore the paperwork from the printer, laid it on the counter, and handed him a pen. "Sometimes people just need to go someplace different." She pointed at the X: "Sign here."

She watched him leave and turned to Lisa, who was hunched over her keyboard, squinting at the screen. "I'm leaving," she said.

Lisa looked stunned. "I thought you were staying till four when Kathleen comes." Kathleen was their boss.

"You can handle it for an hour."

"What if somebody wants something I don't know how to do?"

"Figure it out," Alice said, and left through the front door.

I shouldn't be so hard on her, Alice thought as she walked to her car. Why should she care about hotels in Tel Aviv or buses to Sinai? She knows enough to have the life she wants and how to get it, which is more than I can say for me.

She got into her car and drove to the bar. It was empty except for two off-duty waitresses drinking at one of the tables and Kevin behind the bar. "You're early," he said, setting a Scotch before her. "I missed you this week."

Alice sipped at her drink. "I have a boyfriend."

"No kidding? Not one of the suits you met here, I hope."

She smiled. "No. He's an old hippie, a college professor. He's wonderful."

"So what are you doing here today?"

Kevin was crimping pour spouts with needle-nosed pliers, replacing those with cracked and leaking corks. "Why do you flatten the ends like that?" she asked.

"Ah, let me show you." He took a glass from behind him and poured from a bottle of Scotch with a new spout. "One thousand one, one thousand two." He brought the bottle upright. "I count as I pour, turning time into volume, so that, *voilà*—an ounce." He poured the Scotch from the glass into a shot glass. It came exactly to the white line that marked an ounce.

"I'm impressed."

He poured the shot of Scotch into her glass. "So what brings you in here today?"

She lit a cigarette. "I just needed a drink."

"Is this guy married?"

"Divorced." She watched him crimp another pour spout. "Kevin, what would you do if you were in love with someone and everything was great and you found out they were crazy—they told you they had visions from God or they were from Jupiter or something? How would that make you feel? What would you do?"

He put down the pliers and leaned on the counter. "Well, I get asked questions like this all the time. Usually it's some guy who wants me to imagine being a wronged wife. I'll tell you what I tell them: I don't know. Probably the person they're having me pretend I am doesn't know until it happens. These guys haven't really got a clue what they'd do if their wives found out they have a girlfriend, but they want me to figure out what their wives are gonna do. Give me a break. Do what you want, and pay the price, then figure out what you're gonna do next."

"Is that what you do?"

He grinned. "Sometimes. I'm unpredictable."

"You're a big help."

"Okay, so you're not just another guy. Why would anybody think you're crazy, except for not giving a chance to a sweet guy like me?"

"I can't tell you. But believe me, he probably will."

"So what will you do?"

She stared at the two waitresses in the corner, laughing about what? Men, more than likely. She wished she were like them and knew enough to laugh. "I don't know," she said.

As she drove home she tried to relive the week, to fix it in her mind as strong and real. Something that a single revelation couldn't mar. She couldn't keep the chronology straight. Too much had happened. The week seemed like a complex history, packed with moments:

Erik's father is taking me for a walk to the river while Erik stays behind to fix dinner. His father sits on his heels by the water and looks at me like Erik twenty years in the future, his hair turned silver, the lines of his furrowed brow eroded deeper, the eyes still bright. He says, "My son is in love with you, isn't he?" I say yes, and that I love him, too, and that, no, I will not hurt him. As I come back into the house, Erik is turned away, setting the table in his precise way, still in his apron. I sneak up behind him and grab him round the waist. As he turns in my arms, his arms settle around me and squeeze hard.

We are lying in bed, and I ask him what Debra looks like. He walks naked across the room and brings back two photographs and lays them on the bed. She is beautiful. In the first her hair hangs in long, thick curls. There is something shy about her, a touch of fear in her laughing smile. In the second the hair is cropped close, her smile a crooked, ironic line. She is not looking at the camera, but she knows it is there. "This is the woman I married," he says to me, holding up the first one. He nods toward the other. "That's my ex-wife."

On the same bed, he is smoothing out a map and pointing to the places he wants to take me camping, describing them, lifting his hands from the map as if conjuring them in the air, grinning all the time. "You will love it," he says over and over, and I love to hear him say it, know without a doubt that it is true.

They had spent every moment, except when she was at work, together. Her stop at the bar had been the first time all week when she could have been with Erik but was not. Tomorrow they were going camping in the mountains for the weekend. She wanted to see these places as herself, wanted him to see her there and know who she was. And be glad, she thought. Somehow, to be glad. It was a foolish vision, impossible, but it was the only one she wanted, the only way she could bear to feel so much for him.

She supposed it was cowardly to choose tonight to tell him, with Luther to run to in case things went wrong. It was hard to imagine them going right. But still, she had to do it, as if entering a room where she suspected that someone lay dead. She had to tell him the truth so that it wouldn't have such power anymore and she would know whether this week had been an illusion.

Erik was not in his usual place on the porch. She hurried into the house. Their morning coffee cups were still on the coffee table. Each morning before she went to work she and Erik sat here and had coffee. Alice set the cups on a tray to take to the kitchen but suddenly sank to the sofa, the tray on her lap. She wondered what tomorrow morning would be like. Or next week.

She used to sit here and read novels or poetry. She had no television, never read magazines or newspapers. Sometimes she felt guilty for not knowing what was going on in the world. But it never seemed to change. New villains, new heroes, new disasters—each one like the one before, the lives in pain or triumph, the constant drone of fear. Her great-aunt used to say, "They can't see the forest for the trees—most of the time they can't even see the trees."

Yesterday she'd showed him Donne's "The Good-Morrow"—"one little room an everywhere." It was true. But not an empty room. How would she ever stay here alone again, never saying, "Listen to this poem, listen to me"?

He would be here soon. She had to get hold of herself. Her work shoes echoed on the wood floor, clicked on the kitchen tile. She set the tray on the counter and went into her bedroom, kicking her shoes off into the closet. She hung up her suit and blouse neatly, stripped her hose, bra, and underwear, and dropped them on the floor. She looked at herself in the mirror and tried to imagine herself as Erik saw her, beautiful and desirable. His fingertips moved across her skin as if it were sacred. This morning a customer had told her she looked radiant. She was. She could see it in the mirror even now, despite her fear. He is my lover, she thought. I've never really had a lover until now.

She put on clean underwear and a pair of jeans and dug in her drawer for her most comfortable sweater. She plunged herself into it, pausing before putting her head through the neck, letting the soft knit envelop her face, breathing in her own warm breath.

She heard Erik's rap at the screen door. "Come in," she hollered from inside the sweater.

"It's latched," he called back.

She hurried to the door, saw him through the haze of screen wire like the first time he came. "I'm sorry. Just habit. I had to get out of those meet-the-public clothes."

"I'll try to forgive you. Pretty serious, latching your screen door." He pulled her to him in a strong embrace and kissed her. They stood clinging to each other. He drew back and looked in her eyes. "What's wrong?" he said. "You're a nervous wreck."

"I'm sorry. I'm just a little frightened about telling you about—what I have to tell you about."

131

"Just a little?"

She gave a nervous laugh. "Okay, I'm terrified."

"What is it?"

She closed her eyes and sighed. "I need a drink first; you want one?"

"Sure, I'll help."

"No, you sit. I'll get the drinks and work up my nerve."

"Are you going to dump me?"

"God, no. Nothing like that."

In the kitchen she made gin and tonics and ran through what she was going to say. In school she'd always hated outlines and had written the paper first, coaxing an outline from it when it was done. But now she must say just the right thing at just the right time. She thought of Kevin—"one thousand one, one thousand two."

She scurried into the living room on the balls of her feet. "I was out of limes, so I used lemons, I hope that's okay." She set the drinks on the table and curled up in her usual place on the sofa, her arms wrapped around her knees. "This is hard," she said. She took a long drink. "What I have to tell you is going to be very hard for you to believe. I can't ask you to promise to believe me. That would be stupid. But please keep an open mind."

He squeezed her shoulder. "I'll believe you."

"Don't say that. You can't know that. Just listen, okay?" She took another drink and pushed herself straight. "I'm not like other people."

"I know that."

"Erik, please."

"Okay, I'll shut up."

"I'm not like other people. I'm different. That's why I keep myself 'cooped up,' as you say. I can't let people know what I am because they will think I am crazy. They won't believe me, they'll just think I'm crazy."

She stopped and swallowed hard, fighting back

tears. He squeezed her shoulder. "I need to tell you because I love you. I want you to know all about me. Even if I could hide it from you, I wouldn't want you to love me and not know who I am. Do you understand?"

His face was full of concern. She thought he might cry himself. "Yes, I think so," he said.

Tears filled her eyes. She brushed them away with the back of her hand and set her drink on the table. "First, I want to apologize for lying to you. I wasn't ready to tell you the truth. That story about the boy I killed, I didn't tell you everything about that." She stopped. She could feel the thrum of her heart pounding. Everything was still. Only his hand on her shoulder kept her from flying apart.

"He didn't have a knife, like I said. I tore his throat out. I bit it out with my jaws." She closed her eyes and clenched her fists, trying to stop shaking. She thought she felt a change in the pressure of his hand but couldn't be sure.

She opened her eyes. His brow was furrowed with deep lines. She forced herself to look at him. "When I was thirteen, something happened to me. I don't know why. It just happened. I went out into the woods at the farm, and I changed. I changed into a wolf. Not a hairy man like in the movies, but a real wolf. And in the morning, I changed back again. And I have changed every month since then. I think I will always do this. I was a wolf when I killed that boy. When I was old enough, I came here so I could keep myself closed up and wouldn't hurt anyone else.

"That's why I never got close to anyone, because I couldn't let anyone know. But when I found you, I decided I couldn't give you up." Her voice broke, and sobs shook her. He took her in his arms. She buried her face in his shoulder. "I have been so afraid to tell you. So afraid you will think I am crazy and leave me. Please don't leave me, Erik. Please don't leave me."

He rocked her slowly, back and forth, not saying a word. She slowly grew calm. She felt relieved. It was over. She would never have to tell him again. Whatever else happened, at least he knew who she was. Even if he didn't believe her, at least he knew.

She put her hand on his chest and pushed herself back, looking up at him. "I'm okay now," she said. "It was just hard to tell you." She smiled and wiped her face with her hands. "It must be hard for you, too. You must have questions."

He stared at her, his brow still furrowed as if in pain. "You're a werewolf?"

"Yes."

He shook his head. "You're not joking."

"Do I look like I'm joking?"

He said nothing. He looked down, rubbing his forehead.

She leaned toward him, trying to catch his eye. "Erik?" He looked sideways at her, shook a cigarette from his pack, and lit it.

"Alice, I can't believe that."

"Why not?"

"Why not! You want me to believe you turn into a wolf!" His voice was loud and harsh.

She felt her panic returning. "Why are you angry? Please don't be angry with me. I'm only trying to tell you the truth."

He stared at her, saying nothing; sat up, then stood, pacing back and forth. "You're a werewolf?"

"Yes."

"I don't know what to say."

"Ask me questions." She shrugged one shoulder and gestured at the drinks on the table. "Have a drink." She picked up her own and stared into the glass at a lemon seed floating in the ice. She was losing him, and there was nothing she could do about it. She couldn't unsay what she'd said, couldn't undo who she was. She could feel him withdrawing as he paced back and forth as surely as if those steps were in a line away from her as far as he could go.

She spoke without looking up. "Can I show you a few things? Some evidence."

"Evidence?"

"Yes, evidence." She stood and walked to her bedroom. He followed a few paces behind. It looks like anyone else's room, she thought: underwear on the floor, family photos on the dresser, chiseled perfume bottles circling a red jewelry box. She opened a drawer and pulled out a few news clippings. "Read these," she said.

They reported the boy's death, saying he died from an animal bite to the throat. A feral dog was suspected; people were advised to be on the lookout for such an animal.

"You know about animals," she said. "How likely is it that a dog would come upon a man raping a woman, tear his throat out without leaving any other marks, and run away without touching the woman?"

"If the dog were rabid, it might do anything."

"Why not attack me?"

"Maybe it was frightened off. Maybe you were passed out, and it didn't even notice you."

"Erik, I wasn't passed out, I was there, remember? I killed him. I was a wolf."

He shook his head. "What you're telling me is impossible, Alice. It's simply unbelievable. How do you believe it yourself? It must seem real to you, but it can't be."

She took his hands. "Erik, listen to me. It doesn't seem real. It is real. As real as getting up in the morning, going to school, and teaching a class is to you. What do you want to know about wolves? I know exactly what it is like to be a wolf. No, that's not right. I am a wolf. I am a wolf." She searched his eyes and released his hands.

"Alice, I love you, but do you know how hard this is

to believe? I'm a biologist. You're asking me to believe your entire physiology changes overnight. It's impossible."

"What about a butterfly," she said quietly.

"That's different, a single metamorphosis in the life cycle of the organism."

She gave him a sad smile. "So you'd believe me if I just changed once?"

"It's just not the same."

"I know." She took the clippings from his hand and put them back in the drawer, sliding it closed with her hip. She pointed at the wall beside him. "That's my calendar. See the x? That's when I changed last." She lifted the page to reveal the next month. "That's when I'll change again. Very regular. If you hang around, you can see for yourself."

"You changed last Friday?"

"That's right."

He remembered the bag of dog food. "Is that what the dog food was for?"

"That's right, you saw that. Yes, the change makes me very hungry—the dog food fills me up."

"You eat a whole bag of dog food?"

"I'm a very large wolf, Erik."

"And you lock yourself up?"

She nodded. "Would you like to see my den?"

The basement door was thicker than the front door, locked with a heavy dead bolt. When she opened it, the unmistakable odor of animal urine filled the cool air at the top of the stairs. She pointed at the sheet of metal that covered the inside of the door. "A long time ago, I used to try to dig out. I don't do that anymore. I'm frightened of the stairs."

The only light came from a single bulb hanging from the ceiling. All the windows were covered with boards. "Watch your step," she said. She pointed to one of the windows. "There's insulation behind the boards for soundproofing. I howl sometimes. I can still hear pretty well, but no one can hear me." She looked at him. "I smell everything. It used to be exhilarating when I didn't lock myself up. Now it's just frustrating." She swung her hand in an arc like a hostess. "Look around," she said.

"What for?"

"You're the expert."

"Alice, this is crazy."

"It can't hurt you to look around."

He walked around the perimeter of the room. There was a mark along the wall, the line of an animal rubbing against the walls, marking its unyielding territory over and over again. He knelt and sniffed it. He found a tuft of fur caught in one of the cracks. He removed it, wrapped it in a piece of paper, and put it in his wallet. He crouched at the foot of the stairs and examined the bottom step where the wolf had chewed. He ran a fingertip over the deep impression of large canine jaws in the wood. At the floor drain he found more bits of fur and a small piece of shit he also wrapped up and put in his wallet. As he crouched there he noticed a paw print in the dust by the drain. He held out his hand and compared the print to his outspread palm. The print was huge, larger than his outspread palm, easily more than five inches long and four inches wide.

"My, what big feet you have, Grandma," Alice said.

He looked up at her. She felt sorry for him. His face was still knotted with worry. "If you found that print in the wilderness, Erik, what animal would you say made it?"

Erik stood, still staring at the print. "A wolf."

"That's right. What do you think now?"

He shook his head. "I think there's been an animal down here, maybe even a wolf, but that doesn't mean that you are a wolf." He rubbed his forehead as if rubbing out the creases there might make his confusion go away. "That time with the boy—was that the first time you turned into a wolf?"

Why do things have to be so complicated? she

thought. "No, Dr. Freud, it wasn't. It did start with puberty, though—as all sorts of things do."

They stood staring at one another for a moment. Alice's voice was weary and sad. "Well, you've got an awful choice. You can believe I'm psychotic, or you can believe I'm telling the truth." She turned and went up the stairs. He followed without touching her.

As she locked the door behind them, she said, "You had something you wanted to talk to me about."

"It was nothing. It can wait."

She stood facing the door, away from him. She didn't want to start crying again. He had needed to talk to her, and now he didn't. Now he didn't want to confide in her anymore. She turned to face him. "It was important before, and it's nothing now. What's that all about, Erik?"

"This just doesn't seem like a good time."

"Planning your escape?"

"No." He stepped toward her, took her in his arms, but he only seemed to be going through the motions. His arms felt different from before. She laid her head against his chest, already missing him.

"What did you want to talk to me about?" she said.

He sighed. "Debra came by."

"She came by your house?"

"Yes."

"What did she want?"

"She says the divorce was a mistake. She wants me back."

Of course, she thought. Of course she does. And what chance do I have? She felt like a fool. "How nice for you," she said.

His arms tightened around her. "Listen to me. I love you. I don't want to go back to Debra."

Her head still lay against his chest. Everything seemed clear to her now. "Why not? You think I'm crazy. You don't believe me." Her voice was quiet and matter-of-fact. Why should he believe me? she thought.

"I don't think you're crazy."

She looked up at him. "Do you believe me?"

"Alice, this isn't fair."

"You're right. It isn't. I'm sorry." She began to cry again. "I'm so sorry." She pushed herself away and was afraid to look at him again. Something in his eyes had changed. She had lost him, she must let him go. He was so sweet, he would pity her. She couldn't bear to be pitied. She pushed past him and made for the front door. "I have to go," she said. "I have an appointment with Adams in twenty minutes." She left him standing by the basement door and ran to her car.

Erik walked back into the living room. Their drinks sat in pools of condensation where they had left them. He took them to the kitchen, rinsed them, and put them in the dishwasher. He leaned against the counter. He felt light-headed and dizzy. The silence in the house seemed to drone in his ears. He spread his palm and stared at it, shaking his head. What am I supposed to think? How did this happen? This morning I was so happy, and now I don't know where I am.

He went back into her bedroom, read the clippings again, touched the tiny x on the calendar that marked the day he had met Alice. Only a week ago. He picked up her underwear from the floor and felt the cool nylon with his fingertips. He looked up and saw himself in the mirror. He laid the underwear on the dresser and walked quickly from the house, locking the door behind him.

Chapter

9

Alice darted in and out of traffic on the freeway, her hands wrapped tight around the steering wheel, her arms rigid, pushing her back into the seat. She felt as if she might erupt into the darkening sky. She imagined herself catching one of the other cars with a glancing blow, careening out of control, soaring over the guard-rail into the intersection below. In films werewolves were brought low in their monster forms, fading into humanity as they died. She was sure her death would reveal no secrets, prompt no belief.

She drove too fast for the danger of it. She couldn't kill herself. She'd thought about it before but didn't have the knack. She marveled at people who could do that, destroy themselves in a triumph of the will, a final solution for the passions. She could only flirt with death. I am good at flirting, she thought.

A semi hurled by her, making her tiny car shudder in its wake. She slowed and moved into a less vulnerable lane. Such nonsense, she thought, the poses I strike for myself.

She was not in a hurry to see Adams. She wasn't sure she wanted to see Adams at all. She entertained the idea of simply getting away. Away from her house, her novels, the artwork on the walls, the bed still rumpled with lovemaking, the empty basement. But I would take the wolf with me, she reminded herself. Every moon she would find me.

I just wanted to be believed. The men in the bars tell me all kinds of shit—I know Johnny Carson, I was dead for ten minutes, I have always dreamed of meeting someone like you (with no idea of the nightmare that would be). I always pretend I believe them. It's the least I can do. They don't have to tell me anything. They will never see me again. I ask them to believe nothing, it wouldn't be fair. I don't exist. I'm just a fuck.

Perhaps that's enough, the life I had. Things were okay. I knew what I was doing. I was familiar with the territory. I fall in love in one week, and now I think my life has changed. But I will change again. I can see the date on my calendar, hear myself howling in my own little dungeon. But I can't imagine the future: No, I'm sorry, dear, we can't do dinner on Wednesday, that's my night to be a monster.

It was stupid to tell Erik, but what choice did I have? Change before his eyes and watch him pee in his pants? Maybe rip his throat out? What choice does he have? Love a crazy person, love a monster, the Lady and the Tiger behind the same door. God, I've always hated that story.

She descended the ramp into the city. It looked odd with so few cars, so few people. She knew some people lived down here in these streets. She looked for them now, sleeping in doorways, digging through trash cans, but she didn't see them. It wasn't completely dark yet. Perhaps they only came out at night. Perhaps they were there but she couldn't see them, like wolves in the wild, invisible except for their tracks and their scat, silent except for their howls in the night.

She waited at a traffic light beside a gray limousine. Behind the black windows, there might have been anyone or anything. They owned privacy, or rented it. They could look out and see her staring, but she couldn't see them. Her shiny black reflection looked brittle and metallic. She pushed the gas to the floor. In the mirror, the limo still sat, waiting for the light to change.

"Mental Health Parking" was closed with a chain drooping across the driveway. Sitting in the lot was a rusted cart splattered with tar, black smoke drifting into the air in lazy clouds, but there was no one around, just a tar-encrusted shovel leaning against it. She parked in the street in front of Adams's building. The parking meter displayed a red crescent announcing VIOLATION. As she got out of the car an empty dump truck lurched past her with the spitting hiss of air brakes. She stood by her car and watched it rattle away down the hill, continued to watch as the retreating line of traffic lights changed in sequence, then changed again for no one.

The lobby looked deserted through the windows. The coffee shop was dark except for the clock, a waterfall advertising beer. The revolving door ushered her inside with a familiar moaning sigh. No one waited for the elevators.

She tried to get a grip on herself in the elevator, watching the numbered lights, but they infuriated her. She looked down at her shoes. Why am I so angry? she asked herself. She looked back up at the numbers. "Goddamn," she said aloud.

Luther's receptionist wasn't behind her sliding glass, no tranquil music oozed through the speaker in the ceiling, but the faint doorbell sounded when she opened the door. Luther came out into the waiting room to show her in, as if she were a guest at a party.

"You look angry," he said.

It took him fifteen minutes to calm her enough to speak coherently.

"He doesn't believe me. He thinks I'm a nut case. Meanwhile his ex-wife just came sniffing around saying she wants him back. My timing's perfect. Just when he finds out I'm crazy, he's got her nice comfortable bed to crawl back into."

"You sound very angry."

"No shit."

"Just who are you angry with?"

"Myself."

"Just yourself?"

"Him, too, of course."

"Why 'of course'? What has he done to you?"

"He didn't believe me. Goddammit Luther, he says he loves me. I don't know what that means to you doctor guys, but being believed would seem pretty basic to me."

"But you said yourself you've been deceiving him. Who is he supposed to believe—last week's Alice or today's Alice?"

"Okay, okay, you win. I have no right to be angry with anyone. We psychos just need to stay in our place."

"I didn't say that. I'm just trying to find out who you're really mad at."

"I told you already, but apparently I didn't get the right answer. Do I keep guessing, or do you want to just give me the right answer and save us some time?"

"We have plenty of time. Why don't you try just one more guess?"

"How about you? You're being a real shit."

"Come on, you can do better than that. I'm one of those doctor guys, remember? You expect me to be a shit."

"I suppose you think I'm mad at her."

"Which her?"

"Debra. Debra. Ex-wife Debra. Debra I-don't-love-you-anymore, Darling-I-want-you-back Debra."

"Go on."

"What's to go on about? She's married to a wonderful man, breaks his heart, then expects him to come running back just because she's in heat. It pisses me off. Erik deserves better than that."

"In heat? Is that what you think? You say he's a wonderful man—couldn't she be in love with him, too?"

"Divorce isn't usually considered a sign of affection, doctor. She had her chance, and she chased him off. Now he's . . ."

"He's what, Alice?"

"He can make up his own mind."

"What were you going to say?"

"It doesn't matter."

"Say it anyway."

"I'd rather not. It's stupid."

"Feelings are neither smart nor stupid."

"Okay. Mine. I was going to say he's mine."

They talked on and on about her anger. Alice didn't think it would do any good, this swell and rumble of pointless rage, but this was the game, and this was Luther's party. Still, he listened. She needed that.

"It is only natural," he said, "given your feelings for Erik, that you would resent Debra's advances toward him."

"Resent doesn't quite cover it, Luther."

"I suppose not. Well, what do you plan to do about it?"

"Look, Luther, there's nothing I can do. Erik doesn't believe me. You don't believe me. I can't expect anyone to understand. Frankly, I just want to go back to the way things were before I ever came here."

"You don't really. You want control over these episodes so that you can lead a normal life."

"But I can't do that."

"Perhaps through hypnosis you could learn."

"Luther, this isn't just in my head. Have you got that?"

"Let's say it isn't. Hypnosis is simply an altered state of consciousness, like the meditative trances mystics use to slow their heartbeats, even change their brain waves. How do you know you couldn't affect your transformations?"

"You're reaching, Luther."

"Maybe so. But what about you? Strictly physiological, is it? You call the full moon a physiological stimulus? Why don't you just go to an astrologer?" He paused, rearranged himself on his chair. "Besides, I want to understand you better. You've said you want someone to understand you. To do that I need to understand your transformations."

"I've already told you all about them."

"That's not the same as your experience of them. I want to know the sights and sounds and smells, the kinds of thoughts you have in that state, what these experiences mean to you. Who knows? You might persuade me they're real."

"I'm not so sure I want anyone rummaging around in my mind."

"No one will be rummaging around in your mind. All hypnosis is essentially self-hypnosis. Only you will be inside your mind. Hypnosis is simply a means of focusing your attention on those aspects of yourself that the everyday world distracts you from. It's like a lens that helps you see certain things more clearly and in a peaceful, relaxing way."

Alice was stroking her cheek with the end of her braid, looking at the painting of the woman in the park. She often wondered where the woman would go next, where she had been, who might come to meet her there in the park among the trees.

"Do you really think I might be able to keep from changing?"

"That is a very real possibility."

Alice stared into his eyes. They were kind enough. He meant well. She imagined hypnosis as an enveloping numbness, a state outside of time, a consummation devoutly to be wished. "Okay," she said, "I'm game. I've got nothing to lose."

"I would encourage you to think about how much you might have to gain." Luther stood and gestured toward the psychiatrist's couch. "This will be easier if you're completely relaxed. Perhaps you'd like to stretch out, take off your shoes, make yourself completely comfortable. I'll go lock the outer door to make sure we're not disturbed."

Alice sat on the couch. The leather sighed and gave. As she removed her shoes, she thought, This is like the nights I change, only I remove all my clothes and lie down on concrete. She glanced at the door, undid her bra, and stretched out on the couch. Adams returned, pulled up a chair, and sat down beside her.

"Comfy?" he said.

"Very. I could fall asleep."

"Wonderful. Now just empty your mind of all stray thoughts. Listen to my voice and relax. Take a few deep breaths, and as you exhale, feel all your tensions and anxieties leave with the air you release. As you breathe more deeply, you will reach those small tensions in your shoulders or your legs or wherever they may be and feel them relax as you let out your breath. As you inhale, open your eyes wide and look at the light in the ceiling above your head. As you exhale, let your eyes relax completely. . . ."

She listened to his voice and her breath. It seemed like the ocean or wind in the mountains. He told her to relax each part of her body, one by one. Everything seemed to slow down, to take on a new rhythm, to move in a harmonious dance. She felt herself letting go of the world like the bait in a monkey trap, felt herself come free. She wanted peace. She felt herself moving toward it like the tide moving into the shore in steady, advancing waves.

"At this point, your entire body should be loose and limp and relaxed. If you feel any remaining discomfort, take a few more deep breaths, feeling with each breath the discomfort dissolving and your body growing completely comfortable and relaxed and at peace. Do you feel completely relaxed?"

"Yes."

"Good. Now remember, even though you are in this relaxed state, you are still totally in control of the situation. If for any reason you should want to come out of this state, you simply have to open your eyes and you will be able to act precisely as you want to act, fully in control. Do you understand?"

"Yes."

"You've told me that when you lived on the farm with your parents, turning into a wolf used to be a joyful experience, one you looked forward to, one that made you feel full of life. I want you to go back to that time and place, remember the joyful anticipation you felt at that time.

"Imagine yourself standing on the hill at your parents' farm in the evening, full of that joy you knew then. It is a beautiful evening. There is, perhaps, a light breeze, maybe you can hear birds or animals. Listen to the peaceful sounds of the evening, relaxing you, bringing you peace. You can feel the ground beneath you, safe and secure. If you look, you can see the woods at the bottom of the hill where you have had so many pleasant experiences.

"When you feel ready, you begin to walk slowly down the hill toward the woods. Perhaps you feel the breeze against your skin, and it soothes and relaxes you. With each step down the hill you feel more peaceful, contented with yourself and the world around you. There is no need to hurry as you move down the hill. Each step is safe and sure as you feel the familiar ground beneath your feet. As you descend the hill, each step brings you closer to the woods, each step makes you more joyful and relaxed.

"As you approach the woods, you can see them more clearly, and as you do, you are filled with happiness and contentment. Perhaps you are so close now that you can smell the trees, hear the leaves rustling in the wind. Perhaps you can see a particular favorite tree standing at the edge of the woods. Each step takes you closer to the woods and the trees.

"When you reach the bottom of the hill you will be back in the world where you were happy with who you are and unafraid of changing. Can you see the woods before you?"

"Yes."

"Listen to the sound of the wind in the trees. It is a peaceful sound, peaceful like the contentment you feel being here. Can you hear the wind?"

"Yes."

"When you feel ready, walk into the woods among the trees. Take your time. There is no need to hurry. The woods are timeless and peaceful. As you enter the woods you are joyful and contented, happy to be who you are. Look around you at the trees. You can touch the bark of the trees if you like. You will find the touch comforting, you feel welcome here. You feel the crackle of twigs and leaves beneath your feet. Breathe deeply and smell the earth and trees, everything full of life and growth and harmony. Do you feel yourself inside the woods?"

"Yes."

"It is a beautiful place. When you feel ready, look at the sky. It is growing gradually darker. The sky is turning a rich, deep blue. As it grows darker, you feel more at peace in these woods where you've had so many pleasant experiences. If you look closely, you may see a star or two, the first stars of the evening. As you look at them you feel peaceful and happy.

"One part of the sky is brighter and warmer than the rest. If you look, you can see the moon, bright and clear. It is a full moon, a bright and hopeful light in the sky. Do you see it?"

"Yes."

"What does the full moon mean to you, Alice?"

"It means I am changing."

"Do you feel yourself changing now?"

"Yes."

"Is it a pleasant sensation?"

"Yes."

"Tell me what you are feeling."

"I can smell the world opening up. The scents of the other animals around me. I can smell you."

"What else are you feeling?"

"I can hear the dogs. I can hear the cars on the highway. . . . I hear an awful noise. It hurts my ears."

"Tell me about this noise."

"It whines and doesn't stop. It shouldn't be here. It isn't anything alive. It frightens me. It shouldn't be here."

"Have you ever heard this noise before?"

"No . . . it's a machine. It shouldn't be here. Wait. . . . It's a vacuum cleaner. I hear a vacuum cleaner. But it's not here. It's somewhere else. I can't stay here."

Alice opened her eyes and shivered. Her eyes were wide and fearful. She sat upright on the couch, her hands digging into the upholstery. "It's fading now." She looked around the office, then at Adams. "You almost made me change," she said. "The vacuum cleaner was not in my mind. It's here. I heard it. I was about to change, here, in this office."

"Calm down, Alice. Everything is just as it was. There is no vacuum cleaner here. Listen for yourself."

"What's that way?" she asked, pointing with her left hand.

"Nothing at all. You were in a trance. You're just disoriented."

"Goddammit, Luther. I know I was in a trance. Now, what is that way in this building?"

"Nothing, just more offices. Nothing to be afraid of."

She stood, held out her hand. "Come on, I'm going to show you a vacuum cleaner."

"Sit down, Alice. Calm yourself. It was just an image in your trance."

"Look, Luther, I'm getting awfully goddamn tired of not being believed. You're the one who started this. Now you can either humor me or you can sit there, but if I walk out of this office alone, you'll never see me again."

Reluctantly Luther rose to his feet. "Very well, lead on."

She was already heading for the door. Luther trailed behind her down the long hall like a child trying to catch up to his mother. At the end of the hall, a door stood open. When they were halfway there, Luther began to hear the faint drone of a vacuum cleaner, and a chill went up his spine. Alice stood in the open doorway and pointed at the vacuum and the startled cleaning woman, who now shut it off. "I heard that from your office," Alice said. "You were trying to get me to change, and I heard that vacuum. But I wasn't just imagining it. I was changing, do you understand? You almost made me change into a wolf."

"What the hell's going on here?" the cleaning woman broke in. "I'm just doing my job." She edged toward the desk, placed her hand on the phone as if she might throw it. "I'll call security."

Luther showed her his identification and explained in hushed tones that Alice was his patient. She cocked

her head and eyed Alice. "Well, you got no business in
here. This is Dr. Rutley's office."

Alice and Luther made their way back to his office
in silence. He offered her pills and a tumbler of water.
Alice drank the water but set the pills aside. "Could
you hear the vacuum cleaner?" she asked.

"No, but you're making too much of this, Alice.
Your hearing is just better than mine." He chuckled.
"I'm not as young as I used to be." She did not smile.
"Besides, heightened senses are a common phenome-
non in hypnosis."

"Come on, doctor. Your office is soundproof.
You could hypnotize a piano tuner and he wouldn't
have heard that vacuum. I almost changed. I know
what I'm talking about. I've been doing it for
nineteen years. You almost had a wolf in your
office. Hell, I wish I had so that you'd finally believe
me."

"Alice, I believe that you had all the feelings of the
experience you've described to me. This is actually
very encouraging. If under hypnosis you felt yourself
changing, you might be able to use hypnosis to keep
yourself *from* changing."

"I don't see how that follows."

"Before tonight you thought of this state as something beyond your control, the result of the moon
in the sky. Now you see that it's not that simple.
Think of this state as a place you enter and depart
through a gate, and now *you,* not the moon or fate,
can be the gatekeeper, locking the gate forever, if
you wish."

Alice felt a surge in her chest as if she might cry. She
pulled her legs up to her chest and held them. "Not
change anymore? How would I do that? Do you plan
to hypnotize me every full moon?"

"I can teach you self-hypnosis. Tonight you vividly
imagined the circumstances that precipitate these
episodes and almost experienced one. Through hyp-

nosis you could use your imagination to shape your response to those circumstances in reality."

"Teach me." Alice's tone had changed, but Luther pretended not to notice.

"Certainly. When you come in for your session next week. . . ."

She reached out her hand and placed it on his knee, her body leaned toward him. "No, please, teach me now."

He looked down at her small hand resting on the dark gray gabardine of his trousers, like a dove nesting on a dark bough. "Please," she said again as he looked into her eyes.

Luther sat up straighter, searching for the right thing to do, trying not to see only her eyes, hear the supplication in her voice, feel the pressure of her palm upon his thigh. "Very well," he said, "I can show you the basic procedure tonight, and you can practice at home. But you shouldn't expect too much right away."

When she got home, she called Erik and told him she needed to be alone for the weekend to think about things, and their camping trip would have to be postponed. She tried to make this sound like a positive thing, a healing: when next you see me I'll be as before, and nothing will have changed. In his effort not to sound relieved, he came across distant and wooden. Like a hunter in a blind, she thought.

She lay awake in bed for a long time before she could fall asleep, planning the itinerary for her journey. Tomorrow she would practice. Tomorrow she might learn to change or not, at any time, as she chose. She imagined the wolf leaving her, never returning, an animal destroyed. She remembered the wolf before she locked her up, before she locked herself up. In a sense she had been her only companion in her long confinement. The wolf had done nothing to her except share her pain. Tears came to her eyes, flowed down her cheeks. She would miss her.

Just before she fell asleep, she remembered Luther's scent when she was changing. He wants me, she thought. So professional all these weeks, and he wants me. How sad for him, and touching.

Chapter

10

Luther held the shoot between his thumb and forefinger and trimmed it from his giraffe's nose. He was in his topiary garden, where he came to relax. Inside a circular hedge trimmed to look like an ornate castle, he had fashioned a bear, a turtle, a fox, an elephant, and a giraffe. When he and Eleanor had moved into this house fourteen years before, he'd planted the boxwoods, nurturing them for ten years until they were large enough to shape into his menagerie—trimming, bending, lashing to bamboo shafts—until they became the shapes he'd envisioned years before while doing his residency. Topiary, someone once said, is the art of a patient man. He'd sketched them on a pad at three o'clock in the morning in the dim half-light of the psych ward, having just subdued a violent patient with a massive injection of Thorazine.

When he was still in medical school with only a few hours a week to himself, he'd dabbled with chicken wire forms covered in ivy. But these were the real thing.

He looked at the circular marble walk, the arched entry to the simple maze leading back to the house, the serrated hedge that supported the dome of sky. Topiary, in Latin, means "a little place." This was his little place.

Once he'd invited Eleanor here for a picnic. They'd lain on a blanket drinking wine, and he'd thought how wonderful it would be to make love to her here. But she'd joked with him, saying that they—meaning the animals—would all be watching, and she'd spoiled his fantasy for him. She hadn't been back since except to deliver messages from the house, and since he'd given himself an intercom phone for the garden last Christmas, even that was no longer necessary.

The workman who'd installed the phone in a tiny box set discreetly in the castle wall had understood why the wires had to run underground, but he'd wanted to take a more direct route through the maze. Luther had insisted the wire be buried in the little wilderness, a tangle of briar and ivy surrounding the maze. From inside the maze, Luther had been able to hear the curses of the man as he worked. "Crazy fuck," he'd said after each wince of pain. When the job was done, Luther had rewarded him with a generous bonus and an imported beer at the kitchen table, where he'd written the check. "You make all them animals yourself?" the man had asked him, his gloved hands wrapped around the green bottle, a red welt glistening on his black forehead. Luther had leaned back in his chair and explained the art of topiary as the man nodded and smiled as if amused.

It was Monday afternoon, Luther's "alone time." He saw no patients on Monday, rarely saw Eleanor. He believed that she'd gone shopping, but he couldn't remember what she'd said when she left. They'd roamed the countryside on Saturday looking for antiques, had spent Sunday lounging in bed reading the newspaper, then going to a dinner party at a neighbor's that Eleanor had arranged with no mention to him that he could remember. This was the first opportunity he'd really had to think about Alice and what had happened Friday night.

He listened to the sounds up and down his street—birds singing, wind sifting through the trees, the rumble of a car, and at some distance the strident conversation of a mother and child. He could hear splendidly. He prided himself on it. "Can't you hear that?" he would often ask Eleanor, who would accuse him of imagining things until, as the noise grew louder, she could hear it herself.

How could Alice have heard that damn vacuum cleaner? he asked himself for the hundredth time. He stepped back and looked at his giraffe. The neck was splendid, firm and straight, just the angle he'd hoped for, but he wasn't happy with the head—cocked to one side and thrown back as if straining to reach some invisible leaf just behind its ears. As she said, his office was soundproof, and even though hypnosis could heighten the senses, this seemed more than extraordinary. It could have been a lucky guess, of course. A cleaning woman in an office building at that hour was hardly surprising. But Alice had been so sure, so determined.

Perhaps she was more dangerous than he had assumed. Psychotics, too, often have heightened senses, and their hunches can seem to them to be revelations. He had spent the morning looking through her file, reading the transcripts of their hours together. It was like the journal from a lost expedition, desperate for some landmark other than those that indicated they were only going in circles.

He kept returning to the story of the boy she thought she'd killed. He wondered what had happened with those two alone in the barn. What if she actually had taken his life in some vicious way he could not imagine? What if, in fact, it hadn't been a rape? What he'd thought was simply a hysterical reaction might be a more dangerous psychotic delusion. She might kill someone else, may have already done so. He thought about the young men in the bar she talked about. Didn't he have a responsibility to them as well?

Inescapably, when his mind turned to such thoughts, he saw Alice transforming into a wolf. She bared huge fangs, her eyes glowed red. He shook his head, walked round his giraffe, surveying it critically. It was inevitable, he reminded himself, that her metaphors should lodge in his mind. Nevertheless, even if she were not the monster she thought herself, she still might be dangerous.

It so happened that the medical examiner in Bristol, where the boy had died, had been a classmate of Luther's. Luther had considered calling him about Alice before but hadn't thought it was necessary. He sat down on the wooden swing next to the telephone and creaked back and forth. He opened the telephone box, painted to match the foliage, and set the phone in his lap. The turtle stared at him. He didn't much care for the turtle. Its legs were too long. The sparse foliage on the right front leg made it look like a peg leg. From this angle he could see that it listed to one side as if it might fall over and roll onto its shell, its roots flailing about in the air. He'd thought about transforming it into something else, but he couldn't decide what. Besides, he was pleased with the smooth dome of its shell, like one of those snowball cupcakes he'd liked as a kid.

He made his way past Information, the operator, and a receptionist to get Marvin on the line. Marvin owed him a favor. If it hadn't been for Luther, he never would have gotten through anatomy. The cadavers had unnerved him. "They don't look like they were ever alive," he'd complained to Luther, but

Luther had patiently showed him how to sort out the tangled structures nonetheless.

"Luther, how's the crazy business?"

"Beats dead people."

"I'd rather figure out how they died than try to tell them how to live."

"I don't tell them how to live, Marvin. I just help them figure out what they want."

"That's not how Eleanor tells it. How's she doing?"

Marvin had introduced Eleanor to Luther at a party during their first year at medical school. She and Marvin had dated for several years, until they'd evolved into friends. She'd accompanied him to the med. student parties, where she drank too much like they did and listened to their impassioned postmortem of the morning's test. Luther had talked to her about dreams all night, as they'd lingered by the cheese dip, and when he'd driven her home, he'd told her she was beautiful.

"She's fine," he said now. The swing began to creak at a slightly faster tempo. "Marvin, I've got a favor to ask you."

"Shoot."

"I've got a patient named Alice White who was involved in an attempted rape case down there about eighteen years ago. The boy was killed. His name was Dale. I don't know the last name."

"His name was Blevins. This ain't the big city down here. We don't have too many last names to go around. I remember it. I'd just gotten here. Messy as hell. What do you want to know?"

"Well, this was a major trauma in my patient's life. She's built up some rather complicated delusions about it. It might help me sort things out if I knew precisely what happened."

"If I remember the case, there was nothing very precise about it. You need this information right away?"

"If that wouldn't be too much trouble."

"No problem. Deer season's over. Nobody killed anybody this weekend. I've got nothing to do but paperwork right at the moment. Let me dig out the file, and I'll give you a call in a little bit."

Luther liked Marvin, sometimes wished he were more like him, easygoing, almost complacent, the most unambitious doctor he'd ever met. He often wondered if Marvin still loved Eleanor. She had been so shy back then. If Marvin had been a bit more aggressive, she might have married him instead of Luther. Marvin would have been warmer, less preoccupied. Eleanor never complained, but Luther knew she wished he were a more ardent lover. But he wished the same about her, in his way. He would've liked for her to be swept away, for them both to be swept away. But she wasn't that sort of woman. She was so down-to-earth and practical. He imagined the ceiling of their bedroom dissolving to reveal a spacious transcendent realm into which they might ascend through love. But it wouldn't happen. Their room was a sealed space, his study resting on top of it like a lid.

The phone chirped in his lap, and he jumped. It was Eleanor telling him she was home. "I've got swatches for new drapes," she said.

"I'll look at them later. I'm expecting a call."

"Are you all right?"

"Fine. I'm just expecting a call."

"Well, I'll be here when you're through."

"Okay." He hung up the phone. Later, he knew, he would have to make up for his brusqueness. He wasn't sure why he was so short with her sometimes. She made so few demands upon him, was always so nice.

Luther set the phone aside and went to his fox. He was his favorite. His low crouching stance and his swept-back ears made him look as if he might scamper into the maze at any moment. He trimmed each ear and the bushy tail to a finer point, crouched and studied from every angle, then decided to leave the snout alone.

He imagined Alice in his garden, naked, her long hair undone, falling around her breasts. She would look at him and say, "I love you, Luther." He would look into her large, dark eyes and smile, and she would know that he loved her, too. He did not take his vision in his arms. He gazed at her quietly in the peaceful stillness of his garden.

The phone began to ring again, and he was reluctant to abandon this moment of imagined bliss. By the time he picked up the phone, Eleanor and Marvin were already talking.

"I've got it, Eleanor," Luther said.

"Luther, why didn't you tell me you were expecting a call from Marvin?"

"It's a professional matter, Eleanor."

"Luther, I swear, you are such a pill sometimes. I was just about to ask Marvin about his new girlfriend. I'm assuming, Marvin, that she's the reason you haven't had time to answer any of my letters."

Luther remembered something about a Kelly or a Kathy in the last Christmas card but hadn't given it much thought. He listened impatiently as Marvin talked about this woman and her kids and Eleanor laughed and cooed.

"How old is she?" she asked.

Luther had reached his limit. "Eleanor, Marvin is calling from his office on a matter of professional importance to me, so would you please allow us to tend to our affairs."

Silence sang through the wires for a moment. Luther could barely hear music playing in the house or in Marvin's office. "All right," she said quietly. "Marvin, call me sometime when the doctor isn't in, and we can talk, okay?"

Marvin's voice was soft and gentle. "Sure thing, Eleanor." After Eleanor hung up, his tone changed. "I can see you haven't changed, Luther."

"And what's that supposed to mean?"

"Forget it."

"All right, I'll just do that. Now what did you find out?"

Marvin cleared his throat and shuffled some papers. "Well, did you have something specific you wanted to know, or do you just want me to run through the whole thing?"

"Why don't you tell me all of it."

"Okay. The boy was found in the barn early in the morning by the girl's father, who called us immediately. We were there in about fifteen minutes. There were signs of a struggle. His pants were down. Looked like he was about to mount somebody."

"Where was Alice?"

"I'm getting to that. She wasn't around. Nobody knew where she was. I examined the body and determined the cause of death to be a single bite to the throat by a large canine."

"It couldn't have been a human?"

"Not unless he had a six-inch snout and a jaw as strong as a weightlifter's arm. The throat was gone, Luther."

"Were there tracks?"

"Oh, yes, big ones, like a dog with snowshoes. But this is one of the weird things. There were tracks leading away from the body but none leading to it."

"Couldn't they just have been obliterated?"

"It's a dirt floor. All the tracks were clear, the boy's, the girl's, the father's, and one big dog. The other weird thing is that the girl's tracks lead up to the body, but not away. The only thing I could figure out is that she carried what must've been a hundred-pound dog into the barn, then rides out of there on its back, which makes about as much sense as the rest of it.

"First of all, there were no other bites whatsoever, not on his hands or his arms or anywhere. I've seen a few dog attack cases, but I'd never seen one like that. Of course the dog could've surprised him, then been frightened off by something, but it didn't seem to hang together to me. The strangest thing was the girl. The men who went looking for the dog found her in the woods, naked, sound asleep, her clothes lying around her in rags. When they woke her up, she was hysterical and kept saying that she did it, that she was a werewolf and she tore his throat out. That's all I could get out of her, too. She said there wasn't any dog. We looked for three days and never found it. The tracks came to a dead end where we found the girl."

Luther hung suspended in the swing, staring at the chain hooked above his head, creaking ever so slightly in spite of his stillness. In the sky above, clouds were beginning to build. "Is there anything else?" he said.

"One more interesting detail. Judging from the angle of the bite and the flow of the blood, the boy was on top of the dog when it bit him, like he had it pinned to the ground. Pretty difficult trick if you think about it."

Luther shifted his weight and swayed from side to side. "What happened to the girl after that?"

"We only keep records on the dead, but as I recall, a psychiatrist from Kingsport was called in. He had her in a private mental hospital for a couple of weeks or so for observation. I don't remember where."

"What was the psychiatrist's name?"

"Neally or Nielson or Nelson. Something like that. He's not around here anymore. He left for greener pastures several years ago."

Luther brought the swing to a standstill. "Well, what do you make of it?"

"Officially? Feral dog bites boy. Unofficially, the girl's explanation makes more sense than anything else."

Luther stood, the swing banging against the backs of his legs. "Surely you don't think she's a werewolf."

"Of course not. But when you figure out what happened, you be sure to let me know."

"Psychotics can be quite clever and resourceful," he heard himself saying to Marvin. He stood apart and listened to the rest of his diagnosis in sad disbelief that a woman he loved should prove to be a murderer who would almost certainly kill again. Then, as if they had simply been gossiping on a street corner, he steered the conversation briefly back to Karen or Kelly and her children, made a few inconsequential teasing remarks, then wished Marvin a friendly good-bye.

He returned the phone to its box and gathered up his tools. As he passed the elephant, he noticed the trunk. It was curved up at the end, like a candy cane. Eleanor had called it cute and laughed. He took his pruning saw and sawed off the upward curve so that the trunk was short but straight.

Before entering the maze, he looked around his garden, up at the sky. It would rain soon. That was good. The spring had been a dry one.

In the maze, a slender brown snake abruptly slithered away into the hedge wall like a withered branch come to life. Luther shuddered. He knew they were good for the garden, killing insects, loosening the soil. But he preferred the toads he'd seen in the moonlight, hopping leisurely around the marble walk. He tossed the elephant's trunk over the hedge into the wilderness and quickened his pace as the first drops began to fall. He'd resolved to get to the bottom of things, but now that seemed much deeper than he had anticipated.

Alice wrestled the fabric-covered foam rubber to the top of the stairs and let it go. It slid, unfolded, lodged halfway down between the wood railing and the wall. It was the mattress from the cot she used to take camping. She planned to lie on it today when she put herself into a trance. No amount of concentration could overcome the bone chill of cold concrete. She locked the door behind her, walked down to the mattress, and gave it a kick. It sprang into the air like a diver, belly-flopping onto the floor in a *whoosh* of dust as it glided to a halt.

It was Monday afternoon. She'd spent the weekend

practicing self-hypnosis. It came easy for her. She was used to being alone with herself. Hypnosis was like walking into a daydream and taking possession of it. She simply had to find the way in, the means to move.

She had unplugged the phone. On Sunday someone she'd assumed to be Erik had knocked persistently at the door, but she hadn't answered it. What would be the point of talking with him now? She wanted to be someone different when she spoke with him again, someone who could say, I will never change again—I can be, if you wish it, only who I appear to be.

She'd called in sick this morning. It was true in a way, had been true for years. Today she hoped to learn if she might cure herself. If she could change herself through self-hypnosis—just as Luther had almost changed her in his office—she might be able to keep herself from changing as well.

She descended the last few steps, sat on the stairs, and slipped off her shoes and socks. She stood, the concrete cold beneath her feet, and pulled off her sweater, folding it neatly and placing it on the steps. If she managed to transform herself into a wolf, would she be able to come back? She would die here without food or water, or if discovered, she would be imprisoned or destroyed. This did not frighten her. Any resolution was preferable to the maze in which she found herself.

As she stepped out of her jeans, she imagined she were meeting some invisible lover, like a medieval witch who confessed to being visited by demons. She must have longed to go with them, she thought, instead of lingering in this world, awaiting the stake. She looked around at the featureless gray walls. This room was like the cells monks built to protect the spirit from the flesh. She pulled the string, turning off the single bare bulb. As she lay down upon the mat, she imagined a monk, invaded from within, a hard penis in his hand, arching his back into the darkness.

She lay still, then began to empty her mind as she

had learned to do, imagining each atom of her body finding peace. She could see nothing, hear nothing. The dank smell of the basement soon faded away. She might be anywhere, floating in a void. Somewhere in this place she would find the wolf, and she would come to her. She would summon her, and she would come. She wanted to come, she wanted to be here, she wanted to join her in this empty place.

At first it was as if she could see her at a great distance on the horizon, gradually approaching, at a steady loping pace. She was so far away, she could not be sure it was her except by the undulating rhythm of her four-legged gait. The distance between them seemed not to change, but she grew larger and larger as she watched. She fought the impulse to look away and stayed fixed on the head thrusting forward with each surge of her powerful legs, her tongue hanging loose from the side of her jaws. Her eyes were now distinct, their solid intelligent stare seeking her out. Her breath rushed in and out as her paws thudded and sprang from the earth, at a faster and faster pace, her muscles rippling beneath her thick fur. Her ears cocked back. Her hind legs braced and thrust. Her eyes narrowed as she hurtled through the air. She struck the full length of her body, penetrating blood and bone and tissue in a single crushing impact like the end of a long fall from a great height.

She lies panting on the ground until the room begins to take shape around her in the darkness. She rises clumsily, stretching her back and neck by thrusting her forepaws in front of her, her rear haunches thrust into the air. She keeps her head low, sniffing in the darkness. She smells the woman in the mattress and squats to mark it. More faintly, she smells the man in the dust upon the floor. He has been here, but his scent is almost gone. She follows it around the walls.

She is hungry. In the dim light she can just make out the woman's clothes on the stairs, the thin line of light at the top. She sniffs at the clothes and places her front paws on the bottom step. Thrusting her snout toward the door, she can smell where the woman had been. Crouching low, she moves her front paws to a higher step, one by one. With the wood pressed against her chest, she draws up her hind legs, slipping against the wood at first, then finding a hold on the step above where the clothes still lie. She continues up the stairs. She does not know how she will get down. About halfway up she discovers that a motion like running will work, though she slips and strikes her jaw upon the wood when she first tries it.

At the top of the stairs, there is just enough room for her to stand, her nose pressed to the crack at the bottom of the door. She can smell the food in the kitchen, and beyond, grass, trees, humans, and cars. She begins to dig, at the floor, then at the door. Nothing moves. Her paws slip from the door as if it were ice. She remembers the woman attaching metal to the door so that she couldn't dig through. She turns in a circle, starts down, draws back, tries to lie down, but there is not enough room. She leans far forward, sniffing carefully into the darkness. She thrusts one paw forward onto the first step below and shifts her weight, trying to place her second paw beside her first. But they both slip on the dusty wood. She tries to keep her balance by pushing with her hind legs, but they slide from beneath her. She falls hard on her side, falls to the next step, slips between the stairs and the railing into the air, twisting her spine to keep her head upright. Her left front paw lands on the mattress, skids to one side. She falls forward hard, landing on her chest and lower jaw.

After a time she pushes herself up onto her haunches, throws back her head, and howls, a long, slow, single note. As the echoes return to her, she echoes them, until the darkness is filled with her howl and its answer. She holds the note until her breath gives out, the echo fades, and there is silence.

She rises lazily, walks to the mattress, sniffs it. The woman will come and open the door, walk into the light, and get something to eat. She turns in a circle, lays herself down onto her side as the woman would, rolls over onto her back, her feet in the air. She arches her spine, feeling it stretch. Her limbs push out like spreading roots in rocky soil. The room grows darker. The scents fade and become indistinguishable. She hears nothing but a voice in her head, the woman's voice saying over and over again, I did it, I did it, I did it.

Chapter

11

No one wanted to hold class outside today, the first Monday after spring break. The clouds rolled in suddenly, midafternoon. The sky turned a thick, opaque gray. By class time the rain poured down in a steady hiss. As Erik spoke about territoriality, his students looked out the window, past the clouds, to the beaches most of them had just left several hundred miles south.

After class a short, frail girl named Paige approached his desk, her books clutched to her chest. Erik looked up and smiled at her, then returned to gathering his scattered notes. "Dr. Summers, Kimberly wanted me to tell you she wasn't in class today because she's stranded in Florida. She called me last night. I'm her roommate."

"You're Kimberly's roommate?" Erik tried to keep

the disbelief out of his voice. Kimberly was the one with the beautiful legs and the vacant eyes. Paige was the one who, at the bottom of her last flawless exam, had written a note telling him she wanted to be a wildlife biologist.

She winced a small smile. "We were both soc. majors at the beginning of the semester. They match up people by majors." She shifted her books to one side. "She's hardly ever there, though, so I've pretty much got the room to myself."

"Did she think she would manage to make it back by Wednesday?"

"She's supposed to catch a plane tonight." She glanced out the window and smiled. "She said her ride just up and left her. I think her boyfriend got pissed at her."

Erik had gathered together his things. Any day but today he would have wanted to talk to a student like Paige. Today he just wanted to be alone. He had done well just to make it through class. But she'd made a gesture of friendship by daring a mild obscenity to a teacher, and he didn't just want to thoughtlessly send her away. "What did you do for spring break?"

She smiled, shifting her weight to balance her books on her hip. "I stayed in the dorm. I had some papers I needed to work on. It was great. I practically had the whole hall to myself."

Erik could picture her there, stationed at her desk in the middle of the night. "I hope you didn't spend the whole time working."

She laughed, pushed the hair back from her face. "Oh, no. At night I snuck up on the roof. It was incredible. I could just lie up there and think. Of course there weren't any stars like there are back home, but it was still wonderful. I wrote about it." She glanced nervously out the window. "I keep a journal of my thoughts."

Erik smiled. He realized she had a crush on him. She had probably written about him in that journal.

There'd been others who'd developed crushes on him. There was one who'd brought him blueberry muffins and sat laughing nervously in his office as he'd eaten her gift. He could see Paige sitting in the moonlight writing her thoughts in her small, delicate script. He was touched. "Sounds marvelous," he said.

"I wrote a lot about something you said in class. You said that we are animals, too, and that by understanding other animals, we can better understand ourselves."

Erik laughed. "I always say that. I didn't know anybody ever listened." He picked up his books. "Thanks."

Paige didn't budge. "It's really made me think. I'd never really thought about us being animals before. But once you start thinking about it, it's everywhere, especially in the dorms, the way everybody relates to everybody else."

Erik moved from behind the desk. "I'm glad you're thinking about the course."

She walked backward toward the door, smiling and nodding. He reached past her, opened the door, and held it for her. She hurried beneath his arm into the hall. She stood, waiting for him, flushed and nervous.

"I'd like to talk to you sometime about biology."

"Maybe next week," he said.

Before descending the stairs, she gave him a tiny wave. "See you Wednesday."

Erik smiled and nodded. Only a few weeks ago, before he'd met Alice, he might have suggested coffee. He'd never dated a student, didn't think it was right to pursue someone he had authority over. He probably wouldn't have asked her out or let it go beyond the coffee, wanting only to sustain the flattery a little while longer to distract him from his pain. He liked Paige, even found her attractive. But she wasn't Alice, or even Debra.

The halls were deserted this time of the afternoon. In the classrooms, rows of empty desks were bolted to the floor. Erik stared into one of the rooms. He'd taught in it once a few years ago. He filled the chairs from memory. Most of their faces were distinct, though some were a blur. He couldn't remember any of their names with certainty. He wished he could. He loved to teach, but sometimes it made him feel sad and useless in a way he could never quite grasp. He thought he would feel better if he could just remember their names.

On his office door was a sarcastic note from Higgins in chemistry about the committee meeting he'd missed that morning. Higgins, a plump, elflike man with five children at home, imagined Erik's bachelorhood to be a Rock Hudson movie. Under normal circumstances Erik would've written an equally sarcastic answer catering to Higgins's fantasies and stuck it on Higgins's door down the hall. Today he just left it.

He wasn't sure what normal circumstances were anymore. He slumped at his desk and tried Alice's number again, counting the rings. He hung up at fifteen. He pictured himself in front of the class, Paige hanging on his every word. *Don't forget, we are animals, too.* Dumb animals, he should've added. We call ourselves *Homo sapiens,* as if all other animals, even our own ancestors, had no wisdom. As for himself, he didn't feel particularly wise right now.

He ran over everything Alice had told him once again and tried to make sense of it. *By understanding other animals, we can better understand ourselves.* He and Alice were animals, *Homo sapiens.* She was asking him to believe that she was also *Canis lupus,* a different species altogether. He admired the poetry of magical views of nature in which humans could transform into eagles, bears, or wolves. But that wasn't science. No matter how much poetical truth it might depict, no matter how meaningful it might be to the people who believed such things—or to Alice—it just couldn't be true, any more than gold could be made from mercury or coachmen from mice. What was Alice trying to understand about herself by imagining she was a wolf? What could he hope to understand about her?

Last Thursday, four short days ago, they were at the park. His head lay in her lap. Her face was above his, a tree spread above her, the sky over all. Her face was his connection with all that was beautiful.

"You are beautiful," he said.

"I have never felt so beautiful as I feel at this moment," she said. "Years from now when nothing is left, I'll remember this moment."

Erik had imagined the roots of the tree thrust deep into the earth all around them, holding them aloft in its embrace.

He pushed himself away from his desk. That wasn't particularly scientific thinking, either. Was he going to discount that as well? Hadn't he been transformed? But a werewolf? He couldn't believe it. He couldn't help but be frightened of someone who did.

He left his books. He couldn't look at them tonight. The last three nights he'd seen the lights, her shadow crossing the windows. He sat at his kitchen table, smoking cigarettes and drinking coffee, watching. When the lights went out he continued to stare, imagined her lying down in darkness alone. Why wasn't he there? he'd asked himself. Did he want to be?

Outside, the rain had stopped but still clung to everything. A light wind shook the trees and showered him with water. He decided to take the alley. The water ran down the center trough like a small river. The cobblestones, rounded like the backs of turtles, glistened a dark, rich gray.

He and Alice had walked the alleys. "Back here," she'd said, "you can tell more about the people who live in these houses." In the fringe of grass at the edge of the alley, a sofa and chair sat beside a trash can, as if waiting for guests. Their cushions were pumped into place, though sodden and heavy. He could smell the faint aroma of cat piss in the warm damp air as he passed.

He remembered the smell of Alice's basement. There'd certainly been an animal there, and a large one. But where was it now? How had it gotten there? He'd checked out the paw print. It could have been a wolf's, but he couldn't be sure. The shit was canine. It could've come from a wolf who ate dog food or simply from a dog.

He wanted to talk to her psychiatrist. He had his number in his pocket. This morning he'd looked through the Yellow Pages, remembering she called him Luther. There was only one. He'd called Luther Adams's office and said he was calling for Alice White to verify whether her appointment time this week would be at seven or the usual four. Seven. He'd called back later and asked to speak to Dr. Adams but was told he would not be in today. After he'd hung up he'd written down Adams's home phone on a slip of paper, stuck it in his shirt pocket, and tried to glance over his lecture notes.

Parked in the alley was a bread van, the motor running, the doors wide open. No one was inside. It was filled with a dense web of wire racks. Royal blue plastic trays of rolls and breads and coffee cakes, each with a bright orange sticker, seemed to hover in the darkness.

Erik stopped beside the open doors and smelled cinnamon and gasoline. He looked up and down the alley. There was no one. If this were a carcass on the African veld, it would never sit undefended, until it had been consumed. He imagined jackals in the alley, closing in around him.

Perhaps the psychiatrist would tell him why Alice believed she was a werewolf. Perhaps, he admitted, he could tell me just how crazy she is. He cringed from the word and its implications but knew he meant, maybe he could tell me if she is the woman I fell in love with, the woman I believe loves me.

She didn't like to talk about herself that much, but the look in her eyes, he'd thought, was unmistakable, the way she curled up against him as they slept. He hadn't been able to sleep the last few nights. Tuesday, they'd made love with such passion that when it was over and they lay sprawled over the edge of the bed, they'd burst into laughter. He couldn't imagine such a scene with Debra.

Debra had called on Saturday and again on Sunday. She'd said she didn't want to pressure him, that she understood how hard her change of heart must be for him, that she just wanted to talk. She'd told him what a sweet man he was, told him about the photo exhibit at her museum. "You will love it," she'd said, and he didn't doubt her. She knew him well, even though she had often tried to change him. He'd said he would try to get by to see it.

"You sound depressed," she'd said.

"I am, I guess."

"About me?"

"No, not really. Other things."

"Well, if you want to talk, call me or come by."

He was behind the old folks' home now. It too was deserted. The white metal chairs stood in an empty circle, pools of water in the rust-streaked seats. There was usually a group here playing cards. One woman in particular always turned as he passed and wished him a good day in a small, formal voice.

He wanted to see Debra. He had spent years trying to scale the walls she erected around herself. Now she seemed to be offering to let him inside. He was curious who lived there. More than curious, he longed to know.

But Alice was a darker mystery. How could she believe such a thing and be who she seemed to be? He had seen it in movies but never quite believed it—

that someone could fall in love with a psychopath and not know in some way that there was something wrong. He tried to remember what he'd learned in an abnormal psychology class years ago, but nothing fell into place. Manic-depressive, schizophrenic—those words seemed to have little to do with Alice.

As he opened his back gate, he looked over at Alice's house and saw her silhouette pass in front of the kitchen window. A towel was piled atop her head. He saw the lights come on in the living room, imagined her on the sofa brushing out her wet black hair in long, slow strokes.

His back door always stuck in the rain. He turned the key, leaned against it, and shoved. The kitchen was small and gloomy, but he left the lights off. He found his coffee cup from last night and this morning and rinsed it out in the sink. He filled it with cold coffee and put it in the microwave. When he and Debra had divided up the property, he'd gotten the microwave because Debra had said, "All we ever use it for is to heat up your coffee." The machine made a loud, bleeting wail.

From his living room he could see hers. The houses were mirror images of each other, built the same time, just after the war. Little cottages where GI's and their brides might set things right again. He put his feet on the coffee table and the phone in his lap and called Adams's home. A warm, pleasant woman's voice answered the phone. A faint, hollow sound hissed in the background.

"May I speak with Dr. Luther Adams, please?"

"I'm afraid he's busy right now. May I take a message?"

"Please, this is very important. It's about one of his patients."

"Well, I'll see. What was your name again?"

"Erik Summers. It's about Alice White."

Erik could hear Mrs. Adams's muffled voice saying he sounded like a nice young man. Adams was a distant rumble, but then filled the phone like a wise and melodious voice from the radio.

"This is Luther Adams. May I help you?"

Erik took a deep breath and stared across at Alice's living room window. "You don't know me. I'm Erik Summers. I'm a friend of Alice White's."

"Yes?"

"Well, I'm not sure where to begin, but she told me something rather bizarre, and I don't know what to make of it. I thought you might be able to help me out."

"I'm sorry, Mr. Summers, but I really can't discuss her case with anyone without her permission."

Her case. Erik listened to the hissing sound on the other end of the line. It was louder now that Adams was on the line. "Are you aware that she believes herself to be a werewolf?" Erik said.

"Yes. She told me that she had told you, so I don't suppose there's any harm in my acknowledging that much, but what is it you wanted to speak with me about?"

"I'm frightened for her. Since she told me, she's holed up in her house. She won't answer the phone or come to the door. She didn't go to work today."

"Perhaps she is ill. Perhaps she is simply avoiding you."

"Maybe she is, but couldn't she be dangerous, to herself, I mean? Someone with an idea like that."

There was a long silence. Erik realized the hissing sound was running water. He could hear Adams breathing quietly into the receiver. "Yes," he said. "She might be dangerous, and my conscience demands I should warn you that she might be dangerous to you as well. There is some evidence that she has the potential for violence."

"You mean the boy who tried to rape her?"

"She told you about that?"

"Yes. She said she turned into a wolf and killed him."

176

"Well, there is much that is uncertain about that whole incident. But I've probably said too much already. My advice to you would be to leave her alone if that's what she wants. She is not a well person."

"'Not a well person'? That's all you can say? I love this woman, doctor. I am worried about her. I can't just leave her alone if she needs help."

"Erik, she may not be able to love you in return as you might wish."

Erik could feel her body against him, smell her scent as if she lay in the room beside him. "I'm sorry, I can't believe that."

"I know how hard this must be for you. If you'd like to talk about it further, I'm sure I can work you in tomorrow. Just call my office in the morning."

"I don't think so. Thanks anyway."

Erik hung up before he had a chance to hear any more reasonable words. After he'd talked to Debra on Sunday, he couldn't stand sitting and staring at Alice's closed house any longer and walked to the art museum where they'd gone that first day. He'd roamed through the regular collection. The place had been almost empty. He'd stopped to look whenever something caught his attention—a landscape by Hopper, an Aphrodite by someone he'd never heard of. Some of the galleries had made him walk faster. He'd emerged from one of these and stopped short, startled to see a man seated on a can of tar by the entry. Then he'd seen it wasn't a person at all but a sculpture, called *Hard Hat, Construction Worker*. It was a superdetailed mannequin—deep scar on the cheek, day's beard, sunburned nose. A crumpled pack of Tiparillo cigars stuck out of his shirt pocket, and a tattoo of blooming flowers peeked from beneath his rolled-back sleeve. He was miserable—heavy-lidded, with bloodshot eyes, battered hands, and a look of stupid despair on his face. And of course, he wore a hard hat with American flags. His open lunch box with plastic fruit and synthetic white bread sat between his legs. Every detail was perfect.

Erik loathed it, studying it to understand why. Even the cuffs were properly frayed. It was a perfect specimen, a person turned thing. Or worse, a trophy of the superior man who could look at a man having lunch and say, "One for my collection."

There was a surplus store on the southside that sold camping gear and weapons. It was full of trophy kill. Above the bazooka on the wall, Erik remembered, as he studied the hard hat, was a mounted timber wolf. It was dusty and listed to one side, staring down at the store through glass eyes. Beneath it was a photograph of a man standing beside an airplane in a snow-covered landscape, a rifle and scope in one hand, the dead wolf in the other. The same man, somewhat older and heavier, rang up his purchases.

He'd walked home from the museum, thinking about Alice's books on wolves. He'd read some of them years ago, in grad school. There were worse animals to imagine yourself becoming. He'd gone to the university library and checked out everything he could find on wolves. He'd lain in bed Sunday night reading them. When he'd finally fallen asleep, he'd dreamed.

Alice was standing beneath South River Falls, a high, slender falls. They were camped there, at the top. She was naked, stretching her arms up into the ribbon of water. He stepped into the pool and waded slowly across to her, his eyes fixed on her body glistening in the spray. The water pulled at his legs; he moved in a tense, slow motion. Finally he was behind her and put his hands at her waist. Her skin was cold from the water. She squeezed his hands, leaning back against him. He slid his palms up her wet body to her breasts. She rolled her head back, kissed him, moaning now, low in her throat, as the water hissed and spewed around them. He bent at the knees, and she lowered herself onto him, slowly. He closed his eyes and could hear his heart pounding. They moved together in a motion like the icy water lapping at his thighs.

He opened his eyes and saw, through the water, a wolf in the rocks behind the falls. To the left was another, and another up above. He turned his head back and saw they were behind him as well. He could no longer hear the falls, only the low growl of the wolves as they crouched around him, their snouts thrust forward, sniffing the air. He remembered his hands and felt them buried in thick, wet fur. He turned back and looked into a wolf's eyes, inches from his own. They stayed poised that way for a moment. At first he was not afraid. This was Alice. She wouldn't hurt him. But then she bared her fangs. He could not move, did not see her move, but felt the jolt as she fastened her jaws around his throat. He tried to shout her name, but his voice had been torn away.

He awoke to the sound of his own wailing scream and quickly sat up in bed, searching each shadow until he found a familiar shape.

Thinking of this dream now, he felt his heart race with fear and arousal. He had to see her. He stood up, looking to see if he could catch another glimpse of her through her windows. Maybe she was crazy. Maybe they were both crazy. He'd fallen in love so quickly and so completely; so much passion had startled him. That seemed a long time ago. Sometimes he had trouble believing it had happened.

Maybe she was crazy. Maybe it didn't matter. Maybe he didn't care. He walked to the door and out, closing it behind him.

Alice wove her wet hair into a braid and stared at her great-aunt's photograph of the birches. Her muscles ached as usual after her transformation, but she didn't care. She could change whenever she liked now. It had not been difficult. It was like one of those optical illusion pictures that first appear to be an elegant vase, then a crone. It was simply a matter of changing her perspective. She knew it would be easier the next time, now that she knew she could do it. She was sure also that she could keep from changing, if she wanted to. As Luther had said, she could now be the gatekeeper.

She had thought ever since she'd killed Dale that if, by medicine or fairy godmother, she could keep from changing, she would. She thought she would feel rescued, but she felt stranded instead. I am a werewolf, she thought. How many times have I said that to myself in the course of a day, year after year? What do other people say to themselves? What is this "normal" life I think I want so badly? Where would the wolf go, and who would care besides me?

Erik loves me. I know he does. He came to my door on Saturday and Sunday. The persistent phone calls are from him. I couldn't answer. I wanted things to be like they were before I told him. I wanted the choice of being who he thought I was, a woman he could love, who wouldn't change each moon, who wasn't an animal, who was beautiful forever. But now that I have that choice, I don't know if I can choose it. It seems wrong. I am the wolf, too.

Perhaps he still loves his wife. They've had years together. We've had one week. Now that Debra wants him back, how can he bear to stay away from her? When we talked of Debra at the park, he cried and promised he would never leave me, and I promised the same. It was because of her that he promised, and because of her, he needed me to promise.

She rose and took out a record album but stopped when she saw his shadow cross her window, heard his knock upon the screen door. She stared at the door, imagining him beyond as he had looked ten days ago. He knocked again, louder. She laid the record on the coffee table, walked to the door, and stood in front of it. The screen door squealed as he opened it. The door shook as he knocked again. She turned the lock and opened the door.

She wanted him to hold her, to kiss her on top of her head the way he did when he nuzzled against her and told her he loved her. But he stepped past her and into the room, turning and standing as if he were planted there like a fence post. He is taking up where we left off, she thought. He must be terrified.

"Please hold me," she said.

He took her in his arms and held her close. "I love you," he whispered over and over. "I've been so worried about you."

She pressed her forehead against his chest. "Let's sit down," she said, but did not move. They clung to each other as they shuffled to the sofa and sat, still entwined. He kissed her neck, and she laid her cheek against him.

"I've frightened you, haven't I?"

"Yes."

"I've missed you."

He kissed her cheek and whispered, "I've missed you."

She tightened her arms around him and offered her neck. He kissed her hard, she felt his teeth upon her neck. She took hold of his shoulder and bit. He pushed her back onto the sofa, raised himself slowly, parting her robe. She unbuttoned his shirt as he kicked off his shoes and socks, undid his belt, and struggled with his pants and underwear. They seemed to move faster and faster, all the while staring into each other's eyes. When they were both naked, they froze for a second. His face shone with love and desire. He thrust himself into her. They moved in a strong, urgent motion, again faster and faster, still locked in the same steady gaze, until their bodies shook and their eyes fell closed. Alice took Erik in her arms. He laid his head upon her chest.

* * *

181

A half hour later they hadn't stirred. His body still covered her with a comfortable heaviness. She never wanted him to move. When he spoke she could feel the rumble of his voice against her. "I was worried about you."

"I'm sorry. I just needed to be alone for a while. I'm okay now." She ran her fingers through his hair, watched it fall back into place. "Do you still love me?"

His arms tightened around her. "Yes, I still love you."

That was all she wanted to know. Anything else could be made right.

Without moving, he said, "I talked with Dr. Adams on the phone."

His breathing had changed, waiting for her to speak. She could hear the children outside on their way home from school. She had often watched them from her window, trailing coats and backpacks on the ground or swinging them through the air to watch the colors arc through space. "What did he have to say?" she said quietly.

"He said you were not well."

"Because I think I'm a werewolf?"

"Yes."

"And what else did he say?"

"He said you might be dangerous."

She closed her eyes and felt herself sinking away from him into a familiar well of loneliness. The children were shouting at one another—indistinguishable taunts and challenges. The cadence and tone rang in her ears like a persistent memory.

She put her hands on Erik's shoulders and pushed, opening her eyes to see him above her. "What do *you* think?"

His brow was furrowed in deep lines. His eyes were dark and sad. "I can't believe you're dangerous."

"But you can believe I'm not well?" She did not

mean to accuse him, but she had to know what he felt, what he and Luther had decided about her.

She could see he made an effort not to look away. His weight upon her seemed to lighten. "Yes," he said.

She closed her eyes and felt him push himself upright. The sweat on her stomach grew cold as the air struck it. When she opened her eyes he was sitting at her feet, putting on his shirt. "I'm a little cold," he said.

She sat up, pulling her knees to her chest. "Me too."

"I felt awful when you left Friday." He found his underwear on the floor and slipped them on, still sitting on the couch. She saw his jeans sprawled on the floor, one leg turned almost inside out, and wondered whether he would put them on as well.

"I'm sorry. I had to tell you," she said. He reached for his jeans, struggled with the tangled legs. "I was a little stunned myself," she said, "to hear Debra wants you back."

He looked over at her with the ironic smile he often wore when he spoke of Debra. "Me too."

She thought she should let it all go, that if she were to ask nothing of him now, then everything would be all right; but she couldn't do it. Too much paced back and forth within her.

"Do you want her back?"

He shook his head. "No, I don't trust her."

She had wanted him to say, "No, I love you."

She rested her chin on her knees and looked down her shins at her feet. "I know it was stupid, but I had hoped you would believe me."

He stood, zipping his pants. She looked up at him, and he did not speak, did not move. He doesn't know what to say, she thought. His eyes are full of fear. She patted the sofa at her feet. "Would you sit down?"

He sank down beside her and wrapped his arms around her legs. His voice was kind. "Can you understand how hard it is for me to believe you?"

She closed her eyes and nodded. She found his hands and looked at them in hers. "Can you understand how much I needed you to?"

"No. I guess I can't. But I want to help you in any way I can. I love you."

She looked up, held his eyes, squeezed his hands hard. "Then believe me."

"But Alice . . ."

"You haven't really tried, have you? You've just tried to decide what you're supposed to do now that you know I'm crazy."

"Alice, I'm a scientist. The sort of transformation you've described to me just isn't possible—every cell in the body changing and changing back again."

She touched his cheek, smiled softly. "You are so sure. The penguins, they find their way home each year, and you don't know why, and you love them for it. Couldn't I be like them?"

He looked down, closed his eyes. "That's different."

"Yes, it is." She pressed her hands against her chest. "Every cell, like you said. Everything changes. You can't imagine what it's like." She put her fingers under his chin and tilted his head up, looking into his eyes. "But it's real to me. It's as real as loving you. That's changed me, too. I never thought I would have a life like other people. I thought I would always have to be alone. Do you believe I love you?"

"Yes," he said, and kissed her eyes. They sat with their foreheads together, their eyes looking down at their clasped hands.

She spoke quietly and evenly, a reasonable woman to her lover: "You study animals in the wilderness, migrating and mating and making a place for themselves. Isn't that right?"

"Yes."

"The cells and genes, the millions of events that go on inside every creature—other scientists study that."

"Well, yes, but I'm hardly ignorant about it. You can't separate one from the other."

"But you're not an expert."

"No, but . . ."

She placed her fingers on his lips. "Just try. That's all I'm asking. I don't want you to think I'm crazy. I know everyone else does, and that's all right. But not you. I want you to believe me."

He promised her he would try. Before she could ask him to stay, he asked her if she wanted him to. His tone made her say no; she would see him tomorrow; tonight she wanted to be alone. After he was gone she stood naked in the middle of the living room until she realized she was cold. She picked up her robe and put it on. He'd left his cigarettes on the coffee table. She shook one out and smoked it, lying on the couch, staring into space.

Luther stepped from the shower and dried himself, using three towels, one for his face, one for his torso, and one for below his waist. Eleanor chided him about it, but he didn't see that it should matter to her. It was his body. When he had finished drying his feet, he tossed the towel into the hamper, slid the remaining two towels to the right, and placed a clean towel on the left beside them. Eleanor teased that one night she would sneak into his bath and mix up his towels. He didn't think it was funny. Besides, he would know immediately. They were different colors. He would remember the proper order.

He looked in the mirror on the door. He looked pretty trim for a man his age. He only wished that he wasn't quite so hairy, especially now that it was all turning gray. He especially disliked the silver down upon his shoulders and back, though Eleanor claimed to like it.

What was he to do about Alice? Surely he had a responsibility to those who might be endangered by her illness—including Alice herself. He knew where she lived. He'd driven by one afternoon in the fall, shortly after she'd first come to him. It was the only house in the block where the leaves lay upon the lawn unraked.

He was struggling with the idea of going to see her. Professionally, of course, it was simply out of the question. But what if she did harm herself? What if the self-hypnosis *he* had taught her had led her into a constant delusional state? She might do anything. He imagined himself knocking down the door, taking her in his arms. He shook his head. No, he told himself, it wasn't just that. He had sound reasons for going to see her. He *should* go see her. But things weren't that simple. After that call from her boyfriend, with Eleanor sitting right there, Eleanor was already wondering what was up.

After the phone call, Luther had gone off to shower so he could think. Eleanor would see nothing odd in a shower. He showered all the time.

As he dressed in casual clothes—jeans and a sweatshirt—he thought about how he might plausibly leave the house in the middle of the afternoon without arousing Eleanor's suspicion.

When he came down the stairs to the solarium, he found Eleanor writing a letter.

"Who to?" Luther asked.

"Marvin," she said. "I didn't get a chance to talk to him."

The corners of his mouth tightened. "Wish him well for me," he said.

"Where are you off to?"

"The nursery."

"I thought you cleaned out their stock last week." She looked up at him, over her reading glasses, and smiled.

"Very funny. I saw another snake this morning. I want to get something to control them."

She cocked her head to one side. "I was just teasing, Luther. Don't be so sensitive."

"I'll be back in half an hour."

"I'll be here." She was already turning back to her letter.

He forgot to kiss her good-bye, but he was already halfway down the sidewalk before he remembered and could not worry about it now. The drive would be easy—five minutes at the most—which meant he had at least twenty minutes there—more, actually, for Eleanor expected him to linger at the nursery. When he returned he would drive straight to the garage, where he could pretend to unload his purchases. He smiled at himself in the rearview mirror.

Alice had never seen him in casual clothes. He wondered how she would react. He pushed his sleeves back on his forearms, noted the dark thatch of hair that came down to his wrists, and pushed them back down.

He would have to be careful with her. He didn't want to startle her. He was just in the neighborhood and thought he'd drop by to see how the self-hypnosis was progressing. Of course, she might not answer the door.

What should he do then? Was she suicidal? It didn't seem to him she was, but what did he really know about psychotics except for his stint at the state hospital? They were so knocked out on Thorazine all the time, he had no idea what they were like without it.

The name on the mailbox was written on an index card and taped on with Scotch adhesive tape. The ink had faded to a faint sepia brown. For some reason he found this touching. He reasoned that Alice was the sort of person whose doorbell might not work, and he knocked.

She was wearing a white bathrobe that touched the floor. Her skin looked different here than under the fluorescent lights at the office, darker and more immediate. She offered him coffee.

He sat on the edge of the sofa and looked around as she poured the coffee in the kitchen. The room was not what he'd expected. It was neater and more orderly than he would have thought. He looked at the album cover on the coffee table, the only thing out of place. It was *Stop Making Sense* by Talking Heads, or the other way around. He wasn't sure which. He laid it back on the table when he heard her footsteps in the hall.

"I've had great success with self-hypnosis," she said.

He smiled, burned his lip on the coffee. "Oh, really?"

"I changed myself—and back again, of course." She looked happy about it, even smug.

"You mean you changed yourself into a wolf using self-hypnosis?" He tried to sound as if he were asking for simple clarification.

"Yes." She was placid, unruffled. She believed it.

"I thought the point was to prevent these episodes, not precipitate them."

"But I had to see whether I could do it. It's always just happened to me. I had to know whether I could do it myself." She was leaning toward him, lost in what she was saying. He could see the lovely curve of her bare breast nestled in the shadows of her white robe.

"When did you do this?"

"Just this morning. I practiced all weekend bringing myself just to the point where I thought I would change. Today I let it happen. It was easy."

He knitted his brows and sipped at his coffee, then placed it decisively in his saucer. This had gone too far. "You believe you actually became a wolf this morning?"

Her face froze. She opened a small box on the coffee

table and took out a pack of cigarettes. She lit one and blew the smoke above them. She settled back onto the sofa, her feet on the edge of the table, her robe wrapped tightly around her.

"You're still smoking?"

"They're Erik's. He left them. He was just here."

"He called me today."

"He told me."

"Did he tell you what we talked about?"

"He said you thought I was sick, and I was dangerous."

He didn't like her smoking. He'd quit when the risks became apparent. Watching his weight was a bother, but he had to take care at his age. Seeing her smoke, he wanted a cigarette. He sighed, taking in the smoke from the air. "That's not quite what I said."

"But have I missed the general idea?"

"Alice, he called me, quite concerned. I felt I owed him the truth."

She blew smoke into the air. "I've already told him the truth, Luther. If you thought I was so damn dangerous, how come you've let me run around loose? Or maybe you have your own reasons for wanting to scare Erik away?"

He thought he knew what she was implying but chose to ignore it. "I talked with the medical examiner in Bristol today, Alice, and what he told me has prompted me to reexamine the whole case."

She sat up straighter, cocked her head back. "What did he tell you?"

"Well, I'm not at liberty to discuss a professional consultation in detail, but he did tell me enough so that I suspect you killed that boy as you say, and rather brutally at that."

"You mean you believe I'm a werewolf?"

"Of course not, but I have serious doubts that a dog did it."

"Which leaves me?"

"Precisely."

"Well, have you figured out how I did it?" She bared her teeth. "Did I use these little guys?"

He shook his head slowly. "This is no laughing matter, Alice. I don't know how you may have done it. That's for a forensic expert to decide."

She looked away. Her face was hard and angry. He felt a stirring inside him. Good God, he thought, this is no time for that. He spoke softly. "Alice, you are a very sick woman. There's no denying that. And now that the incidence of these episodes is increasing, I must recommend more serious treatment than I alone can give you."

She stared at him for several moments, her mouth resting against her clenched hands, the cigarette smoke rising before her eyes. "A mental hospital." Her voice was sad and hollow.

"Yes."

"And if I don't go willingly, you and your forensic expert will have me committed."

"Alice, listen to me, I am only trying to do what I believe is best for you. You came to me. You asked me for help. I'm trying to do that the best I can."

She looked away again, closed her eyes for a moment, then opened them. "Would you like to see?" she said quietly.

He knew what she meant. He didn't know what to say. He could feel his heart rate increasing, a tingling at the nape of his neck.

She put out her cigarette. "It would be simple. I could put myself under. You could sit and watch. It wouldn't take more than ten minutes. What do you say? I might not even kill you."

He took one of her hands and laid it between his. He looked into her eyes. Her face was set and hard, but her eyes were filled with tears. "Alice, you know I only want what is best for you. Let me take you to the hospital right now. I have a friend there I'm sure can help you."

Her face crumpled in pain. She yanked her hand away and clenched it, striking at his chest and hands. "God damn you!" she sobbed. "God damn you!"

He put his arms around her, pinning her arms against him. She shook with crying but did not try to break free. He held her for several minutes in silence, rocking her gently back and forth, her head against his chest. He could smell her hair. He let his lips rest against it. He kissed the top of her head. "Everything will be all right," he said. The part along the top of her head, the narrow furrow of flesh, filled him with tenderness and longing. He kissed it, lingering there, his eyes closed. "I love you," he whispered. "I love you." He caressed the smooth curve of her back with his open palm, the bare skin at the back of her neck.

She pushed her hands against his chest. "Please let me go," she said.

He could not just release her now, now that she knew how he felt. She looked up at him, and he leaned toward her to kiss her, but she turned her mouth away. He kissed her cheek, mumbling against it, "I love you, Alice. I love you."

Her voice was cold and matter-of-fact. "Let me go, and get out of here. I don't want to hurt you."

His passion evaporated. He remembered the boy Marvin had described to him. He dropped his arms and stood, filled with shame. "I am sorry," he said. "I am so sorry."

She looked up at him and gave him a small, sad smile. "I know," she said. "Now go."

Chapter

12

When Erik left Alice's, he drove downtown to the medical school to see Rupert Brand, a friend of his from grad school. Rupert was now a geneticist doing research Erik could only pretend to understand. Rupert pulled his gray hair back into a ponytail and wore a Mickey Mouse earring in his left ear. Well pressed, neatly clipped M.D./Ph.D. students battled each other to work with him. Geniuses came to this school because his name was in the catalog.

Erik waited in the hall outside Rupert's office. Through the open door he could see five white-jacketed students ringing Rupert's chair as he sat at a computer terminal, his back to the door, alternately pecking at the keys and pointing at the screen, talking all the while. "Can anybody tell me why we got screwball results like this?" he said loudly without turning around.

One of the students said something too faint for Erik to hear. Rupert turned in his chair and looked up as if the student had just muttered an obscenity. "What's your name?" he said, though they all wore names like tagged items in a department store.

"Chandler, sir."

Rupert rolled his eyes. "How many times do I have to say this: Don't call me 'sir,' don't call me 'doctor' or 'Professor' or 'Your Most Exalted Holiness of the Cosmic Gene.' My name is Rupert. All this goddamn bowing and scraping. I feel like I'm in a Charlie Chan movie. Is that clear?" Five heads bobbed up and down. Chandler gave a slight smile. "Now about this idea of yours, Chandler. It sounds pretty ridiculous to me, but I'm sure your four colleagues here will be glad to tell you about that in painstaking detail."

As Rupert glanced around at the other four, Erik caught his eye and Rupert grinned. "All right, people, go enjoy spring. Geneticists ought to have sex once in a while. I'm going to talk to an old friend." Rupert rose from his chair, and the students parted as he strode into the hall and gave Erik a bear hug. As the students filed out and down the hall, Rupert hollered after them, his arm around Erik's shoulder: "Chandler, get to work on that idea. I'd like something to look at by Friday."

"Yes, sir!" Chandler called back.

Rupert shook his head and led Erik into his office. "They get smarter and more subservient every year. Go figure." They sat on soft leather chairs. "What's up? I heard you were getting divorced. Does this mean we're friends again?"

"Rupert . . ."

Rupert held up his hands. "That's okay. Debra didn't like me. I didn't like her. Fact is neither one of us is very likable. Hell, if I'd been you, with a woman who looked like that, you wouldn't have seen me, either. How is she doing, anyway?"

"Okay, I guess. I'd rather not talk about it." Erik took out a cigarette and lit it.

Rupert leaned forward. "Oh, thank God, you haven't quit. Give me one and all is forgiven. You wouldn't believe how hard it is to bum a cigarette in this monastery. I used to bum off my students—I know some of them smoke, you can smell it on them like formaldehyde—but no, they all sneak these days. The stairwells are full of butts, but they don't want their cronies witnessing such depravity. They brag to each other about how many miles they run each morning. It makes me want to throw up."

Erik lit Rupert's cigarette. "Still too cheap to buy your own?"

"I see it as a means of controlling my intake." He took a deep drag and held it before sighing it out.

"Are you still living with Cindy?" Cindy was an art major and the last girlfriend Erik knew about. He and Debra had had them over for a disastrous dinner party a couple of years ago, the last time he'd seen Rupert. Cindy had told Debra that museums were mausoleums for dead art. The evening had gone downhill from there.

"No, she went to Montana with a lesbian who made sculptures out of melted Barbie dolls. Kind of interesting stuff, actually. I'm living solo at the moment, trying to build my record collection back up. Cindy made off with all the blues."

"I can see your life hasn't changed."

Rupert wagged a finger in the air. "Not so. Changes all the time, so I don't get bored. What about you? What brings you to the land of Dr. Goodwrench?"

"I've got a scientific question for you."

"For real?"

Erik nodded.

"Shoot. I haven't heard one of those since we used to get drunk every Friday after anatomy lab." He rose, shut the office door, and returned to his seat. "I don't want this to leak out. These androids wouldn't know a scientific question if it bit them on the ass."

Erik sighed and plunged in. If anyone whose opinion he respected would listen to his questions without telling him he was crazy, it was Rupert. "I know a woman who claims to be a werewolf. I want to know if that's by any stretch of the imagination even remotely possible."

Rupert picked up a pad and pencil. His expression was perfectly serious. "Define werewolf."

"She claims to turn into an actual wolf—*Canis lupus*—every full moon from sunset to sunrise. She says she's done this since she was thirteen, that the process takes only a few minutes, and she has no idea of how or why it started."

"She wasn't bitten by a slavering beast under the blood red moon?"

"No."

"Which is why you're seeing me."

"Right."

"Very unusual, a woman werewolf. In the movies they're all men. Is she pretty?"

"Yes, very. What does that have to do with anything?"

"A pretty woman is always relevant. You're in love with her, right?"

"Yes."

"Damn, I love it when I'm clever. So what does she do when she turns into a wolf?"

"She locks herself up in the basement."

"No insatiable blood lust? No glimpses of pentagrams on the palms of her next victims? No consorting with gypsy fortunetellers or vampires?"

"Nothing like that. She says she mostly paces and sleeps, and eats a bag of dog food."

"Not very romantic. Pretty dull life for a monster. I hope you've been livening things up for her the rest of the time."

"So is it possible?"

Rupert shrugged. "Sure."

"You're kidding."

"Why not?"

"But, Rupert, what possible mechanism could there be for such a thing, and why in hell on the full moon?"

"I know it's goofy, but you could slow your heart rate if you wanted to learn how—on Groundhog's Day if you had a mind to. Change is something I've learned to expect with humans. It's what we do."

"But a werewolf?"

"Look, Erik, I've been a science nerd all my life. I read Asimov and Clarke at lunch while the other guys beat each other up. Now I'm actually doing shit I read about then. Sure it's possible. Fucking anything's possible. Would you like me to splice a gene for you before you go? Give me enough time and money and I'll make you the Frankenstein monster—and without those tacky bolts in his neck."

"Then you don't think she's crazy?"

"I didn't say that. I think she's probably a very serious nut case. She must be *very* pretty."

"But you just said anything is possible."

"Sure it is, but not everything's equally probable. I'd say a nut case is a whole lot more probable than a werewolf."

Erik stared blankly at the computer screen. The columns of number, letters, and symbols made no sense to him at all.

"Look," Rupert said. "If you want to believe her, then go ahead. If we can imagine it, it just might be true. Hell, I sometimes think it's true *because* we imagine it, but not too often. I haven't done that many drugs."

"So you're telling me I should just choose to believe her or not."

"What's wrong with that? What have you got to lose? I take it since you're talking to me that you haven't actually had the opportunity to witness this little performance. Why don't you hang in there till the next full moon? *National Geographic* could make you a very famous guy, and her, too, of course."

"Swell. Is that what you'd do?"

"No. I'd send her to a shrink, but then I'm not in love with her."

"She's already seeing a shrink."

"Then talk to him."

"I already have. He says she's seriously ill and probably dangerous."

"You sure know how to pick them, Erik."

"Thanks."

Rupert took Erik's cigarettes from Erik's shirt pocket, lit himself another, and laid two more on his desk before replacing the pack. "You're really upset about this, aren't you? I'm sorry I'm not any help. I've always been pretty much of a jerk. All my ex-wives tell me so. Look, maybe it'll work out. You tried loving a relentlessly sane woman, maybe it's time for you to try a little craziness." He repeated the last four words, singing them to the tune of "Try a Little Tenderness."

Erik had to smile in spite of himself.

Rupert leaned forward on his chair. "You sure you don't want to talk about Debra? You look like you've got more on your mind than being in love with a beautiful werewolf."

"She says she wants me back," he said.

"Now? After you're divorced?"

"That's right."

"Does this have anything to do with your new girlfriend?"

"Hell, I don't think so. She started this before she knew about her."

"Well, why, then?"

"I don't know. She says she realizes now how important I was to her."

Rupert made a small grumbling noise in his throat. "Well, I'm probably not the best person to talk to about Debra, but all I've got to say is watch out when people 'realize' things. They get dangerous. They don't mean to be, they think they've finally seen the light. Usually they're just showing their own movies, but sooner or later the film breaks."

"I know. I know." Erik stood up, walked to the window, and looked at the street fourteen floors below. "I used to lie around in bed all the time, wishing she'd call me. Sometimes I'd get drunk or stoned and try to convince myself it never happened, that I could just go out and get in my car, drive home, and there she'd be, just like before. I'd even call her up. Half the time I wouldn't say anything. I didn't have to. You could hear it in her voice, the way she said hello, that things were different, that her life didn't have anything to do with me anymore."

He turned from the window and looked at Rupert. "And now she says that somehow all that wishing came true, and I feel like I'm back on that bed again, hurting all over, and my car's right outside the door."

Rupert stood and put his arms around him, and Erik cried on the starched white cotton of Rupert's shoulder as they swayed back and forth before the window.

"What about the wolf woman?" Rupert said quietly. "Does she love you?"

"Yes."

"My best advice? Stick with her. You can't go back. You'll be lying on that bed again in no time."

Rush hour seemed to be starting early because of the light but persistent rain. Erik waited in a long line of cars to escape from downtown. The way home took him within a block of Debra's museum. By the time he got there it would be about a quarter to five, closing time. He could see the exhibit she'd told him about, perhaps talk to her about what was going on in his life. He swallowed hard as he finally lurched into motion, a cop beckoning him more quickly than the traffic could possibly move. He glanced into his eyes in the rear-view mirror. He needed someone to talk to.

Erik entered the museum through the back entrance where the offices were. Sue and Sandy looked up and smiled at him. "I wasn't expecting to see you around here," Sandy said. She used to give Erik meaningful glances and ask him to dance at museum parties. Erik had always assumed this was to annoy her boss.

Sue came around her desk in a fluster, as usual. "Oh, Erik, I'm so glad to see you."

"How are you doing, Sue, and the dogs?" Sue's favorite topic of conversation was her dogs. According to Debra, only Erik was foolish enough to actually inquire about them, and for that reason Erik was Sue's favorite man in the world.

"Hamlet has had a cold," she said. "But he's better now. Luscious, well, she's just old."

Erik nodded and smiled. This was the usual state of affairs. The young Hamlet was usually afflicted with some ailment, and Luscious had been old for years now. Hamlet was a Great Dane and Luscious a chihuahua. They were the stars of a menagerie Erik knew to include rabbits, turtles, several species of birds, and at least one snake. Cats, because of the birds, were outcasts, though she did feed several wild ones from the steps of her back porch.

"You here to see Debra?" Sandy asked, a playful edge to her voice.

"And the new exhibit."

"Oh, you'll really like it," Sue spoke up.

Sandy pointed to the stairs behind them: "She's down in the workroom."

Erik nodded to them both and quickly made his way to the stairs. Sandy winked at him as he passed, a gesture he didn't want to interpret at the moment.

The workroom was half of the unfinished basement, the other half was filled with junk donated to the museum by well-meaning individuals too important to offend by throwing their gifts away, no matter how useless. Erik's favorite was a large moldering stuffed peacock whose head had been broken off and glued back on at an angle that made him look drunk. Someone had placed him at the helm of a battered kayak with a gaping hole in its side that hung from the ceiling. The workroom itself was piled with scraps of lumber and Plexiglas. A Mozart piano concerto played loud and thin from a small clock radio. Debra was standing at a drafting table under a fluorescent lamp cutting something with a razor knife. For a moment he stood and watched her profile, her large eyes intent upon her work.

"Hi, Debra."

She turned from her work, startled, but broke into a smile immediately. "You came," she said.

"I know it's kind of late, but I thought I could take a quick look."

"Don't be ridiculous. I'll give you a personal tour." She had taken his arm and was standing at his side, smiling up at him. At one time he would have bent to kiss her cheek.

"Don't let me take you from your work." He gestured toward the drafting table.

She laughed. "I was just redoing some of the labels. They were crooked, as Sandy's labels always are. But as you say, who the hell reads them anyway?" She smiled up at him. "I'm so glad to see you."

He didn't know what to say, so he just nodded and smiled.

"Let's go up to my office where we can talk."

She went to the radio and clicked off the Mozart and waited for him to join her at the bottom of the stairs. The stairs were too narrow for them to ascend arm in arm. He followed behind her. He remembered the perfume, but he couldn't recall the name. He'd bought it for her years ago because he found it exciting. She must have bought this bottle herself. Or it could have been a gift from someone else.

As they emerged into the office upstairs, Sue and Sandy looked at them with undisguised curiosity. Debra said, "You two can go on home. I'll lock up after I show Erik the exhibit."

Sue scurried to gather together her things. Sandy slung a backpack over one shoulder. "See you, Erik," she said with a leer, and left, while Sue was still frantically stuffing paraphernalia into her purse.

"There's no hurry," Debra said to her through a clenched smile as Sue chased a skittering lipstick to the edge of the desk.

Erik walked behind Debra down the hall to her office. He liked to watch her walk. She was most sensuous when moving through a room, bent on some purpose, but with a gliding, liquid movement. She looked over her shoulder and smiled at him as she bent to unlock the door. She always seemed to know when he watched her.

Debra's office, like the museum, was small and modest, furnished mostly with castoffs from more prestigious state institutions. The deep plush carpet, a rich powder blue, had been a coup—a scrap from a remodeled office at the courthouse. Debra had charmed it from someone at a cocktail party.

"You're all wet," she said.

"It's raining outside. I had to park a couple of blocks away."

"I'm flattered."

"You said the exhibit was exceptional."

"It's okay, Erik, if you wanted to see me as well."

"All right. I wanted to see you."

She smiled and took a jug of red wine from a cabinet and two plastic glasses. "We had some wine left over from the opening," she said as she poured and handed him a glass. "To old times." They touched their glasses together with a dull click and drank. Down the hall they could hear the echoing clatter of Sue closing and locking the door behind her.

Debra was wearing what Erik called her museum

director's clothes, tailored and precise. She took off the suit jacket and hung it on the back of a chair. She was wearing a gray silk blouse he'd never seen before, the color of a mockingbird's wing. "It's been hot all day in here."

Erik looked around the office. His photograph sat on the corner of her desk where it used to sit. The last time he'd been here, it had been removed. He wondered where it had been in the meantime.

"You're awfully quiet," Debra said.

"This is very strange for me."

"It doesn't have to be. We're old friends, aren't we?"

Erik smiled faintly. "You might say that."

"We don't have to talk about anything important right now. We can just see each other, take things slow."

At the thought of taking anything anywhere, Erik's heart froze, though he could not avoid the thought of holding her in his arms again. He'd thought of it often enough before, and now she wouldn't resist him. "Why don't we look at this exhibit?" he said.

As they walked down the hall, she became the director conducting a tour for a friend. "Have you seen the photo exhibit at the art museum?"

Erik winced, but she didn't notice. "Yes."

"How did you like it?"

"I liked the photos. The interpretation was a bit overblown."

"Oh, Erik, you're such a romantic. I thought it was brilliant."

"To each his own."

"Well, you'll like this," she said as she flipped on the lights in the exhibit hall. "Nothing but photos and titles."

He did like it. It moved him more than he was prepared to be moved in his precarious state. As each image touched him, the ache joined the pain of losing her that lingered inside him like a wounded animal in a cave. From the corner of his eyes he could see Debra watching his reactions, but he couldn't hide them. She left his side for a few moments in front of a photograph of an old man with a cat. The cat pushed the top of her head against the old man's grizzled chin. Both had their eyes open, looking off in different directions. The man's hand lay against the cat's side as if caressing a baby. Both were smiling. When Debra returned she refilled his wineglass and put her arm around his waist. He slid his arm around the unfamiliar gray silk and felt the curve of her waist in his palm.

"I'm glad you like it," she said.

"I do. Very much."

She laid her head upon his chest. "I've missed you," she said in a small, quiet voice.

He pulled her closer and kissed the top of her head. "I missed you, too." He could not decide whether to take her in his arms and kiss her or to shout out his anger that she had waited till now to tell him what he had always wanted to know.

She looked up at him, as if to decide, but he did not move. "Don't rush me, okay?"

She smiled and nodded, kissed her palm, and laid it on his cheek.

He followed her through the streets that used to be his neighborhood. He took little notice of things. He didn't want to know what had changed and what had stayed the same. He didn't want to know how he would feel if he let himself enter into this world again. He watched her taillights, her silhouette at the wheel, and followed her.

This time he found the beer opener with no trouble and poured beers for them both while she changed. "You said you wanted to talk to me about something?" she called from the bedroom.

"That's right," he called back.

She entered the kitchen tucking in her T-shirt. She wore jeans, and her feet were bare. It was how she dressed on Sundays when she wanted to relax. She took the beer from his hand. "Hungry?" she said.

She cooked for them while he sat on the kitchen counter and told her about Alice. He didn't know what he expected from her, but he told her everything, trying to be accurate in every detail.

She listened attentively, interrupting him only for clarification on some point of fact. They were calm. They did this well. She had often discussed her research with him and he with her. They might have been discussing the fate of jackass penguins or the diaries of a pioneer woman over a hundred years dead.

He talked through dinner, and when he had finished she was loading dishes into the dishwasher and he was making Scotch and waters. He realized, with a start, that it had been one year and two months since they'd last lived together, had done what they were doing now.

"Thanks for listening," he said. "You're really the only one I can talk to about something like this."

She closed the dishwasher, started it, and dried her hands on a towel. She took a long sip from her drink and held it in front of her as she leaned one hip on the counter. "You want to know what I think?"

"I guess that's why I came over here."

"I think your girlfriend is crazy and that you ought to come back to me."

He knew that was what she would say. "Why?" he said. "So that you can decide you're tired of me again?"

"That's not fair, and you know it."

"What's so unfair about it?"

"Goddammit, Erik, yes, divorce was my idea, but tell me you didn't want out. I want to hear this. You moved out, remember? Come on, tell me how perfect

204

our marriage was until I ruined it and broke your heart, ending your life of ecstasy."

He leaned back against the counter and crossed his arms. He looked through the doorway into the living room. Everything but the carpet, the sofa, and the walls had been changed. Even the drapes. The only sound was the rhythmic *swoosh* of the dishwasher. "You're right. Things were pretty bad."

"So it's not just my fault that things turned bad."

"I didn't see you shedding too many tears."

"You think because I don't weep and wail that I don't care."

"No, I think because you divorced me that just maybe you didn't care."

"Whatever you decide to do about me, Erik, this woman believes she turns into a wolf at the full moon and tears people's throats out. She is not well. Think about it."

"I will." He was quiet now, sad, and a little drunk, staring at the tile floor, tracing the familiar pattern.

She came over, stood in front of him, and took his arms in her hands. She looked up at him. In her ragged clothes and barefoot, she seemed small and childlike. "Think about me, too?" she asked.

"It seems I can't help that."

She leaned her weight against him and guided his arms around her waist. "Erik, you know you want me. Just one kiss?"

He kissed her hard. She opened her mouth and thrust herself against him. He took her by the waist and lifted her onto the counter. He kissed her throat, his hands gripping her thighs. He pulled up her T-shirt and took her breast in his mouth. Moaning softly, she wrapped her legs around his hips and her arms around his head. "Carry me," she whispered in his ear.

They undressed standing on opposite sides of the bed. Her silhouette in the darkness was familiar and exciting. He knew the touch of her skin, knew the way she would move beneath him. The sheets were clean and crisp and cold. He tried to see her face in the dim light, but her eyes were pools of shadows.

"I love you," she said.

He thought of Alice, now distant and inaccessible as well, and took Debra in his arms, breathing in the perfume at her throat.

"I want you," she whispered, and he entered her.

Chapter

13

Debra stabbed into the air and found the button on her alarm clock that gave her five or ten minutes more sleep depending on whether she rocked it right or left. She began each morning with a decision. She rolled her head to the left and expected to see Erik beside her.

At first she thought she'd dreamed his being here. Nothing in the rumpled covers or the pillow showed he had been here, that he had made love to her.

She put her hand between her legs and felt the dampness. She propped herself up on her elbows and saw the two glasses on either side of the bed, the cigarettes in both ashtrays, a small piece of folded paper with her name across it propped up next to the lamp.

She turned on the lamp and spread the sheet of paper out on the bed:

Had to leave to teach a class. Will try to call later.

Love,
Erik

He doesn't say anything about last night, she thought. He must feel guilty or scared. She looked at the clock: 8:20. If she remembered right, his class ended at nine-fifteen. If she hurried, she could beat him home. He wouldn't mind if she showered or not. She smelled of him.

She put on the T-shirt and jeans from the night before and called Sue at home, telling her she was sick and wouldn't be in, giving instructions for each person in her absence. Sue urged her to take vitamin C. The kind made from rose hips was best, she said.

She stopped at a 7-Eleven and bought two bottles of the best wine they had, which wasn't very good, but that didn't matter. Erik wouldn't mind. Years ago they used to laugh about being "decadent" together, getting drunk and fucking like crazy. I'll even suggest a joint, she thought. He'll love it. She usually didn't like it; it made her feel silly and out of control. On an impulse, she also bought two packages of Twinkies and a huge bag of potato chips.

Erik had a fear of lost keys. She quickly found a spare front door key under an empty flower pot and let herself in. She left the door open. The room smelled stale and musty. It was different from the other day. She was alone now and could study just what sort of life Erik had constructed for himself without her. Books about one kind of animal or another sat on chairs, on the floor, on the tables. The largest stack was beside his chair. She scowled. They were all books about wolves. Beside them, the Sunday newspapers sat in a pile, unread except for the comics, the reviews, and last week's TV schedule, which lay on the arm of his chair beneath the remote control. She lifted up the cushion and found two felt-tip pens, one red and one blue, and laid them on the table by the chair.

She dug a cigarette from one of the packs beside the chair and lit it with the lighter she knew would be lying there, just like the ones in the bathroom, the bedroom, the car, the kitchen (on top of the microwave), and his desk. She sat in the chair. The only other times she'd ever been in this chair she'd been sitting on Erik's lap, seducing him, though she hardly thought of it as seduction since he never said no. She'd told him no many times. He always seemed to pick the oddest times to want her, in the morning before she went to work or late at night when she was tired. The chair was worn to the shape of his body. She felt swallowed up in it, like Jack in the Giant's house. He sat here for hours, sometimes reading, sometimes staring off into space thinking of God knew what.

What does he think of this girl? she wondered. She knew it wasn't casual. Erik didn't know how to be casual about such things. Sometimes in their marriage she'd wished he didn't love her so much, didn't miss her so much when she came home from out of town, expecting her to throw her arms around him. It made her feel smothered. Twice she'd had affaris with other men. She felt terribly guilty. At the same time she believed the affairs had been good for her, reminding her of her essential identity, making her feel free. They were short affairs, no more than two or three weeks. She broke them off even though both men had wanted to see her again. Erik never knew anything about them, never even seemed to suspect.

Why am I doing this with Erik now? she thought. For love and what else? Did it matter what else? She shook her head. Of course it mattered. She didn't want to be the bitch, the Dragon Lady. She did have to admit that she wanted to win Erik back, in part, to see if she could. That he'd fallen for someone else made her want him more than ever. Did these things make her a bitch? Did these things take away from the fact that she loved him and wanted him?

She rose from his chair and went into his bedroom. The bed was low, the covers a mess. He never made the bed. He compared it to ironing pajamas. Slipping off her shoes, she lay on his bed and held the pillow against her chest, burying her face in it, breathing deeply. The room was brighter than their bedroom at home, light leaked in through the window blinds. She wanted him to make love to her in this bed, his bed. She wanted him to make love to her and no one else. The clock by the bed said 9:15. He should be home in fifteen or twenty minutes. She would wait for him here.

She went into the kitchen and found a corkscrew. She opened one of the bottles, washed a couple of glasses, and took them back to the bedroom. She stripped off her clothes, got under the covers, and finished her cigarette, sitting up in bed. Half a joint lay in the ashtray. She smiled to herself. This was perfect.

Alice stood at her kitchen sink, staring into Erik's house, wondering whether she should call in sick again. It was nine-fifteen. She went in at ten on Tuesdays.

Erik's car was back. He must've been home sometime between four, when she'd finally gone to bed, and now. He must've walked to school as usual and would be walking home now. Where had he been last night? She remembered the two photographs of Debra—beautiful, competent, a woman who would never go crazy, would never bay at the moon.

Why didn't I ask Erik to stay with *me* last night? she thought. Why did I send him away? Does it matter so much that he believes me now that I can change or not, whenever I want to?

She picked up the phone and called in sick. She hung up and started to cry. Of course it matters whether he believes me or not, knows who I am, woman and wolf. She wiped away her tears and looked up to see Debra through Erik's window, opening a bottle of wine.

She stared until the image disappeared, then rushed to her door, across the yard, and into Erik's living room through the open front door. The screen door slammed shut behind her. The scent of strange perfume filled the air. She could hear someone rustling cloth in Erik's bedroom, heard the sound of bare feet on the floor.

Debra stepped into the living room wearing Erik's bathrobe. She wore a faint and distant smile as if receiving a guest. Her eyes moved up and down Alice and seemed to say "I thought you would be taller and prettier."

She held out her hand. "I'm Debra, Erik's wife. You must be Alice."

Alice stared at the hand—long, thin, and delicate. "I've seen your pictures," she said, her arms at her sides.

Debra folded her arms and held her smile. "I'm afraid Erik isn't here right now. May I give him a message?"

"I know when Erik's classes are. That's why I came over, because I saw that someone was in Erik's house. Does Erik know you're here?"

"Of course. This morning, when he left my house, he left me a note saying I should meet him here and told me where to find the key."

They stood for a moment in silence. Alice looked around the room to get her bearings. It was still Erik's room, but she didn't seem to belong here anymore. Debra's expression remained the same. Finally Debra spoke.

"I'd ask you to stay, but we sort of have plans. I'll tell him you came by."

Alice drew back, then looked at Debra quizzically. "Is this how it's done? I don't know how to do this. We pretend that nothing is happening, that we don't feel anything?"

Debra set aside her smile. "All right," she said. "I know that you're Erik's girlfriend, but he is my husband. You are a very pretty girl, and I am sure Erik found you very attractive. He's been very lonely. But Erik and I have spent years together. He wants me back, and I want him. I'm sorry you have to be hurt."

Alice laughed. "You're sorry I have to be hurt? How about Erik? How much do you care about him? You divorced him. He's not your husband anymore."

"We made a mistake. I'm afraid you just got caught in the middle."

"Erik can't be that stupid. You don't want him back. You just want to prove you can do it. You'll just fuck up his life even more than you already have."

"Who in the hell are you to talk? Erik told me all about you. That's all Erik needs is to play nursemaid to some crazy bitch who howls at the moon and eats dog food."

Alice felt a rush of hatred. She'd never felt hatred before. She hadn't really hated Dale. She couldn't— he was dead. And as she now realized, hatred was wanting someone dead.

"I think you'd better leave," Debra said.

Alice stepped forward and pushed her onto Erik's chair, grabbed the poker from beside the fireplace, brought it down hard across the arms of the chair, and leaned down so that her face was only inches from Debra's. "Yes. I'm crazy! Don't fuck with me or I'll tear your throat out and scatter your guts around the room!"

She straightened up and peeled off her shirt, stepped out of her pants, all the while holding the poker aimed at Debra's chest. "And the reason I'm crazy is that I'm tired of no one believing me, even 'your husband,' as you call him, so I've picked one person to believe me without a shadow of a doubt, one person who will believe I am what I say I am. That person is you."

Debra could see the clock just over Alice's shoulder. Erik would be home any minute. She had to stall until then. She had no doubt that Alice intended to beat her to death with the poker. She was too frightened to imagine why Alice was stripping off her clothes. "Alice, I apologize for what I said. I understand that you're upset. I certainly would be upset if I were in your position."

"What in the hell would you know about 'my position'? I'm crazy, remember? And you're sane. Both of you. It's all a matter of changing those healthy little minds of yours, and I'm supposed to just fuck off."

Debra kept her eyes on the poker that Alice held poised and ready. "Erik will be home any minute," she said. "Maybe the three of us can talk this out."

Alice brought the poker down on the arms of the chair again and shouted, "No! I'm tired of talking and thinking and waiting for nothing!" She was breathing heavily, and her face was distorted with rage. She straightened up and took long, deep breaths, steadying herself. "So. Now I'm going to give you a gift to celebrate your reunion with your husband. I will show you the truth, and see how *you* like it. No one will believe it but you and me, and I won't even be here. Anyone else will call you crazy. They can put you away. You may even become crazy." She held Debra's eyes and whispered, "I may even kill you."

Alice lay on the floor and closed her eyes; the poker rolled from her hand. Debra could not move, could not take her eyes away. Alice's body quivered for a few seconds, then shifted and moved like the coils of a huge snake, reshaping itself as Debra watched. Thick, dark fur sprang from the flesh like sweat. The face thrust into a large snout and bared teeth. The limbs contracted and bent. It wasn't the hurried march of a time-lapse flower. Each cell was changing, quickly, completely simultaneously. Debra felt dizzy and nauseated. The animal rolled over onto its feet, shook itself, and looked into her eyes. Debra jerked her head down and clamped her eyes shut, willing it away, falling into darkness, as she heard the low rumble of a growl, felt the animal's hot breath sniffing at her, then passed out.

The wolf smells the man has mated with this woman. This place is his place, filled with his smell. Filled with her own woman's smell. She follows the scent, marking his path and hers.

Her woman has also mated with the man. Her woman's anger pushes at her chest. She whimpers, breathing in the man all around her. She comes back to the sleeping woman, pushes at her face with her snout, still whimpering. She tilts back her head, and the sadness howls through her in a long, aching bellow.

The sleeping woman's eyes come open and meet hers. Her woman had wanted to kill this woman lying helpless, her throat bare. This is not her way. She bares her teeth, and the woman beneath her closes her eyes in submission, shaking with fear.

She hears the man approaching and follows the scent and sound. The kitchen door opens, and he stands in the open door with the light behind him. She stands stiff-legged, does not move except for the tentative sway of her tail. She sniffs the air and smells his fear, sees it in his eyes. She feels her woman wailing inside her, pushing at the backs of her eyes. She ducks her head, pushes the man aside with her shoulder, and finds the sky. Wind ruffles her fur. It has been a long time. Fences surround her. She runs and leaps, lands in sand and gravel, slips and skitters, digs into the earth and runs down the fenced path to hide and find the woman who will come and take her from this place hemmed in by human smell and sadness.

Chapter

14

Erik knelt by Debra and took her head in his arms. She didn't seem to be hurt, but she was trembling, staring straight ahead, mumbling incoherently. He had never seen anyone so frightened. He could not imagine why he wasn't more frightened himself. He had just met a wolf in his kitchen. Alice's clothes lay in a heap at Debra's feet.

"It's okay," he told her. "I'm here."

"Erik," she managed in a whisper, and clutched his arms hard.

"I'm going to call for help. I'll be right across the room."

Slowly, as if she feared he might vanish once she let him go, she loosened her grip.

He dug through his pockets and found Adams's number. "I'm calling about my wife, my ex-wife," he told him. "She's damn near been frightened to death. She saw a wolf, doctor, in my living room. And I saw it, too."

"We can discuss this at the hospital, I'll meet you there. They'll be expecting you. Do you need an ambulance?"

"I can drive her." He looked over at Debra, still staring blindly ahead of her.

Three hours later Erik had yet to discuss anything with Adams. He sat in a large room, near the ICU and just down from the psychiatric ward, called the Snack Bar. Vending machines lined all four walls, tables and chairs filled the middle. For the first two hours he had shared the room with the Seymours', three generations of them, while they waited for word of one of their youngest, who had drunk from a jar of paint thinner. They were gone now. The boy was going to live. They had all gone to lunch. They asked Erik to join them, but he stayed because he still didn't know anything about Debra.

She hadn't said a word on the way to the hospital. She stared through the windshield with a determined, fearful look, apparently studying with her mind's eye what she had seen in his living room. He didn't dare ask her any questions. When they reached the hospital, he led her inside. She stood passively by the reception desk, the same look in her eyes, until Adams came and led her away.

He knew the animal he'd seen in his kitchen was a wolf, though the meaning of the look it gave him was a mystery. The clothes were Alice's. He had seen her wear them. Hell, he had taken them off her. They smelled of her. She had been wearing them. But where had she been? Where was she?

She didn't answer her phone, even though her car was in front of her house when he brought Debra to the hospital. She might have unplugged the phone. What would he say if she answered?

He rose and pushed the large white button on the refrigerated food machine. Sandwiches on white bread, cartons of whole milk and juice, pudding, and bruised apples clicked by him. The Seymours had just about wiped out the yogurt, but Erik was still able to buy a pineapple-cherry yogurt for a dollar. The plastic spoon bin was empty, but he found a plastic fork.

He sat and ate, tried desperately to understand what had happened. Was Alice, perhaps, what she said she was? She'd asked him to try to believe her. He had found the effort impossible. Belief wasn't something he could cajole himself into. What was it Rupert said—"If we can imagine it, it just might be true"? Trouble was, he could not imagine it. Until now. Until he'd felt the shoulder of a wolf against his thigh, pushing him aside. In the middle of Virginia, where there hadn't been wolves since the eighteenth century.

That Alice had something to do with that wolf being in his house seemed clear—her clothes on the floor, her disappearance. But what was the connection? She'd told him she changed into a wolf from sunset to sunrise the night of the full moon. But that was twelve days ago. He was suspicious that the evidence he now had didn't fit what she'd told him. Was it some sort of elaborate ruse to prompt him into belief? And why bring Debra into it? What would have happened to her if he hadn't arrived when he had?

And what was he going to do about Debra now? She was his wife. He was her husband. He had stepped into the role immediately, calling her work, taking care of the insurance. He was terrified of what might have happened to her. He knew that fear might obliterate her, crumble her identity so that she might as well be dead. He could not bear the thought of that happening to Debra, could not imagine a more horrible thing for her—she, who took such pride in her strong grip on things.

But it's me, he thought, who somehow has to make sense of all this. It's me who has to make up his mind.

He wished he had stayed with Alice last night. He wished that he hadn't gone to bed with Debra. He wished he knew what he wanted. He loved Alice. He was sure of that. But she was, as she herself had said, a werewolf or crazy. Such a choice made him feel dizzy. How could he leap into such an abyss for someone he'd known for twelve days? Where was she? What was she thinking and feeling? She must've figured out that something was going on with Debra. Perhaps she didn't want him to find her, didn't want to have anything to do with him. But he had to do something.

He stared at the tines of the plastic fork and licked them clean, threw the yogurt cup and fork into the trash, and looked around him. But all I can do, he thought, is sit here with this goddamn row of machines.

Dr. Adams entered the Snack Bar with his right hand extended. Erik rose and shook his hand, and Adams sat down.

Erik looked down at him. "Can I see her now?"

Adams smiled and gestured with the back of his hand toward Erik's chair. "Sit down. She's fine. You can see her in a little while." They remained poised for a few moments. "Please," Adams said, and Erik sat down.

"How is she?" Erik asked.

"We've talked for quite a while. She's fine. Somewhat disoriented as yet, but I am confident that will pass. She can probably go home in the morning."

"Is there some reason I can't see her?"

"No, no, none at all. I do need to talk with you for a few minutes, though. I need to know as much as possible about what happened at your house this morning, if I'm going to help your wife. Now, just tell me in your own words what happened last night and this morning."

Erik did not like the man's smile. It hung in the air like the Cheshire cat's. "What does she say?"

"I'd rather hear your version first, if you don't mind."

Erik leaned forward. "I do mind. As you know from our recent phone conversation, I've been having a rough week. Now, my wife is in the psych. ward, and her doctor wants to play Kojak. I am not your patient, doctor. I want to know what Debra said happened to her this morning in my house."

Adams dropped the smile and nodded his head. "Okay, at first she said that she saw Alice White change into a wolf, that the wolf did not harm her in any way, but sniffed her crotch and left. When pressed, however, she could not describe this supposed metamorphosis in any detail. I have calmed her down a great deal by persuading her that the metamorphosis was a hallucination, a hysterical reaction to the very real threat that Alice White presented to her." Adams made a tent with his fingers. "She also says that you two had sexual intercourse last night. Is that correct?"

"Yes," Erik said, and sat back in his chair. "I saw that wolf, too," he said. "It practically knocked me over in the kitchen."

Adams drew a pad and pen from his breast pocket. "Did you see Alice White change into a wolf?"

"No, but there was a wolf in my kitchen."

"What kind?"

"Hell, I don't know."

"You're an expert, right? A wildlife biologist. And yet you can't tell me what kind of wolf you saw in your kitchen? Maybe that's because you didn't see a wolf at all."

"I am telling you. This was no dog."

"Now it's 'not a dog.'" Adams held up a forefinger. "But let's just say you did see a wolf. There are domesticated wolves, are there not? And I would say that all the evidence points to Alice White being the owner of such an animal, perhaps trained as an attack animal to carry out her psychotic delusion that she is a werewolf. Given her feelings for you and that she had every reason to suspect you had renewed relations with your wife, I would say that it is probable that she intended to kill Debra. Debra said she did threaten her with a poker before she stripped and the animal appeared."

Erik twirled the salt shaker around with his fingertips. "So Debra hallucinated the wolf that bumped into me and ran out my back door?"

Adams's voice was kind and gentle. "I'm not saying that. Alice had an animal with her, apparently. But a pile of clothes doesn't mean she *is* the animal in question. You saw Debra, Erik. Who knows what she saw? But I don't think she's the one who can tell us. I have no doubt she had a terrifying experience and that Alice White had something to do with it, but I don't think we need to start believing in werewolves to explain it."

Adams looked away and seemed to be somewhere else for a moment. "I wish she were a werewolf. That would make everything easier." He looked back at Erik. "I should tell you that I notified the police about this, and they'll probably want to talk to you."

"But as you already pointed out, I didn't see anything but an animal in my kitchen."

"Yes, but I suspect they'll want your help in locating Alice White."

"She's gone?"

"Her car's gone, and no one's at the house. The police say it looks like she left in a hurry."

"Did they check the basement?"

Adams cocked his head to one side. "Yes. It was empty. They think she was keeping an animal down there."

Erik looked down at the table. "She was," he said. He didn't want to talk about Alice anymore. They sat silently, Adams's questions apparently over. "Can I see Debra now?" Erik said.

"Certainly," said Adams, rising to lead the way, "but please don't say anything at this point about wolves or Alice."

Erik followed behind him, watching the white flutter of his physician's jacket, trying to put Alice quite deliberately out of his mind. No matter what he believed now, it seemed, Alice had intended to kill Debra. He had brought them together. He had betrayed Alice and enraged her. He would have been responsible for Debra's death.

He felt numb. He had never wanted so desperately to do the right thing, had never been so confused as to what the right thing might be. When they reached Debra's room, Adams stepped aside. Erik pushed the door and entered the cool darkness, where she lay in the far bed.

The bed closer to the door was stripped of linens and closed up like a snail. Debra rolled her head toward him, her eyes drooping from tranquilizers, and smiled. "Hi, Erik."

"Hi, Deb." He took her hand and sat on the edge of the high bed.

"I guess I scared you." Her voice was childlike.

"Guess you had quite a scare yourself."

She squeezed his hand. "I'm okay now." She looked at their clenched hands. "Dr. Adams says I can probably go home tomorrow, if there's someone there with me." She looked up at him. "Will there be someone there with me?"

"Of course," he said.

She closed her eyes and smiled. Soon her grip had loosened, and her eyes fluttered with dreams. Erik kissed her forehead and went back into the hall.

Adams was gone, and a policeman had taken his place. They sat in the Snack Bar, and Erik lit a cigarette. "How long have you known Alice White?" the policeman began.

* * *

Luther couldn't understand how he had been so wrong about Alice. Granted that he felt a certain affection for her, but to have failed to see the potential danger of her illness from the very beginning seemed to him now to be inconceivable.

He'd canceled his appointments for the day. After the ordeal at the hospital and with the police, he couldn't face anyone. He'd told Eleanor, "I have to be alone," and had taken a drink to his study. It was gone now, and he was wondering whether he should risk Eleanor's questions by going to the kitchen to fix himself another. It embarrassed him to have been such a fool. Debra might have died. The trauma alone, no doubt, had done incalculable harm.

He'd been in quite a state when he got back from Alice's last night. He didn't know what had come over him. Why had he even gone over there in the first place—to a patient's house? And then to have made advances. He winced to think of it. Fortunately Eleanor had still been writing letters when he'd returned and hadn't asked too many questions. He'd said he was tired after dinner and gone off to bed. Whenever he'd fallen asleep, Alice had shown up in his dreams to seduce or destroy him. He had finally fallen into a deep sleep when Erik called.

He was glad Erik had had the presence of mind to call him. Now that he knew what he was up against, he'd handled the situation rather well. Now, finally, this Alice White business was out of his hands, though he didn't have too much confidence in the police. They'd said there was no evidence of any crime. The dog or wolf or whatever it was hadn't hurt anyone. Alice had every right to go anywhere she wanted. There was nothing they could do. Luther was outraged. Threatening people with a vicious animal wasn't against the law? He shuddered to think what would have happened to him if he had gone to her house on the full moon, as she'd suggested. He remembered her saying, as he'd held her in his arms, "I don't want to hurt you."

He heard the garage door opening, Eleanor's car starting, then the garage door closing. Where was she going? She always told him where she would be. He found these reports annoying, actually, and only half listened, but it was a bad sign that she'd simply taken off without saying a word. She was probably angry about something. He would take her to lunch tomorrow, perhaps take her to that overpriced antique store she liked so much. For now, he was glad to have solitude.

He emerged form his study and looked up and down the hall of closed doors. He whistled as he walked to the kitchen. It began to dawn on him that a tremendous burden had been lifted from his shoulders. Alice was gone, and it looked as though Debra would be all right. She and her husband were even getting back together. They made a very handsome couple. All in all, things had turned out much better than could be expected.

The kitchen was spotless. Eleanor was an excellent housekeeper. He filled his glass with ice and opened the liquor cabinet. Inside, propped against the bourbon, was one of Eleanor's peach-colored envelopes with his name on it. He smiled to himself. When they were younger, she'd written him love letters. He still had them around someplace. He poured his drink, sat at the table, and opened the letter.

Dear Luther,

I am leaving you. I finally decided this morning, though I have been considering it for a long time. I no longer love you. I am not even sure I ever did. I married you because you were good for me. You were so intelligent. You would teach me how to think. I thought you would transform me, if not into the son my father always wanted, then at least into the wife of the son-in-law he'd always wanted. Eventually, I learned that I already could think quite well before I even knew you. With that realization I had to decide if I loved you or not. You couldn't just be my good medicine, once I was cured.

While I was desperately trying to decide whether I loved you or not, I recalled something you said when we were first dating: "I think I am falling in love with you." Then, of course, I was carried away, but remembering it now, I was struck by the stupidity of what you were saying, and the same stupidity in my trying to decide whether I loved you. No amount of thought would change that I did not.

I do not know whether or not you still think you love me. It seems to me your thoughts have been focused on your patient, Alice. No doubt you think you love her as well. Perhaps you have been unfaithful to me. More likely, you have simply thought about it.

I don't know who you are anymore. I don't believe you want me to know. You don't seem to want to know who I am. You seem content with the ideas you've adopted about me—a wife appropriate to your orderly life. I confess that once I wanted nothing more than to fulfill those ideas, but I have found that an idea cannot be loved or love.

Don't bother trying to locate me. I have some savings and plan to travel for a while. I will write you when I have made more definite plans.

I know you probably think me cowardly for not talking this over with you face to face. Frankly, I couldn't bear to hear the theories you would formulate to explain my behavior, ignoring whatever feelings I might have. I am sorry things have come to this.

Good-bye,
Eleanor

Luther read the letter over several times, trying to make sense of it, but it seemed to shift and blur, saying one thing and then another, none of which made any sense to him. He tried to find his image of Eleanor, tried to imagine these words coming from her mouth, but she was transformed, lost to him. She had vanished. He stared at the dark oak grain of the table until tears could fall and the room had become dark and quiet.

Alice had driven as far as she could without eating. It had rained all the way through Maryland, and Pennsylvania was buried in fog. She headed a train of cars behind a nervous man driving a van full of children. He would brake at nothing and send the children laughing and hurtling through the van. Then they'd return to the windows and wave at Alice, shoving each other out of the way, mugging for their audience. The oldest child, a girl of about eight, made a sign on a piece of notebook paper—WEAR LOST—and held it up for Alice to read. The van made an abrupt lurch and swerve, and the children disappeared from the windows for good.

Alice didn't want to be conspicuous, so she looked for someplace large that would be filled with customers. She followed the signs from the interstate and sat in a Denny's sipping coffee, staring at the menu, unable to decide. Table toppers announced specials for senior citizens. Alice was the only customer in the crowded restaurant under fifty.

At the table beside her, two women had a loud conversation. One of them, the younger, a lean dark woman in her mid-fifties, did most of the talking, speaking into the older one's hearing aid. "They operated on her brain, you know. Had to cut open her head with a saw. I think they both knew she wasn't going to make it, but you know doctors. Never say die."

"Now, there's always a chance, you know. Look at

Margaret. Dead, they said, with the cancer. And that was five years ago."

The younger woman waved Margaret away with the toss of her hand. "This was a brain tumor. Eloise said it was big as a grapefruit. Anyway, she died while they were operating on her. But what I wanted to tell you about was what happened after. They shaved her head, you know, cut off all that hair. She'd let it grow for years and years. Well, a month later, Bill gets a big brown envelope in the mail from the hospital marked 'Personal Effects,' and guess what's in it?"

"You can't be serious."

"I'm telling you—it was stuffed with Eloise's hair. Bill just about went crazy. Called up the hospital, cussed them up one side and down the other, and they didn't any more care than the man in the moon. Cecily told me all about it. Said Bill was going to sue."

"I can't believe such a thing. How did Cecily know about it?"

"Bill and Cecily are an item, haven't you heard?"

The older woman shook her head in dismay. Alice looked around at the other customers who, like herself, had all been eavesdropping. Like the old woman, they could not believe such a thing. Alice could picture the long gray coil of hair spilling out into the grieving man's hands. She brushed her cheek with the end of her own braid. Personal effects, personal causes. She would like to think, if she were Bill, that she would be grateful for the hair that probably only he had seen hanging loose in the evenings as she brushed it out, evidence of the years.

Returning to solitude would be hard, Alice thought. Even the conversations of strangers blocked her way. When the waitress came, Alice could only manage to point at one of the pictures on the menu and nod that, yes, she wanted her coffee cup filled.

She hoped to make it to the St. Lawrence before dark. There was a campground there she remembered as a little girl when the whole family would go to visit her great-aunt. She sipped her coffee and stared out the window. The afternoon sun had finally burned through the fog, but the light was still heavy and damp. She thought about Erik, the fear in his eyes. Did he believe her? she wondered. Doesn't matter much now one way or the other.

Tears came to her eyes, and she wiped them away with a paper napkin. She had been unable to stop crying for more than a few minutes at a time. God damn him, she thought. I love him so. She saw herself whirling through the air in his arms, heard his voice saying, "I didn't think you were ever going to get here," felt her arms around him as she told him the first time, "I love you." She was glad she had told him. At least he knew that much. He couldn't doubt that.

The waitress timidly set her plate before her. "Are you all right?" she asked.

Alice nodded and managed to smile.

"Would you like ketchup or mustard?"

Alice shook her head.

The waitress put her hand on Alice's arm. Her face was full of concern. "If you need anything, just give me a holler." She squeezed Alice's arm, filled her coffee cup, and walked away. Alice watched her move from table to table filling cups, talking to strangers.

Alice had decided to seek temporary refuge with her great-aunt Ann. During her week with Erik, she'd gotten a letter from Ann after a long silence. Howard was dying. She wanted to see him, to comfort Ann, to be in the presence of a sadness greater than her own.

She might even tell Ann about the wolf. It didn't seem such a difficult thing anymore. The worst had happened. Ann wouldn't flee from her, would let her be crazy if that's what she was. It wouldn't matter. Alice planned to cast her lot with wolves.

Near Ann and Howard's house in southern Ontario was a huge provincial park where wolves lived protected from traps, poison, or gunfire from airplanes. Alice planned to enter that wilderness and learn to be a wolf. She wasn't sure what the wolf knew from her, whether her reading about wolves would have "educated" the wolf. The wolf seemed to have educated her. Once she and Willoughby were out in the woods with her dog, Fay. Fay was eating grass. Wiloughby kept trying to stop her. "She'll throw up," she said. Alice knew how Fay felt and said, "She needs to throw up. Her stomach probably hurts. Just because you'd rather have a stomachache than throw up doesn't mean Fay does."

Her actual memories of the wolf were fragmentary, like memories from childhood, vivid but unconnected. She remembered a moment standing in the stream on the farm, the air heavy with honeysuckle. She remembered digging at the floor drain in the basement where she had heard the squeak of mice. These memories were largely of sound and scent. She could hear and distinguish the faintest sound. Smell had a shape—she didn't know how else to put it—it was as if she breathed in line and color. Her heightened senses before she changed were nothing to the wolf's. At least she would have the senses to find her way in the wilderness.

Still, she knew she might die in the effort. Wolves didn't take kindly to strangers, especially ones who didn't know the rituals of the wilderness. But surely the wolf knew as well as she did the life of a stranger and would learn how to deal with its risks.

Her mother had always warned her to beware of strangers. She remembered once when she was five or six and they still lived in the city; her mother gave her an umbrella. She waited impatiently to use it, but every time it started to rain her mother said they had no place to go and what kind of fool would *want* to go out in the rain, anyway?

So late one afternoon after school, while her mother was in the basement doing laundry, she silently took her umbrella and stepped out the front door into a downpour. It had started suddenly but came down in an inviting roar.

She hurried down the steps to the sidewalk. She walked briskly for a block, then slowed down to enjoy it. The rain on her umbrella was the best sound she'd ever heard. The water cascaded around her; it was like being beneath her own waterfall. She turned down a street with hardly any trees so the leaves wouldn't block the rain. She turned again. Soon there were no trees at all, and it was just her and the rain. In a loud voice she started singing "Itsy Bitsy Spider."

A voice called to her. She turned to see a black man standing on a drooping front porch. "Child," he said, "what you doing out walking in the rain?"

"I got a new umbrella," she said.

"That's a mighty pretty one, too. You trying it out for the first time?"

She nodded.

"You look like you having a pretty good time. Your momma and daddy know you out here with your new umbrella?"

She shook her head.

"Whereabouts you live?"

"1815 Grove."

"And which way is that?"

She pointed back the way she had come.

He nodded. "This walking in the rain looks pretty good. You mind if I just walk along with you a little ways?"

"Have you got an umbrella?" she asked.

He put on a large floppy hat and stepped from the porch to her side. "I don't put much stock in umbrellas, always getting in the way. Me, I wear a hat." He took out a cigarette and lit it, his hands cupped around his mouth and the huge brim drooping over his face. "Now you see, if I was toting a damn umbrella, I couldn't light my cigarette."

"But your clothes are getting all wet," she said.

229

"That's half the fun of walking in the rain, changing into them nice, dry clothes when you get back home, maybe have a little hot chocolate with marshmallows in it. You like hot chocolate with marshmallows?"

She thought they were walking back the way she came, but she couldn't be sure. She knew the way to school. She knew the way to the store. This wasn't either one of them.

His face ducked under her umbrella. It looked funny tilted to one side. "I said, do you like hot chocolate with marshmallows?"

They had stopped walking. "Yes, sir," she said.

He made a face. "Don't be sirring me. Name's Lawrence." He held out a huge black hand.

She held out her hand. He took it with two fingers and a thumb and gave it three shakes. "What's your name?"

"Alice White," she said.

"Pleased to meet you." He straightened up, and they continued walking. She tilted her umbrella to one side so she could see him better.

"Yes," he was saying. "Ain't much that beats a cup of hot chocolate with three or four marshmallows floating in it."

"My momma only lets me have one," Alice said. "She says they're nothing but sugar."

He laughed. "Yeah, that sugar's some pretty bad stuff all right. I bet your momma don't think much of candy bars, neither."

"My daddy buys me a candy bar sometimes and tells me to eat it before we get home."

He laughed a long time at this. She liked his laugh. Most grown-ups laughed as if they thought they weren't supposed to. They walked on. He didn't say anything. The rain was still coming down hard. She still didn't see anything that looked familiar. The water was starting to come through her umbrella in a cold mist, and her shoes and socks were soaking wet. "Are we almost to my house?" she said.

"1815 Grove? It'll be up here just a little ways."

She was beginning to get scared. Her momma must be out of the basement by now, wondering where she was.

"Which way you going?" he said. "It's this way."

She turned and followed him down a street she thought she'd seen before, but she couldn't be sure. They turned again, and he stopped. "There she be," he said.

She looked across the street, and there was her house. He stuck his head under the umbrella again and handed her fifty cents. "Look both ways now, and buy yourself one or two of them candy bars next time you go to the store."

She stared at the two quarters in her palm.

"You tell your momma you found these quarters in the rain. Don't be saying nothing about me, okay?"

"Okay." Again he took her hand in his fingers and shook it.

"Be seeing you, Alice," he said.

"Bye, Lawrence," she said.

Her mother yelled at her for a solid hour, as Alice held the quarters balled up inside her fist. She went to her room as ordered, her umbrella taken away and hidden on a high shelf. She put the quarters in the box where she kept her stamps from Canada, the ones with pictures of the queen.

Now, through the restaurant window, trucks whined up the grade heading north. The sun would hang in the west for another few hours. She left half her meal uneaten. She paid her check and bought a Snickers and an Almond Joy. The air outside smelled like a wet forest.

Western New York was a different world. As she approached the Canadian border she was all alone, no cars, no gas stations, just the low trees and long grass of the marshlands.

The image of Debra standing before her in Erik's robe returned to her. She struck the steering wheel

231

with the palm of her hand. What had made Erik do it? Was he so drawn to Debra, or was he repulsed by me? Did he love her more, or me less? She couldn't love him more than I do. But that's not enough, is it? He needs . . . How do I know what he needs? I'm not like other people. I'm an animal. She could still smell his fear of her.

The campground was empty. She pitched her tent by the river and sat on the pier, eating her candy bars. This place was called The Thousand Islands, the river was filled with them, a house or two on each one. A Greek freighter moved slowly upriver. She imagined herself in the upstairs bedroom of the yellow house the ship was passing now, lying awake in the moonlight, watching the shadows of the masts as they moved across the wall, the ship so close that sailors might jump from her deck to the balcony. He will be happier with Debra, she thought. They understand each other.

PART
THREE

Now remember courage, go to the door,
Open it and see whether coiled on the bed
Or cringing by the wall, a savage beast
Maybe with golden hair, with deep eyes
Like a bearded spider on a sunlit floor
Will snarl—and man can never be alone.

—Allen Tate
"The Wolves"

PART

THREE

Chapter

15

Six weeks later, in mid-May, Debra sat in her kitchen and watched Erik through the screen door as he crawled around on all fours. He was weeding their herb garden. The garden had been her idea. They had planted it in early April, the week after she'd come home from the hospital. He had cleaned the whole house while she was gone, even waxed the floor. He was still scrupulous about doing his share of the chores around the house. Debra knew this was mostly to assuage his guilt at being there at all. It had rained throughout April, and the herbs now flourished. "They will add spice to our marriage," Debra said as they watched the rain fall, and Erik smiled and said nothing.

At first she had flirted with him like that, wanting

him to flirt back, wanting him to say he would marry her again. When the conversation took this turn, it ended with Erik's silence. Now she no longer flirted; she just got through the day, waiting for something to happen.

The semester was over; he had just turned in his grades. All the previous semesters they'd been together he had been elated on the last day, had always wanted to go out to celebrate. Today he had slipped into the backyard. She knew he wanted to be alone. He was scared. She was scared, too. So much had happened—a cataclysm had leveled everything. She thought of the phoenix rising from the ashes but knew that was false. They hadn't been reborn. At least their marriage hadn't. They occupied the shell of it. At least they didn't fight. They were too distant to fight. What would be the point of fighting with someone who didn't love you anymore?

He must feel he is betraying someone, himself or the girl. She corrected herself. The girl had a name, Alice. He had betrayed her, and now he was betraying himself. And I, she thought, have been betraying him.

She had never told him what she had seen that day six weeks ago. As Dr. Adams questioned her, she'd remembered what Alice had told her: "No one will believe it. They can put you away. You may even become crazy." She saw that Alice was right. It had been a warning, not a threat. When Adams had offered her a hysterical hallucination in place of the truth, Debra had taken it. She'd seen that until she gave Adams a truth he could believe, he would hold her prisoner.

She was ashamed that she'd kept Erik prisoner by concealing the truth. This wasn't like concealing her affairs. They had less to do with Erik than he would ever realize. But this was *his* truth. He should've been the one to see what I saw, she thought. He wouldn't have fled. I think he would have loved her all the more, another animal he could be sentimental about.

A couple of weeks ago she and Erik had gone to the park. It had been her idea, a romantic outing. He was even more distracted than usual. His eyes wandered around, then fixed on a spot beneath a huge ancient tree. He was oblivious of everything for at least a minute, then jerked himself back. He pointed away from the tree and said, "Do you want to go over that rise?" Debra believed that if she could have seen through his eyes for that minute, she would have seen him and Alice, together, as palpable as that tree.

On the other side of the hill, they spread a blanket. Erik sat cross-legged on the corner and said, "Tell me what you saw that day."

She knew what day he meant but said, "What day?" stalling for time.

"The day that put you in the hospital," he said.

She thought of picking a fight with him. It would be easy. She was his wife, and he was in love with another woman. But she wasn't his wife, and he was in love with another woman. Why fight about such a thing? Weeping was quite enough. She wanted to tell him the truth but couldn't bring herself to do it, to let go of him once and for all. Instead she said, "I saw a woman and a wolf. Other than that, I don't know."

"But you must have seen something," he insisted. "Did you ever see them together? Could you hear the animal in the next room?"

He was bent forward, waiting for her answer. He knows, she thought, I have the truth if only I would give it to him. He had come back to her because he felt responsible. The only way she could keep him was to sustain that feeling. She said quietly, "I don't want to talk about this, Erik. Not just yet."

He hesitated. She could see he was tempted to press on, to shrug off his guilt, but in the end he looked away with the same dead stare she'd seen so many times these last few weeks. "Okay," he said. "I'll drop it."

She watched him now, digging up weeds, so careful and precise, digging deep for the roots. He is thinking about her now, she thought. He loves her. This thought didn't pain her anymore. She remembered what else Alice had told her: "You'll just fuck up his life even more than you already have." Maybe so. She certainly wasn't making him happy. He didn't belong here anymore.

She rose from the table, walked into the bedroom intending to change her clothes for dinner. Instead she lay down on the neatly made bed, stared at the ceiling, and cried.

Erik pushed the trowel into the earth, loosening the soil around the taproot of a tall dandelion. He tugged gently, but the root broke off two or three inches below the surface. He cursed and dug with his trowel and fingers.

He was thinking of Alice. There had been brief stretches of time over the last six weeks when he hadn't thought of her, times when he didn't seem to think of anything. They would end with a jolt of remembrance and him locked up in his office, crying. All emotion, especially joy, reminded him of Alice. At first he'd tried to deaden himself, but he couldn't. Now, each day he woke thinking of her, thought of her all day, dreamed of her at night if he could sleep, or thought of her if he could not.

He had memorized each day with her, even the moments where nothing happened, nothing was said. He remembered how he felt: standing in line with her at the drugstore buying batteries for a flashlight, smiling at the shelves of boom boxes and film behind the dour cashier, I put my arms around her waist as she was getting the money out of her wallet. She leaned her head back against my chest, and the cashier laughed. "You two gonna get arrested," she said.

The mint was taking over everything, as he knew it would. He rubbed a sprig in his palms and smelled, wishing he could hold out his hands for Alice to smell it, too. He decided to let it have its way. Like most everything else, he had neglected this garden. He managed to do his work—teaching classes, grading exams, revising a paper and delivering it at a conference on endangered species at the end of April.

His work had given him someplace to hide, an excuse for being alone. With the semester over, he dreaded being caught out in the open. He felt safer alone. He took long meandering walks, striking out for neighborhoods where no one would know him, though he often walked by the house still rented in his name and Alice's abandoned house next door. No one knew where she was. Junk mail spilled from her mailbox.

He harvested some dill, though he and Debra already had a huge bunch of it in the refrigerator, waiting to go bad. Neither one of them had the energy to cook anymore. They went out to eat, sat in movies holding hands. They still didn't like the same films, but they didn't bother to argue about them anymore. It just didn't seem to matter.

Debra, in a gesture of peace, had invited his father over for dinner a few weeks ago. They cooked together in silence, passing back and forth in the narrow kitchen without touching. After dinner, when Debra had left the room, his father said, "You look miserable, Erik."

"I am."

"Then why don't you go find her?"

"I don't know enough yet."

"Surely there's someone who has some notion where she's gone."

"There is, and I'll talk to them, but I mean I have to know more about something else."

His father tilted his head in the same way he himself did when asking a silent question.

Erik said, "I have to know about wolves, Dad. She's gone where there are wolves. I can't tell you how I know that, but if I'm going to find her, I'll have to know how a wolf thinks."

In his mind, he had found Alice over and over again. Sometimes she'd been insane. Sometimes she'd been a werewolf. Sometimes she still loved him and sometimes not. Sometimes, but these were few, she forgave him.

He had decided that no matter what the truth was about Alice, he still loved her. He had to see her again. She couldn't be that hard to find. She had so few connections with other people. She must have gone someplace where she had been before. He thought of the penguins returning to their particular place on the planet each year. What would be Alice's place? What was his own?

For the last several weeks Paige had come by his office often, flirting in her earnest, idealistic way. He had let her know he was married, for that seemed the easiest way to discourage her. But after she turned in her final she tried to engage him in a philosophical discussion of the ethics of adultery. She said she'd read Bertrand Russell and wanted to know what Erik thought. She asked him why he didn't wear a wedding ring. While they were talking, the last student finished his exam and left.

As he stood in the empty hall with Paige, Erik tested himself with the thought of seducing her. All he had to do was say, Yes, there's nothing wrong with adultery. He could see she was quite prepared to do the rest. She was young, pretty, adoring—the perfect distraction for a confused middle-aged man.

"What are your plans for the summer?" he said, changing the subject.

"I'm living off campus now," she said. "I've got my own place: 705 Boulevard, number ten."

"You should like that."

"Would you like to come over?" she said. "Just for a little while."

"Paige, I am flattered and tempted, but I belong to someone else."

She looked down at the floor. "Your wife," she said.

He tilted up her chin, smiled at her, and said, "No. Someone else."

He stood now and dusted the dirt from his knees. He lit a cigarette, looked down the row of backyards and fences. He remembered the wolf pushing him aside, leaping his fence, and running out of sight. It was Alice. It had to be. Something in the eyes he couldn't measure or explain had been her.

He glanced at his watch. It was dinnertime. He and Debra would eat out again. He finished his cigarette and flicked the butt into the alley, turned, and walked back to the house. He would tell her tonight that he must leave.

She was getting dressed when he came in. He loitered in the kitchen until she was through, then changed himself.

He met her by the front door. "Have you seen my sunglasses?" she said.

He shook his head. "Maybe you left them at work."

"I wore them home, Erik."

"Maybe they're in the car."

"No, I know I put them right here."

Erik looked at the empty table she pointed to and didn't say a word.

"Here they are." She scooped them up from the mantle and put them on. "Okay, I'm ready."

Erik led the way to the car. When they were both strapped in and Erik had started the car, he said, "How was work today?"

"I had lunch with Hodges. He was his usual charming self."

He didn't look at her. He studied the road, then the rearview mirror. Hodges was a pig. His company was under indictment for falsifying EPA reports. Once, at a museum opening, Erik had lectured him on the impact of pollutants on the Chesapeake. Debra hadn't been amused. "Why would you subject yourself to lunch with Hodges?"

"He's on the board, Erik."

He merely nodded. There was no point in reviving the old arguments.

She moved the mirror to adjust her hair. "Do you feel like celebrating the end of the semester tonight?"

He shrugged. "What did you have in mind?"

"I thought we might go to a movie later."

"Okay."

She twisted the mirror back toward him, and he reached up and readjusted it.

"Is there anything you'd like to see?" she said.

"I don't know. What haven't we seen?"

"How about the new Woody Allen?"

"Sounds fine."

They rode for a few blocks in silence. "Where do you want to eat?" he said.

"Anyplace. It doesn't matter."

"I need to know where to drive the car, Debra."

"I don't know. Just pick a place. I promise to eat."

He turned uptown to Third Street, where there was a diner they liked. They drove the rest of the way in silence.

Over the menus, he said, "I need to talk to you."

Debra smiled up at the waitress who had appeared out of nowhere. "Chef salad," she said, "with oil and vinegar."

"Cheeseburger and French fries," said Erik.

When the waitress had gone, Debra looked around the room. It was not a real diner, but someone's idea of what a diner should look like, like a rich girl dressed up as a hobo for Halloween.

When she looked across the table at Erik, he said, "What made you think you wanted me back?"

She smiled. "You must've thought so, too. You wouldn't have come back otherwise."

"Maybe thought had nothing to do with it."

She closed her eyes. "Okay, okay, felt. Thought was your verb, dammit. Sometimes you are such a sanctimonious prick."

Erik's mouth flew open, but he could think of nothing to say that didn't make him sound like a humorless sanctimonious prick. He tried to make it a joke. "I thought that was what you loved about me."

She took his hands and shook her head. "Not that," she said fiercely. "I never loved that. I'm not good enough to live with a saint."

"I'm not a saint."

"I know. But you try to be. You don't have to be perfect, Erik. We all do the wrong thing sometimes."

They were silent a moment, looking into each other's eyes. "This isn't working," he said.

"I know."

"We're too different."

She looked down. "Don't say that. It's just over, that's all. Isn't that enough?"

The waitress stood a few paces from the table with their food, waiting for Debra to finish. Erik and Debra noticed her at the same time. "Would you like ketchup?" she asked Erik, and he nodded.

They bent over their food and ate. Erik could think of nothing to say. Their waitress sat at the counter, totaling checks. Her uniform was a sleeveless white blouse with her name stitched across her breast and a short flared skirt such as skaters wear. She perched on the edge of the stool, balanced on her outstretched toes. Her young, slender legs were beautiful.

He looked at Debra, her head still down. He could tell by the way she speared her food with her fork, slowly and deliberately, that she knew he was watching her. "I'm in love with Alice," he said.

She picked up her napkin and put it back down. "I know," she said without looking up. "I've known it all along."

"I'm going to try to find her."

She looked up, wiped away her tears. "I'm glad you told me. I've been waiting." She smiled sadly. "I feel almost relieved now." She took his hands. "We don't have to fight this time, do we?"

He shook his head. "No, we don't have to fight anymore."

They paid the bill and drove home. They passed a row of turn-of-the-century homes turned into offices, painted with cheery pastels like buildings at a theme park. "My God, how ugly," Debra said, and Erik called it "pastelification." They talked about the way the neighborhood used to look, how it might look if someone cared to restore these buildings with some sense of their history. It was the sort of conversation they used to have. They rolled down the car windows, and Erik drove with one hand upon the wheel. They might have been strangers, out on a date.

At home Debra changed into a worn, faded caftan that had once been a gaudy Indian print and sat beside Erik on the sofa. "You know what I think?" she said.

He smiled. "No, what?"

"I think you wanted me back for so long that you didn't know how to stop. When I threw myself at you, you had to catch me."

"I wouldn't say that."

"Of course you wouldn't. You're too sweet, and probably too confused. It's okay, Erik. Even if you still love me, you don't have to be married to me anymore. You're not happy. This isn't what you want."

He pulled her to him and held her. "This feels nice," she said. Silently he rocked her in his arms. Her head lay upon his chest. She said nothing for several minutes, then slowly pushed herself away. "There's something I have to tell you," she said.

He felt an inexplicable surge of panic. He stared at her and waited. From the pack on the table she shook out a cigarette. As she lit it she said, "I should have told you earlier, but I didn't know if you wanted to hear it or what you might do. I guess I didn't know what I wanted you to do." She laughed, then looked as if she might cry. "I'm not making much sense." She gave him a tight smile, and her hand trembled as she put her cigarette to her lips.

He laid his hand on her shoulder. "What is it, Deb?"

"It's about Alice and what happened that day." She took a deep drag and composed herself. Erik could see she had something to say that had been coming for a long time. She spoke as if she'd been turning the words over and over in her mind to get them right, to find out what they were. "That day scared me very badly. I don't remember much of anything I said or did after I got to the hospital except Adams telling me that what I saw was a dog or a domesticated wolf or a hallucination. I wanted to believe him. That seemed the easiest thing for everyone. It didn't seem to matter so much what I saw or didn't see. But I've changed my mind since then, and I think it probably matters a lot. She did change into a wolf. I saw it happen. There wasn't any dog. I wasn't just being hysterical. I'm positive. I know what I saw."

She sighed deeply and brought her trembling under control. "And there's something else. Before she changed, she was furious with me. I think she would have killed me if she could. I'd been awful to her. But after she changed into a wolf, all that anger seemed to go away. I was terrified of what I'd seen, but I knew she wouldn't hurt me. I don't know how, but I was sure of that. I don't think she means anyone any harm." Debra shook her head and added softly, "It must be awful for her, to live with something like that." She looked into Erik's eyes for the first time since she had started speaking. "I think you should find her, Erik."

Nothing Debra said surprised him. As he listened it was as if already he knew everything she was saying but was waiting for someone else to say it. What surprised him was that she would be the one to tell him. "Why are you telling me this?" he said.

"Because I've lived with you for the last month and a half. You love her, and she loves you. I remember what that feels like. You're not happy with me. You keep pretending you are, and I keep pretending you're not pretending. It's stupid."

He pulled her to him and held her. "I guess you're right. I'm sorry."

"Don't be sorry. You just tried to do what you thought you should, and you couldn't do it. It wasn't right. I should've told you before."

"I probably wouldn't have believed you. I didn't believe her."

"You believe me now?"

He thought a moment. "When I came in that back door and saw that wolf, I knew immediately it was Alice. I don't know how, but I did. I tried to talk myself out of it because I was scared."

"And ashamed?"

"Yes, that, too."

"Are you going to go look for her?"

"Yes."

She looked up at him. "In the morning?"

He nodded.

"Good. I don't want you to think I've gotten too noble. I do expect you to make love to me one more time before you go."

With Eleanor gone, Luther had indulged in his own habits. He now took his evening cocktail in the topiary. In a few months it would be too hot, but for now it was cool and comfortable in the May evening.

He supposed he should eat something, but the thought of cooking set him to brooding. He'd lost several pounds since Eleanor had left. It would shock her to see the consequences of her actions. He knew he shouldn't have become so involved with the girl, but, after all, he hadn't slept with her. He didn't even know or care where she was. It was Eleanor who'd made a big to-do of it. Nothing had changed between *them*. If only he could get her into counseling, she'd have to see that she was throwing away their marriage over nothing.

But she'd written him a short letter saying she was filing for divorce. There was no return address. The postmark was someplace in Maryland. Who in the hell did she know in Maryland?

He'd called Marvin to see if he might have some advice. He always seemed to have such a great influence over her. But she had already called him. "She sounds happy," he said. What an asinine thing to say. Of course she *sounds* happy. She's chucking all her responsibilities and behaving like a child. Who wouldn't sound happy? Marvin refused to give him the phone number, saying that Eleanor didn't want him to have it.

He glared at the house beyond the maze. Last night he'd gone to almost every room, starting with the basement and working his way up. He'd sat on the chairs, looked out the windows. All those curtains. Eleanor was always showing him pieces of fabric and asking what he thought. He'd learned to act decisively and point to one as if its superiority were self-evident. He'd found some of his choices, now turned into curtains, but he'd also found some of the weaves he'd denounced.

In a small room on the top floor, little more than a gable window closed off with a low door, he'd found her writing desk. Eleanor had had it for years. Her grandmother's, he thought. He'd sat down at the tiny desk. His knees had barely fit beneath it. Under the hinged top were several plain gray notebooks. He'd opened one and seen Eleanor's swooping hand with its elaborate capitals and deep loops filling the page. It was her journal. These were all her journals, going back for years. She'd kept one when they'd first met, but he'd had no idea she'd continued.

He'd paged through them without reading. Sometimes a single entry would fill page after page in a steady unchanging hand. Sometimes a page would contain only a line or two or quick stabbing letters, smeared from the journal's being snapped shut before the ink was dry. He was stopped by the words *Marvelous Dream About Luther* written in large bold letters across the top of a page. Below it he'd found in neat lines like the compositions Luther had written in college the following:

> *He is calling for help from somewhere outside, and I am in the house watering the plants. Finally, when I've reached the top floor and am watering the ivy in his window, I see him below in the topiary.*
>
> *I rush down the stairs and through the maze, though the usual turns don't work, and it takes a long time. When I get to the topiary, all the animals are gone and they've been turned into women. Luther's in the middle where the fox is now, embracing a tree. When I look closer I see Luther's naked and the tree looks like a woman, like Daphne turning into a laurel.*
>
> *Luther is screaming because his penis is stuck in the tree/woman and as soon as the transformation is complete, it will be cut off.*
>
> *I don't do anything. I can see immediately that there's nothing I can do, but I don't want to watch, so I leave through the maze, which somehow leads to the beach, where I go swimming in the ocean.*
>
> *It's tempting to tell Luther, just to see the look on his face, but of course I won't.*

Luther had stared at the page, trying to see in the neat placid blue letters the feelings Eleanor had as she'd written this on the page. She seemed to be laughing at him. He was, she had told him repeatedly, someone she admired, someone intelligent and capable, but here he was ridiculous.

He'd looked up from the page and out the window

and realized it overlooked the topiary. She must have looked out the window as she wrote and imagined him there.

Sitting in the topiary now, he looked up at the gable that held Eleanor's desk tucked away in the corner of the house. She was not looking out at him now. No one was.

Luther stood and let the swing sway behind him as he walked among his animals. He'd let them go since this business with Eleanor. He never felt like tending them. And now this dream of hers. It was horrendous. He had read no more in the journals, full no doubt of more things she'd chosen not to tell him despite the temptation of seeing the look on his face.

He opened the ivy-covered door of his toolshed and went inside. The smell of damp wood and dirt calmed him. On a high shelf was a dust-covered box. He opened the end and slid out an electric hedge trimmer. It looked like a boxy plastic swordfish. He'd never used the thing. Eleanor had given it to him several years ago for his birthday or Christmas. He couldn't believe she thought he'd want such a thing. She'd offered to take it back, but he kept saying he would find a use for it. He certainly didn't want her to cry about the damn thing again.

On the wall, a coiled orange electric cord hung like a lariat. He took it down and plugged it into the outlet by the phone box, then plugged the other end into the trimmer. He squeezed the handle, and it made a whirring sound.

He went to the fox and sliced away the stray shoots from the ears and snout. The blade made a chirping sound as it cut through the wood. Down the block he could hear the whine of someone's lawn mower, some stranger pacing back and forth. Maybe some friend of Eleanor's. She seemed to know everyone in these houses—Mr. This and Mrs. That.

He brought the blade down on the fox's neck. The blades made a clattering noise as they bit into the thicker wood, jumped, then bit deeper, severing the head. He kicked it aside and swung the humming blades parallel to the ground, cutting the animal down at the knees as the machine bucked and strained in his hands.

He attacked each one of them—the bear, the elephant, the giraffe, the turtle—the careful sketches turned into plants, until the blades jammed in the turtle's foot with a loud whine and the trimmer became so hot that it burned his hands and the air reeked of burning plastic.

Chapter
16

The wolf rolls over, stays close to the ground, sniffing the air. She is in a thicket. The woman has just left her. Just beyond the thicket, the earth drops away. The wind blows up from below. The scents are layered thick. Wolf. Human. Deer. Rabbit. Other scents she does not know. She has never been here before. She crawls out of the thicket. The sky is large above her. The sun is low in the sky. She marks the thicket and looks over the edge of the cliff. A lake shines below. She follows a path winding away from the thicket. It is strong with human smell. She hears a stream and moves toward the sound, marking often, stopping to listen and smell this strange land stretching far in all directions. Nothing is familiar except the path back to the thicket and her own scent.

This is a human path. The woman's smell is fresh.
The other human scents are heavy but old. She follows
the path down to a stream. The path continues along
the bank toward the lake she saw from the cliff. She
descends the bank to the water, marking a pile of
stones at the water's edge.

She stands in the stream and drinks, watches the
water rushing round her feet, her fur trailing into the
current. She ducks her snout into the water and
douses her face with spray, drops and rolls over, rises
and shakes a glistening shower into the air. She trots
upstream until she catches wolf scent and climbs the
bank to a road, broad and black. The hot dry smell
makes her nostrils burn. The wolf scent comes from
across the road where high grass is thick and the land
slopes down.

She remembers cars, long ago, roaring out of the
darkness, bright lights blinding her. She ducks her
head and moves one paw, then another, onto the road,
sniffing the air for cars, ears cocked to catch the sound.
She moves with a sideways gait, turning her head one
way and then another until she is across the road. At
the bottom of a steep slope she circles around a marsh
to a path cut through the high grass, a narrow path
with little human smell.

She smells many wolves. They have marked this
place together. They moved through here in a line of
young and old, male and female. The last, an old
female, is a scent she knows. She zigzags back and
forth across the line of scent, trotting into the wind at
a steady, ambling pace. Scent mark strong at her feet
sends her skittering to one side. She lowers her body,
creeps to the scent. Tracks cross the path and lead
down a dry wash. It is one of the line of wolves, but
this scent is fresher. He is very old. His right rear leg is
stiff and comes down heavier than the rest.

She follows the tracks to a boulder still wet with his
mark. She rubs her shoulder in the scent. She moves
on down the wash, stops, listens. Bird sound, water, a

car far away, then a sound she has never heard before—wolves yipping to one another, each voice different. She whimpers in her throat and veers away from the wash, listening to the wolves, moving toward the lake she smells up ahead, keeping the same distance from the sound. At the edge of the woods she finds a way between two huge boulders down to the water. Crouched in the shadows, she looks across the water to see three wolves running helter-skelter. The old wolf with the stiff leg is prancing, his head up high, a stick in his jaws. Two young wolves dart in and out, snapping at the stick, tumbling into the old wolf. The stick flies into the air. One of the young wolves leaps and grabs it, running in quick circles around the others.

The wolf watches, breathing in their wolf scent. Each is different. The two young ones are brothers. The wolf lies on her belly, wagging her tail, her snout resting on her paws. She can see a path along the shoreline that leads to where the other wolves play but knows she cannot take it. She is a stranger. This is their place.

The light is fading, and the air grows cold. The wind gusts across the water. She cocks her head back. There are other wolves close by, different from these three.

She stands, leaning into the wind, her ears high. A small sound, muffled, like mice under the basement drain, but wolf. The scent is sweet and heavy. She whimpers, takes quick stuttering steps from side to side. It is mother and pups, deep inside the den.

She turns and breaks into a run, following her own scent up the wash and across the road and down the stream to the thicket at the top of the hill where the woman waits for her.

The woman is sad. She does not want to come anymore, but she is afraid to go away. The wolf loves the woman, but the woman smells like death. The wolf enters the thicket, paws at the woman's clothes, rubbing her shoulder against them, then lies down and

253

waits, breathing everything in deep. She throws back her head and howls to the wolves, even as the woman comes and it all fades away.

The wolf stands in swift water, brow furrowed and intent, watching for fish. The sun is overhead, and the day is hot. The woman comes some mornings. Other mornings she does not. She never stays long. The wolf remembers her on the bank of the stream, aching with sadness, as lonely as the wolf, throwing stones into the water.

She lunges at a brown shadow in the stream. Her teeth clamp on nothing, and the fish slides past her flank. She shakes the water from her face and waits again. She is hungry. She has not eaten in two days. Her snout is just above the rushing water. She can smell beaver piss and fish blood. Black flies swarm around her face. In the water she can see her own eyes looking back.

She lunges again, seizes a fish, and bites hard. The fish body falls back into the water, rushes downstream in the current. She chases after, but the water is too deep and strong. She swallows her one bite and moves upstream above the fresh blood smell and waits again.

She watched the pack's den early this morning when the wind was right. The pups come out into the clearing below the den most days. She watches them play. The mother hunts. Her mate stays with the pups, who pull on his tail or pile on top of him. He rolls them over with his snout and licks their bellies. The stiff-legged wolf and the two young wolves from the litter before hunt with the mother. The old wolf knows where the deer are and leads the way. When there has been a kill, the pack vomits up deer for the pups.

The wolf sees a fish shadow far upstream. She stares at it as it moves downstream, watching carefully as it vanishes and reappears in the glare of the sun on the water. She braces herself and seizes its head in her jaws, biting down only slightly, holding it firmly as it thrashes back and forth. Trotting to the bank and up to a flat rock, she bites off the head and swallows it, picks up the rest, and gobbles it down.

The wolf lies watching the pack. The mother is showing the pups how to catch a rabbit in their forepaws. She brought the rabbit into the middle of the clearing, dropped it, caught it, dropped it, and caught it again. The rabbit is young, breathing fast, running in small circles. The pups yelp excitedly, impatient for their mother to kill the rabbit, but she does not. One of the young ones starts to move toward the stunned rabbit, the mother nips at him, and he lies back on his haunches, his head high, his tail swaying back and forth. The mother lets the rabbit go and walks away to the front of the den where the other wolves lie watching the pups.

The pups circle the rabbit, then one, the largest with the long snout, charges at the rabbit, knocking it down with his forepaws. He crouches, snarling and yipping, but does not pounce. The rabbit rolls to its feet and bolts for the dense brush at the edge of the clearing. Long-snout stumbles after, but the rabbit is gone. He wanders back into the clearing where the rabbit had been, pawing the scent and yelping.

The mother, stiff-legged, her head down, walks over to the pup, pins him as she had pinned the rabbit, and nips his snout. The other pups watch silently. She turns away and disappears into the den.

The other pups go to long-snout, who lies with his stomach flat on the ground, his head on his paws. The pups lie on top of him. Soon they are asleep in a pile.

The wolf watches them sleep for a long time. She rises and heads toward the road. She has seen rabbit there in the high grass.

There is a new wolf with the pack. She is from another litter. When she came to the clearing around the den, the pack danced around her and howled. She rolled on her back, and the mother licked her belly.

The wolf, crouched in the shadows, threw back her head and answered the howl, greeting the pack. The pups answered her. The others fell silent, standing stiff-legged, sniffing the air, growling low. The old wolf nudged the pups with his snout, pushing them toward the den. The mother walked to the lake and howled long and harsh. Stay away. The wolf lay on her belly out of sight and did not make a sound.

At dusk the new wolf hunted with the pack. The old wolf stayed with the pups. They tried to follow the hunt, but he nipped at them, turning them back to the clearing. He ran in circles around them. They stumbled after him. He stopped, let them get close, bolted again. They did this over and over again. After a time the pups lay in the middle of the clearing and went to sleep. After dark the pack returned with no blood smell, no kill.

Now it is morning, and the new wolf is leaving. The pack weaves in and out, rubbing up against one another. The pups race about, yipping furiously. The new wolf howls, and another pack calls from across the ridge at the other end of the lake. The new wolf and the pack answer, and the two packs call back and forth. This time the wolf remains silent. The new wolf trots off toward the other pack.

The wolf moves along the line of pack scent, then down the wash. At the bottom she turns away from the den and trots down a narrow path. The wind blows in her face. She runs hard, scoops up a stick from the path, and throws it into the air, catching it, running furiously. She stops, drops the stick on the path, and marks it.

A kill, she knows, is just ahead. The smell is old. She follows the scent and digs under a fallen tree marked by the old wolf. She pulls out a bone and gnaws it in her folded paws. It is old and splinters dry in her mouth. She is hungry. The young rabbit she pinned and ate at dusk is gone. She cocks her ears and listens for the pack. They do not want her here. Their scat rings this place.

The deer are too fast for her alone. The rabbits and the fish are hard to catch. Sometimes she finds kill on the road, but it is not enough, and she is afraid of the cars, which come more often now. She is always hungry. The woman never comes anymore, but if she does not eat soon, she will have to find her.

She stops gnawing on the bone and hears the pack moving toward her. She drops the bone and trots away from the sound, circling round the lake toward the hill where the pack scent is weak. She stops and turns, her legs spread wide, her head down, listening, but the wind blows the sound away. She looks across the water and sees them, on the far side of the lake, sniffing the air, their snouts thrust forward. She is looking into the old wolf's eyes. The entire pack turns and stares. She straightens up, returns their stare. The wolf and the pack do not move. Their eyes study her. She waits. They break into a run, the mother in the lead, moving quickly through the grass beside the lake toward her.

The wolf runs low and fast, her breath coming quick and hard. She can hear the pack behind her and off to the side where the narrow path leads down to the water. They call to one another. Her chest aches. These paths are theirs. Their scent and sound surround her. She slows to a loping run, zigzagging back and forth across the path, looking for her scent.

She finds her mark on a fallen tree and leaves the path where their scent is strong, plunging through the wet grass high around her face. She churns through the mud toward the dry, hot smell. Her paws sink deep. The pack follows, but slower now, whining and yelping back and forth. She reaches the gravel slope and scrambles out into the open onto the road. She hears the roar of a car, can feel it in the ground beneath her paws. She looks back to see the pack peering out from the tall grass, stopped. The car appears at the top of the hill and screeches, sliding toward her. She darts into the woods where a twisting path climbs the hill and the scent of humans lingers faintly over everything.

Chapter

17

Erik's house still smelled of piss. He'd planned to deal with it in the summer at the end of his six-month lease. He'd come for his clothes, but nothing else had been touched since the day Alice had changed into a wolf in his living room and run past him out the back door.

His clothes were now piled in the back of his car. Debra had helped him pack this morning. He'd sat up most of the night reading about wolves, watching her sleep. For the first time in years, he wasn't angry at her. They had finally let go at the same time. "Here," she'd said as he was leaving, "take this."

She'd handed him a lightweight cylinder the size of a breadstick wrapped in green-and-white cellophane. "What is it?"

"It's a road flare. I got a bunch of them free. You break it, and it gives off light, in case you break down."

He'd laughed, and she'd made a face.

"Thanks," he'd said, and kissed her cheek.

On the floor of his closet he found his toolbox underneath a pile of coat hangers and fallen shirts. His father had given the tools to him when he was still in high school. All the handles were hardwood and the metal cold-forged steel.

He took the flashlight from the kitchen, went out on the front porch, and sat down. Alice's house was still and dark. The grass was shaggy and choked with weeds. He lit a cigarette, moving his eyes from window to window, each one locked. By the time he finished his cigarette, he'd decided on the back door because it was the least visible from the street and the other houses, and the lock was a spring-loaded bolt. He climbed over the fence and into her backyard.

He pried the facing loose and slid his chisel between the door and jamb, caught the bolt, and pushed it back. He turned the knob and leaned hard against the door. The first two times the bolt slipped from the chisel and held, but the third time he fell into Alice's kitchen and collided with her table. The dark house echoed with the commotion. The stale air streamed across his face and out through the open door behind him. He shut the door quickly as if all evidence of Alice might disappear through that square of light. He turned on the flashlight and moved the beam slowly around the room.

Cups and saucers sat on the counter, the mold grown lush and spilling over the top. There were three. He wondered who had drunk from the third. He turned the beam into the living room and followed it into the darkness, where he parted the curtains and raised the blinds. The light was the color of the pale oak floors. His cigarette butts were still in the ashtray, though the afghan had been folded and lay neatly across the back of a chair. The last time he'd seen her they had made love, then he'd fled. He didn't want that to be the last time.

He went into the bedroom and let in the light there. He even raised the shade in the bathroom and the one covering the small high window in her closetlike study. He returned to the kitchen, opening the blinds and, after some hesitation, the back door. He returned to the living room and opened the front door. The breeze through the screen door surged toward the kitchen.

"I thought you were my mother."

"I'm sorry. I've gotten you out of the shower."

"Tub."

"Tub. . . . Look, I'm sorry. I'll just come back later."

"Can I help you?"

"Actually, I was going to invite you to lunch."

Erik winced and closed his eyes, leaning his forehead against the screen, then turned and went into the bedroom. The bedclothes were knotted in a ball in the middle of the bed. In the shadows it looked as if someone might be curled up there. He sat on the edge of the bed and opened the bedside table drawer.

Matches, paper clips, pens, index cards, a sewing kit, candles, rubber bands. An out-of-date university ID underneath it all showed her smiling to herself in an aqua square, sharing an irony only she would understand. He took the ID and put it in his pocket. He pushed the drawer to with a clatter as everything slid to the back.

Dust lay thick on the glass top of her dresser, and light glinted from the chiseled surfaces of perfume bottles.

"I like the way you smell."

"I guess so, since I smell like you."

"You smell like you, too. I like it."

He opened the jewelry box, the trays unfolding like red velvet stairs. The compartments were almost empty except for broken chains and earring backs and the earrings he had given her, tiny silver penguins. He dropped them into his shirt pocket behind the ID. In the bottom of the box was a letter from Canada addressed to Alice in a hand remarkably like Alice's own. The paper was thin and blue, the ink black, in strokes that could only have come from a fountain pen. The letter was signed "Ann" and dealt mostly with Howard's health and her fear that he was getting worse. But at the end he read, "I know that you are lonely, dear. Believe me I know what that is like. If you come to visit, perhaps we can talk. I was quite lonely until I found Howard. I find myself thinking of those times often these days." Part of the address was torn away, but the town was Whitney, Ontario. It was dated March 1. He put the letter in his wallet.

He moved on to each room, each drawer. Each object was charged with meaning but was not a clue. He found nothing else to take. At the end of his search, all the shades and curtains drawn, he returned to her dresser and looked at his shadowy figure in the mirror. He picked up the perfume bottle and sniffed it, then put a drop upon his finger and rubbed it on his nose, breathing deeply.

He put his hand over his shirt pocket and clutched through the fabric, the artifacts there, feeling each one and remembering in its shape the way it had made him feel. His face contorted as if in desperate prayer. He had to find her. He had to touch her again.

Adam's receptionist had been cryptic as to when the doctor might return to the office. No, he wasn't ill. A personal matter had come up. His home phone rang unanswered throughout the morning, then stayed busy. Erik drove to the address in the phone book and knocked on the door. The house was huge. He knocked harder, and the house reverberated with a cavernous thud. He put his hand on the knob, turned, and pushed. The door swung open slowly into an entry hall opening onto three hallways, all of them dark. He stepped inside and called out, "Dr. Adams. It's Erik Summers."

Slow, shuffling steps approached, then Adams appeared in the middle hallway. He was dressed in the same suit he had worn six weeks ago. It was now limp and hung on him as if it had grown heavier.

"Erik," he said, "come in, come in. I was just having a cup of coffee. Perhaps you'd care to join me?" His voice was a tired parody of his usual professional joviality. He gave no sign that he thought it the least bit odd that Erik would walk into his house.

"I hate to barge in like this, but I need to talk to you about Alice White." Erik spoke to Luther's back, for he had already turned and gone back the way he'd come. Erik followed through several rooms where satin and polished wood shone in near darkness. They emerged into light in the kitchen.

The empty cabinets stood open. Plates with food still upon them covered the counter in teetering stacks. The table was covered with dirty glasses and empty bottles. On the stove where a teakettle steamed was a jar of instant coffee in the middle of a dry, dark brown pool. A spoon lay beside it. Luther pointed. "The coffee's over there. You'll have to wash yourself a clean cup, I'm afraid, and I don't have any cream." He sat down at the table with his own cup, and Erik noticed his feet were bare.

Luther slumped on his chair. He picked up his tie and looked at it. "How do you like my new tie? It's the first one I've ever bought for myself. My wife, Eleanor, used to buy new shoes to cheer herself up, though she hasn't done it in years." Erik sat down at the table with his coffee, but Luther's eyes remained fixed on his tie.

"Are you all right?" Erik asked.

Luther looked up sharply. "Of course I'm all right. A certain measure of grief is unavoidable for a man in my circumstances. I am a professional. I certainly know how to handle my own feelings." He looked over at the counter, glaring at the mess. As he spoke he ran his tie through his hand as if he were petting a cat's tail.

"I want to talk to you about Alice White," Erik said.

"I heard you say that when you came in," Luther snapped at him. "Why don't you just forget about her? Hasn't she done enough to ruin your life?"

"Ruin my life? She hasn't done anything to me."

"Of course she has. Wish I'd never heard the woman's name. All this mess started because of her."

"All what mess?"

"Why, my wife's left me, of course." He swept his arm around the room. "My God, look at this place."

Erik turned Luther's words over in his mind. After a silence he said, "You are in love with Alice?"

Luther drew himself up and spoke to the empty room. "Absolutely not. I was infatuated with her. She is a very attractive woman. But I am a married man. I was absolutely faithful to my wife. I never lost my grip on things." He glared into his coffee. "Eleanor doesn't believe that, of course, or she never would have run off." His shoulders slumped and shook, and he began to cry.

Erik found a paper towel, gave it to him, and crouched beside his chair. When Luther's crying subsided, Erik said, "I know how you feel. I love Alice. I've got to find her."

"What do you want from me?" Luther said quietly.

"You were her psychiatrist. You must have some idea where she might go if she were in trouble."

Luther sat for so long that Erik began to wonder whether he was going to answer. He looked up with a pinched, urgent expression. "If you find her," he said, "I want you to have her tell my wife that absolutely nothing out of the way passed between us, absolutely nothing at all."

Erik nodded his head. "All right."

Luther thought a moment. "She might go to her great-aunt's. She seemed to be the person she trusted most."

"Was that her aunt Ann?"

Luther waved his hand in front of his face. "I can't remember. It was just her great-aunt, that's all. I'm sure she must've said the name, but I can't remember. It's all on the tapes if it's that important."

"Did she live in Canada?"

"I don't know. All I remember is her great-aunt." He looked Erik in the face. "I didn't always listen to her, you know. I just stared at her, like a schoolboy. She must've known how I felt."

"She never mentioned it."

"Not to you, of course. But she must've known."

Erik rose to his feet. "I'll pass on your request to her if I find her." He pushed in the chair and put his cup by the others. "I'll show myself out."

After leaving Adams's, Erik called Rupert and told him he needed to talk. Rupert had suggested they meet at Texas Beach, an access to the James River at the end of Texas Avenue. They used to go there to drink and fish and smoke and talk. Rupert was late as usual. Erik had been early. It was now six o'clock. Erik sat on the rocks and watched an osprey, not more than ten yards away, dive and rise with a fish clutched in its talons. Upriver the sun was setting over the water and glinted off the cars on the bridge.

He had planned to bring Alice here in the summer. Days were filled with such plans, jostling against each other, one after the other. They made him giddy. He'd imagined her moving through the water, his hand squeezing her wet thigh, holding her in the current. She, smiling into his eyes, beads of water on her face. She had told him that she loved the water.

Even though they'd spent every possible moment together from the moment he had appeared at her door, he had carried such images around with him, made new ones every day. They came back to him now, like photos of someone dead.

He hefted a rock, held it with his index finger curved along the edge, whipped it out across the water with a quick sideways throw.

"I hope you didn't invite me out here on another quest for the fucking Perfect Rock," Rupert said at his back.

Erik's stone skipped twice and sank.

"Fuck you, Rupert."

Erik turned to see Rupert with his hands up, a bag-clad pint in one hand and a pipe in the other. "Don't shoot bwana, bring gifts, fuck you up real good, make your juju strong."

Rupert sat down beside Erik and offered him the bottle. Erik took a drink and handed it back. "Doubt all you want, but when I find the Perfect Rock, you'll be sorry."

Rupert loaded the bowl and lit the pipe. "I heard you were back with Debra."

Erik took the pipe, took a toke, and held it in his lungs. He exhaled and watched the smoke drift across the water. "We tried it for about a month. It didn't work. I'm trying to find Alice."

Rupert took a drink and traded Erik for the pipe. "Is Alice the wolf woman?"

Erik had been examining a pile of stones at his feet, tossing them one by one over his shoulder. He stopped, lingered over one, then threw it into the river, where it skipped twice, then sank. "It's real, Rupert. She really is a werewolf. Debra saw her change. I saw her as a wolf."

Rupert's eyes gleamed in the setting sun. "No shit."

Erik told him everything that had happened since he'd talked to him last, told him all that Alice had said, told him about Luther and about Debra.

Rupert squinted at him and took a cigarette from his pocket. "You're really serious about this, aren't you?"

266

"Absolutely."

"You *saw* this wolf in your kitchen?"

"That's right."

"I thought she only transformed into a wolf by the light of the full moon."

"Apparently that's changed."

"What does the shrink, what's his name?"

"Adams."

"What does he say?"

"He says Debra was in shock, that I saw a big dog."

"This guy doesn't know Debra very well, does he?" He shook his head. "Fact, it sounds like the good doctor's got a loose connection to his battery. I don't suppose you got a sample of this Alice's blood."

"It never came up."

Rupert shook his head. "Why should I believe this shit?"

"Because I'm your old friend, and I'm telling you, and I need to talk to somebody about it who doesn't think I've got a loose connection to my battery."

Rupert watched Erik for a moment, then took a long drink from the bottle. "Okay. Why not? At least till the bottle's empty. Have you tried this story out on anybody else?"

"Not the whole thing."

"Good, then you probably still have a job. They think I'm flaky, but I'm Dr. Koop compared with you. How do you think she got to be a werewolf?"

"I figure the obvious—a freak mutation or a recessive gene."

Rupert shook his head. "There's too much folklore about werewolves for it to be a freak. Now that we have the fire, it's hard to miss all the smoke. Of course, it must be pretty rare. It would be pretty hard to hide in prison, for example. What percentage of the population is in prison?"

"How in the hell should I know?"

"I used to know. I'm a geneticist. Statistics are us."

"So what's your point, Rupert?"

267

"My point is that nobody has documented a werewolf in prison, in mental hospitals, in the army—all those places where we stick people even if they don't want to be there and then watch their every move. That tells me it ain't too common. Hell, her closest relative might've died of the plague." Rupert took another drink and offered the bottle to Erik, who waved it away. "Any leads?"

"A great-aunt."

"Is she a wolf, too?"

Erik shrugged. "I don't know. I think so. But it's just a hunch. The whole thing's crazy."

"So what are you going to do now?"

Erik looked out over the water. "I love her. I haven't really known her that long, but I still know I love her. I was too stupid to know it when I needed to, but I know it now."

"You fucked up," Rupert said.

Erik tossed a rock over his shoulder. "I know."

"And I know you know," said Rupert. "That's why I'm telling you. You just fucked up, that's all. You didn't kill or rape anybody. It wasn't exactly an easy situation to deal with. This is your first werewolf, mine, too. Give yourself a break."

"I don't even know where to look for her."

"Maybe she wants to try being a wolf for a while. Being human hasn't exactly treated her right lately."

Erik examined another rock and threw it in a long, high arc into the river. "It's not that easy being a wolf."

"Some places, I bet it ain't bad."

"Someplace protected."

"Exactly."

Erik hefted a rock and stared into the water. "I've thought of that."

"Here, give me that goddamn rock." Rupert seized it and turned it over in his hands. "What the hell's wrong with this one?"

"It's not flat enough."

"What do you want, a fucking Frisbee? Watch this, okay?" Rupert rose to his feet, flexed his knees, then moved like a whip being cracked in slow motion or a snake that had learned to dance. The stone took a flurry of quick, tiny steps across the water, more than Erik could count, before it finally sank well out into the river. Erik had never seen him skip a stone before.

"See?" Rupert said. "*That* was the fucking Perfect Rock, and *I* just threw it in the river. But if you look long enough, I'm sure you can find another goddamn Perfect Rock around here someplace. Just don't ask me to help you look."

"How do you do that?"

"Do what?"

"What do you mean, 'do what'? Skip a goddamn stone like that?"

"I told you. It was the Perfect Rock."

"Screw you, Rupert."

"Okay, you force me to confess it. I surrendered my soul to Satan in exchange for the gift of skipping stones."

"Satan had you long ago." Erik took the pipe and lighter from Rupert's hand. "Come on, how do you do it?"

"Okay. Honor bright. I perfected my method about fifteen years ago under the influence of something Thai, I believe. I had been reading *The Odyssey,* and I was skipping stones in this very river in the moonlight, which should be along shortly, when I began to see a naiad out there and supposed I was flirting with her. In fact, it came to me—in a flash, as they say—that naiad foreplay was what this stone-skipping business had always been about, and we moderns were just too stupid to know it.

"Well, charged with this erotic image, you might say, I became, in a matter of hours, the stone-skipping master you see before you. I then swam naked for a while and had an experience too personal to recount that I'm sure would qualify as surrendering my soul to

Satan in any bona fide Satan expert's handbook. And may I hasten to add that it was damn well worth it, and I would do it again, frequently."

Erik laughed and handed Rupert the pipe. "So you're telling me that to improve my stone skipping I need to make it with a naiad."

"No. I think *you* need to find Alice." He huddled around the pipe, trying to shield the flame from the wind.

Erik looked into the river and imagined Alice in the water, moonlight glistening from her skin.

Rupert's face glowed in the light from the bowl. "You know what I like about Odysseus and Penelope? They were separated for twenty years and still had the hots for each other." Smoke leaked from the corners of his mouth. "Isn't that great?"

"Won't you join us for breakfast," said Mrs. White. "It's just Egg Beaters. Bob can't have eggs on account of his heart. But we've got plenty."

Mr. White smiled up at Erik as if apologizing for his heart. He sat on the same overstuffed chair he'd sat on before. Nothing had changed, except the stacks of newspapers and magazines were a little higher, and folding trays were set in front of their two chairs.

"I would love some," Erik said, and took a chair.

Erik had already considered what these people might be like as in-laws, and he approved. Alice's mother was what Erik's father would call "jumpy as a cat," but she had apparently decided she liked Erik and smiled at him in a way that reminded him of Alice. Alice's father seemed to Erik like a penguin full of disoriented goodwill, and he was charmed.

Bob White picked up the remote control and turned off the set in the midst of peanuts bathing themselves in chocolate. "Have you heard from Alice?" he asked. At the sound of her husband's voice, Ruth White paused at the kitchen door and looked back at Erik. Her back was straight, her chin held high and still.

"I'm afraid not." He looked from one to the other. These were the only other people he knew of who were close to Alice, who loved her as he did. "I want to find her, though," he said. "I thought you two might help me."

"Well, it's for damn sure the police aren't going to find her," Bob White said. "They act like young women just disappear every day."

Ruth stepped back into the room. "Now, Bob."

"Don't 'Now, Bob' me." He scowled at her. "I thought you were going to fix breakfast. Rick and I need to talk."

"His name's Erik, dear."

"Rick, Erik, what's the difference? I know who he is. He's Alice's boyfriend, and I need to talk to him, so why don't you just go to the kitchen like you said you were going to and let us talk."

Ruth White had listened to this with a thin, stony smile, her hands slowly clenching into small fists at her sides. She turned and disappeared into the kitchen, her palms thudding against the swinging door.

Erik and Bob White watched the door slap back and forth till it came to rest. "I'll catch hell later," Bob said, "but there's things I need to talk about I can't say in front of her."

Erik felt the same way he did when some student taking Intro told him she was pregnant. He nodded and listened.

"I'm getting old," Bob White said. "I don't always remember things. But I know my little girl. When I don't know her anymore, then I'll be ready to die." He studied Erik. "Do you know what I mean?"

"I think so."

"Well, I hope so." He dug around on the TV tray and found a package of small cigars. "I quit smoking cigarettes and started smoking these damn things. No telling why." He lit a cigar and asked if Alice had told him about the farm outside Bristol.

"A little bit."

"Did she tell you about a boy named Dale getting killed there?"

"Yes," said Erik. The older man's face was set in hard, humorless planes. It seemed incredible to Erik that this man had seemed a jolly little penguin the last time he'd seen him. Now his daughter was missing, and he was afraid.

"Well, I think she had something to do with it. I hate to say that about my own daughter, but she hasn't been the same since it happened. And I think this taking off now has something to do with that.

"My daughter did some strange things growing up, but I figured we all do. If she wanted to spend the night wandering around in the moonlight, hell, I'd wanted to do that a million times and never did. So why should I stop her?"

Erik was incredulous. "You knew that she went out on the full moons?"

Bob White scowled and shifted on his seat. "'Course I knew. This is my daughter we're talking about here. Her mother didn't know. I always covered for her. Ruth would say, 'I hear something, Bob, I hear something,' until I'd go check. I'd tell her that Alice was sleeping like a baby, though the bed was empty and the window was wide open."

"You were never curious where she went?"

"Of course I was curious. I followed her. She went to the woods all by herself and took her clothes off."

"Did you see what she did out there?"

Bob studied him. "Did she tell you?"

"Yes."

"Would you tell me?"

"You don't know?"

Bob shook his head. "No, I didn't watch her. She was absolutely beautiful—as beautiful as her mother at that age. But this wasn't Ruth we're talking about here, but my daughter. I didn't feel right about watching her like that. She wanted to be alone, so I left. I kept an eye on the woods the first few times it happened, and saw she was safe enough out there. It was a farm. There was never anybody around." He grimaced. "Except that one night, when that boy tried to rape her." He held Erik's eye and leaned forward, his elbows braced on the arms of his chair. His voice was quiet and matter-of-fact. "She killed him. I'm sure of it. It makes no sense otherwise, the way she's acted ever since, afraid of everything. She was never like that before.

"I should've fired that boy long before. He was constantly sniffing after Alice. He was trying to rape her all right. I have no doubt about that. But it wouldn't matter to Alice whether he had it coming— if she killed him. She wouldn't be able to let it go. She'd let it eat at her." He stopped and swallowed hard. He stared for a moment at the mantel, where photographs of his son and daughter stood surrounded by bric-a-brac. "Then she starts up with this werewolf business, and goes to the mental hospital. I knew she was telling the truth when she said she killed him. But what am I supposed to do? Dig her grave? I was just glad to get her back home.

"I tried to talk to her when she got out of the hospital, but there was no getting through to her. She was hell-bent on being 'cured,' and she just wanted me to leave it alone. I couldn't blame her. She didn't want to go back, and I didn't want her to go.

"The first full moon after she got out she made some excuse to be out all night, and I figured I'd find out what she was doing out there in the woods, even though I didn't feel right spying on my own daughter. So I followed her. But she went right on through the woods to this abandoned factory, all fallen down. She used to play around it when she was little even though her mother told her not to. Well, I watched her climb up and down into this chimney. So I go into the factory to see where it comes out, and there's this big furnace door locked with her bike chain, and I can't get in.

"You tell me. What would you do? Haul her out and send her back to that place she didn't want to go? This time, probably for good? There wasn't anything wrong with her. She'd been home for two weeks, and I knew it was still her. Nothing had changed about her except now she was lonelier. The only thing that place did for her was make her lonelier, and she's been lonely ever since." He smiled and blinked his eyes. "Till she found you. That Sunday you two came over, I hadn't seen her like that since before she went to that place. I remember that, what she used to be like. I forget things, but I don't forget that.

"So I never said anything, even to Ruth—the only thing I never told her in thirty-eight years. I don't know whether I did the right thing, but I wanted you to know, because I think you're like me." He waved his hand back and forth in the air. "It doesn't matter to you. You love her no matter what—and maybe it will help you find her."

Erik nodded his head, and his eyes filled. Bob reached out, grabbed his hands, gave them a quick hard squeeze, and let them go. He sniffed and hollered at the kitchen door, "Ruth, we're getting hungry in here!"

A muffled, "Hold your horses!" drifted back.

"Where are you going to look?" Bob asked Erik.

Erik wiped his eyes. "I don't know. I thought she might have been in touch with her aunt Ann. Alice had a letter from her."

Ruth appeared with plates of food and set them before the men.

"Ruth," Bob said, "Erik thinks Ann might know where Alice is."

Erik thought he saw her wince slightly at the name, but then she smiled. "Really? Why do you think so?"

Erik shrugged. "It's just a wild guess at this point. She seems to be the only person Alice was close to, except for you two, of course."

"As far as Ann's concerned," Bob said, "'we two' are dispensable."

"Bob," said Ruth, and turned to Erik. "Alice and Ann were always close," she said with the precision of someone struggling to be fair.

"She's your aunt," Bob said, slumping onto his chair. "I'll remain neutral."

"Bob's jealous," Ruth said to Erik, "but he's too stubborn to admit it."

"I have never been jealous of Ann and Howard. They've been jealous of me. They always wished Alice was theirs. Tell me I'm wrong." Bob had gradually risen on his chair so that now he sat bolt upright on the front of the seat, his chin thrust forward and his arms braced as if he might rise to his feet at any moment, knocking the tray aside.

Ruth tossed her head. "Why should I? Telling you you're wrong never did a damn bit of good, and it's not going to do any good now. Once you get an idea in your head, it might as well be set in concrete."

"Is Howard Ann's husband?" Erik asked in a voice as loud as theirs.

They turned to Erik and looked sheepish.

"Yes," said Ruth. "They married the same year Bob and I met. My mother took me to the wedding. Ann must've been about twenty-two, and Howard was ten years older. Broke her heart when he passed away."

"He's dead?"

"Last month. Bob and I couldn't afford to go to the funeral. We told Ann she could come and stay with us, but she declined, of course. She likes where she is too much. She likes to stay put. They've lived in that same house since 1959."

"If Alice knew Howard was dying," Erik said, "wouldn't she go see him?"

"That's what we thought," Bob said, "but Ann says she hasn't seen her. We called her first thing."

"Could I have her address anyway? Even if she

hasn't seen her, she might be able to think of some-place Alice would go."

Bob snorted. "I think she's there with Ann, and she's just not telling us. I've thought so all along."

Ruth shook her head. "Now, Bob, I can't believe Ann would do such a thing."

Bob held up his index finger. "Tell me one thing she wouldn't do if Alice asked her to."

Ruth smoothed her skirts and set her mouth in a thin line. "Bob, we're being rude." She turned to Erik and smiled sweetly. "How's your food, dear? May I get you more of anything?"

"No, thanks."

"I'll take some more coffee," Bob said.

"You've had quite enough already."

"It's decaf, for Christ's sake."

"The acid isn't good for you."

He pushed aside his tray and lit another cigar.

"And you're smoking too much, besides," Ruth said.

"I eat eggs that taste like plastic. I've forgotten what salt tastes like. And I can't remember the last time I had a drink. The least I can do is smoke these silly cigars."

"Suit yourself," Ruth said.

"The breakfast was delicious," Erik said. "Thank you very much. I wonder if I might have that address now?"

Ruth rose to her feet. "Come along," she said, "I'll find it for you. It's on the top shelf, I think. I might need you to reach it for me." Erik heard the TV come on behind him as they left the room.

She led him into a large dark room stuffed with things. "Watch your step," she said. "Bob says I never throw anything away." She crinkled the corners of her mouth in a way Erik now found familiar. Alice and her mother both apologized with that expression, for crimes more imagined than real.

Along one wall was a span of cabinets. On top of

them were tiny statuettes—several were dusty ballerinas. A woman in violet petticoats looked down demurely, a fan spread across her smile. Beneath the cabinets were stacks of shoeboxes.

With a plywood snap, Ruth slid back one of the cabinet doors. A silver canister of film fell to her feet and rolled across the carpet. Boxes marked "Photos," trays of slides, and photo albums packed the shelves.

Erik retrieved the canister and handed it to her. "Lord knows what this is," she said, and stuffed it back into the clutter. "We haven't taken any pictures in years." She pulled an album from the middle of the stack and spread it open on the bed: Alice's braid was here pigtails, and her legs were adolescent. She wore a swimsuit and stood between an old man and a woman who looked like Alice, her dark hair streaked with gray. "This picture's about twenty years old," Ruth said. She reached out with her fingertip and touched her daughter's cheek. "She and Ann used to braid each other's hair. They'd spend hours, seemed like."

Erik could imagine the braid hanging down Ann's back like a heavy black rope spiraled with gray. "I think she may know something about Alice," he said.

Ruth glanced up at him, then back at the album. As she turned back the pages, Alice grew younger.

"When she was born, I said to Bob, 'She's Ann all over.' And Bob said, 'Won't she be a pretty thing, then?'" Ruth's eyes filled with tears, and she plucked a tissue from a box on the bedside table. "Excuse me," she said. "Bob says I cry over everything." She dabbed at her eyes as she bit her upper lip. She sighed and threw the tissue into the trash.

Standing on tiptoes, she pulled an address book from the top shelf and jotted down an address. She put the paper into Erik's hand and squeezed. "She lives outside of town. She's been there for almost thirty years. Ask anybody, they can tell you."

Bob and Ruth followed Erik to the curb. "Are you going to Canada?" she said.

"I'm leaving today."

She stepped forward and hugged him quickly. "Find my little girl," she whispered in the brief moment they were close.

"I will," he said, and got into the car.

As he started the engine, Ruth hollered out, "Do you need any money for gas?" Erik shook his head and, smiling and waving, pulled away.

Erik went to the bank and closed his account, went to Sears and replaced the bald tires on his car, went to the grocery store and bought food he could take with him in the car. He'd already told his chairman a month ago that he couldn't teach this summer, had hinted he might not be back in the fall. He drove out to his father's to tell him he was leaving.

"Where you going?"

"Canada."

"What does Debra think about that?"

"Debra and I have split up."

"Seems to me I've heard this song and dance before."

"This time's for real. I'm going to find Alice."

His father nodded and looked off at the horizon. "I like Alice," he said. "But I wouldn't count too much on her taking you back, son."

"I know."

They stood together like that, silent for a moment, then his father clapped his hand on Erik's shoulder. "If you find her, be stubborn. I wasn't near stubborn enough with your mother."

At home Erik heated up a can of chile and opened a beer. He spread the atlas on the kitchen table as if it were a placemat. He ate as he turned to Ontario and found Whitney. It sat next to a large provincial park. He read the name over several times. It was familiar. His scalp and neck tingled. He went to his chair and found David Mech's *The Wolf* in the stack of books on the floor. He turned to Algonquin Park in the index. There were three lines of entries. It was the site of much field research on wolves. They had been protected there since 1959. Erik could hear Rupert's voice echoing through his thoughts: "Maybe she wants to try being a wolf for a while," and Ruth saying, "She's Ann all over."

He finished his chile, gathered up his books, and threw them into the back of the car on top of his clothes.

It was two in the afternoon. He estimated he would reach Whitney around eight in the morning.

Chapter
18

As Erik drove through farmlands in the moonlight, he arranged the facts along the dash like protective saints. The great-aunt was a werewolf. He braced his knee against the steering wheel, poured a cup of coffee from the Thermos, and set the cup on the dash. The steam made a ghost-shaped patch on the windshield. It made no sense that there would only be one werewolf. There must be ancestors who had been werewolves. What Alice was had to be there in her genes—not supernatural, but a trick of nature. He could see their spiral in his mind's eye, looking like any others.

His headlights reflected from eyes in the tall grass along the road. Probably rabbits or raccoons. Why hadn't she told him more about the great-aunt? he wondered. She'd talked as if she were the only one.

That was what struck him, even before he knew—the loneliness. It must have struck Adams, too.

He rolled down his window, leaned across the car, and rolled down the other. The wind whipped through the car, sending up a cloud of charge slips and candy wrappers. The air beat against him in a reassuring roar. He imagined her sliding her haunches around the walls of that basement until the concrete was smoothed and glossed by her fur, then waking up a woman, naked on the concrete floor. He put his coffee cup to his lips and let the steam blow across his face. I couldn't have stood it, he thought, all those years, walled up like that, walled up even when she was a woman, hiding herself from everyone.

He stopped at a rest area, soaked his head in the water fountain, and smoked a cigarette. He looked around at the empty picnic tables, the row of idling trucks, trying to see some sign that Alice had been here. He was following a chain of ideas. He wanted to sense her trail, to know she had been here, to know which way she had gone. He looked again at the atlas, at the highway numbers he'd already memorized, and drove on.

By sunup he was in Canada, winding past woods and hills and tiny blue lakes on a two-lane road. He stopped at a roadside table by a lake and walked down to the shore. A swarm of black flies encased his head like a helmet. He lit a cigarette and puffed furiously. They hovered outside the cloud of smoke. He liked this place in spite of the flies. He could see why Alice had come here. It must feel to Alice as if she had climbed out of a pit into the open air.

He reached Whitney at nine. The highway he'd been traveling, the main street of town, was torn up for repairs. No throng of orange-clad workers guided the traffic through. Most everyone but Erik seemed to know where they were going and didn't seem to mind the muddy, rutted road. He stopped at a drugstore and bought insect repellent. "Could you tell me where

Howard and Ann Rawson's place is?" he asked the clerk, a small gray-haired man who'd already been nice about Erik's American money.

"You a friend or relative?" The clerk leaned against the cash register with a kind, unhurried expression.

"Not exactly. I'm engaged to their grand-niece."

The man broke into a grin and stuck out his hand. "Alan Wickert—I've known Alice since she was this high." His left hand hovered by the counter. "Alice didn't say a word about being engaged. Congratulations."

Erik shook hands. "Erik Summers, pleased to meet you." He smiled with false complacency. "Alice isn't expecting me. It's a surprise."

"Go through town," said Alan Wickert, pointing to the west, "the second curve, there will be a gravel road on your left. The house is about five kilometers. You can't miss it—the road's a dead end, you know." He plucked a package of mints from the display on the counter and handed them to Erik. "Give her these—from Alan. And tell her I best be invited to the wedding. Since she's broken my heart, you know." He laughed and waved as Erik left, realizing after he'd driven away that he should have said something about Howard—perhaps this boy and Howard had been close.

The house at the end of the gravel drive was a large wood building with heavy beams stained red. There were no outbuildings except a small shed. Erik guessed it must have been built as a hunting lodge some fifty or sixty years before. Now the screened porch was lined with pots of pansies, impatiens, geraniums, and marigolds.

A woman stood at the screen door. The silhouette was nearly the same as Alice's, but he knew from the slight slump of the shoulders that this must be Ann. She had probably heard his car approaching, spitting gravel and dust, for the last five minutes.

He felt anxious as he walked up to her, wondering how he could find Alice through her. His trail ended with this old woman. If she lied to him, he had no place to go next.

"Ann Rawson?" he said. "I'm Erik Summers. I'm here looking for Alice White. It is very important I find her."

"How do you do," she said, and held open the door so that he might step onto the porch. She leaned on a slim birch cane intricately carved with an Indian design of birds and fish and the sun. "I'm afraid I can't help you. I haven't seen Alice in a good while."

"Please, you can't imagine how important this is to me. I love her very much. I want to be with her." He bent forward to catch her eye. "I know that she is a werewolf."

Ann Rawson looked at him for a few moments, a sad smile on her face. "I *can* imagine, young man. I can imagine, perhaps, more than you. But she's not here. I am truly sorry."

Erik had hoped to startle her with his knowledge, but he could see she was not easily startled. "I know I am being terribly rude. Alice's parents told me about your husband. I am very sorry."

She looked past him into the woods. She spoke as if to herself. "Thank you. He was old. He had a good life. I will miss him very much."

She turned toward the open door to the house, and Erik took the package of mints from his pocket and held it up. "Alan at the drugstore asked me to bring these to Alice. I wonder if you would give them to her."

She looked at the mints and then into his eyes. "Then I guess Alan has made it pointless for me to continue lying to you—which is a relief to me, I can tell you." She shrugged her shoulders. "But I still can't tell you anything."

"I've driven all night. Just give me ten minutes."

She studied his face. "You do look awful. I can't

very well just send you packing." She gestured toward the door and nodded at him. "Would you care for some tea?"

"Thank you very much," he said, hurrying inside.

She gestured to a circle of chairs before the fireplace. "Have a seat," she said.

He followed her into the kitchen. "I've been sitting down for hours in the car. I need to stand for a while."

"Howard had that theory," she said. "Truth is, he couldn't stand to be waited on." She struggled with a box of matches. "Would you do this, please?" She held her hands before her as if they were not a part of her. "I have arthritis."

Erik lit the stove, filled the pot, and put it on the flame. Finding an ashtray on the counter, he put a cigarette in his mouth and offered one to Mrs. Rawson.

"No, thank you, I don't smoke," she said.

"I'm sorry. I assumed you did, since there were cigarettes in the ashtray. Do you mind if I smoke?"

Mrs. Rawson smiled at him. "And you're clever, too, aren't you?"

"I hope not too clever." Erik lit his cigarette.

"Oh, we're all guilty of that one sometimes. Alice told me she'd quit till she met you."

"Where is she?"

Mrs. Rawson sighed and frowned. "I hate this, but I have to respect her wishes. She knew you might come. Though she wouldn't admit it, I'd say she hoped you would. But still, she's ordered me—I think that's a fair description—not to tell you anything that might help you find her. She said if you showed up, I was to say I hadn't see her. There's no sense in telling you that—you wouldn't believe it anyway. But I can't say any more than that, knowing how she feels."

"Alice is justifiably very upset with me right now," he said. "I betrayed her."

She smiled. "How odd it seems for someone of your

generation to announce such a thing. As I told her, I thought 'betrayal' was too strong. She kept so much from you, then expected you to trust her."

"You talked with her about me?"

She was setting out the tea things on a tray, one item at a time, very slowly, with her left hand. Her right remained upon her cane. "Of course," she said, measuring the tea. "She has a broken heart. What else is she going to talk about? She kept apologizing because 'I have my own troubles,' but hers make mine no worse, and perhaps I can make hers better." She turned to Erik.

"Perhaps *I* could make hers better," he said.

She cocked her head back. "Perhaps."

The teakettle whistled, and she reluctantly allowed him to pour the water into the pot and carry the tray into the living room.

"I will serve," she said. "Now, would you please sit down?"

Erik searched the room for some sign of Alice. "You haven't said anything about what I said—that I know Alice is a werewolf. She is, isn't she?"

"I thought you said you knew."

"I do."

"How do you know she's a werewolf and not just insane?"

"She told me, and someone who has nothing to gain from my knowing the truth witnessed her changing and told me."

"This someone, would this be Debra?"

"Alice told you about her?"

Ann laughed out loud. "You might say that."

"It's over between me and Debra. She even encouraged me to find Alice." It occurred to him that Alice might be in the house, might actually be listening to their conversation.

Ann ran her finger along the handle of the teapot. "Howard had an 'adventure' once, a schoolteacher who was always having him split kindling or fix drippy faucets. I don't think he was attracted to her so much as she made him feel so useful." She looked up. "Men like to feel useful." She gave Erik an ironic smile. "And safe."

"I'm not afraid of Alice anymore," he said.

"Why not? Let's say Alice is a werewolf, as you say. Doesn't that bother you? She turns into an animal."

"I'm a biologist, Mrs. Rawson, I know that she's an animal regardless. I don't buy the 'crown of creation' idea."

She laughed again, but Erik wasn't sure why. "That's all well and good, but doesn't it bother you that the woman you love turns into a different animal altogether, one that might find you a delectable snack some night?"

Erik was silent. He felt as if he had run a great distance and finally come to a stop. "Yes," he said. "It does. But I don't believe she would hurt me."

She began to pour the tea. "But you can't know, can you?"

"Perhaps you could tell me."

"How would I know such a thing?"

"Because you are a werewolf—just like Alice."

She looked up from the teacups. "Well, aren't you a clever young man. Sugar, lemon, milk?"

"Milk. Then you admit you are a werewolf?"

"Well, I'm not sure it's something one 'admits,' but yes, I'm a werewolf. Now would you *please* sit down. You remind me of Howard, always hovering around. Serving tea to him was a nomadic experience. He loved it when I was sick and he could wait on me to his heart's content."

She set his tea beside him, then lowered herself gradually onto her seat. Erik waited for her to get her tea from the table and hold it in her lap before he spoke. "Since you were a werewolf, it only makes sense that she would come to you seeking refuge."

"Except that she didn't know before she came. I

only told her when she came to me and 'admitted,' as you say, what she was."

Erik was stunned. "You're joking."

Ann shook her head slowly. "I know. It's awful. I should have told her. But I couldn't be absolutely certain that she was also a wolf. You must remember we rarely saw one another after she started changing, just a few days at a time on holidays. You don't just write a letter about such a thing—'Dear Alice, your auntie is a werewolf, are you one, too?' No, it has to be crept up on bit by bit to see how the other person takes the bait, so to speak.

"She suspected, of course. Her wolf part would certainly have known, but it's hard to get the two parts together sometimes." She arched her brows. "In fact, it's hard all the time. It's a constant effort, in a way, though it's certainly not something that 'trying hard' will help.

"Alice hinted to me once when I visited at Thanksgiving that she knew I was like her. They had that little farm then, and we'd gone out walking. She said: 'It will be the full moon in three days.'

"I said, 'I'll be back home by then.'

"Then she gave me a look and said, 'What do you do, Auntie, during the full moon?'

"I should have told her, I suppose. But here she was frisking along beside me like a pup. I was afraid of being her teacher. I'd found my own way, but nothing made it right. You must understand there's no book of etiquette for us. We don't even exist." She tossed her hand in the air as if she could make herself vanish.

Erik remembered his questions. "Didn't you have someone? An ancestor who was a werewolf? How is it passed on?"

She smiled. "You *are* a scientist. No. I had no one. I suspect my mother's grandfather. He was what they called a mountain man in Wyoming. He left his wife and young son and lived in the wilderness. I never met him. I only heard the family stories. He died quite

287

young, from strychnine poisoning. Some Indians brought the body into town. That's how the wolves were wiped out, you know—strychnine."

She stared into the cold fireplace. "I should have let her know. I can see that now. It was cowardly not to. Nothing like that boy who attacked her ever happened to me. It must have been awful to live with that." She tilted her head to one side. "It was selfishness, too. Howard and I had our own little world. But then, she had no one."

Erik leaned forward, his hands spread before him. "Please, help me. I don't know where to begin or how to look. If she's a wolf and doesn't want me to find her, I don't stand a chance."

Ann shook her head. "I feel so sorry for both of you. I wish Howard were here. He'd have a great deal to say to both of you."

She looked into the fireplace again. "I thought with Howard gone I might be a little more 'self-possessed' or something, but I still jabber on to him. Not out loud, of course—that would be altogether too dotty— but in my journal." She laughed and set down her teacup. "At least my writing's gotten better.

"When I was a girl, after the change, I wrote the most incredible nonsense, called *Memoirs of a Werewolf,* with this elaborate drawing on the title page of me as a wolf howling at the moon over a castle. 'Course I'd never seen a castle in my life, so mine was rather plain, like a couple of giant coffee tins stuck up on top of stony crags. 'Stony crags,' as a matter of fact, was my favorite locale in those pages. My specialty was saving the world, or saving some beautiful man, or, in my most inspired moments, both at the same time."

She smiled to herself. "Howard read it one time, years later. He had unearthed it when we moved here. He asked me first, of course. He was always so careful with my privacy. Anyway, he brought it into here, built a fire, and commenced to read the whole thing, which must have been over a hundred pages. He roared. I thought I might have to rush him to the hospital, he was laughing so hard.

"Well, you can imagine. Even though I'd written it when I was just a girl—I'd never *intended* it to be funny—and certainly not as funny as Howard found it to be. But then he did the damnedest thing that changed it all around—he was always doing that—he started crying. I could just barely hear him. I stood in the kitchen and listened, trying to fathom what it meant. Then it hit me that I should go to him. And do you know what he said?" She shook her head, still amazed. "I asked him why he was crying, and he threw his arms around me and told me he loved me more than anything."

She took up her tea, sipped, and made a face. "If I'd learn to drink instead of talk, I might once before I die drink a hot cup of tea."

She looked up and smiled affectionately. "You are a very nice man," she said. "I can see why Alice loves you. You remind me of Howard—too serious by half, but sweet and very, very kind. It's hard to have too much of that.

"I wouldn't be so hard on yourself about Alice. When Howard found out what I was, of course, it took him a day or two to get over it, as it would anyone— and he knew me longer than you knew Alice. Anyway, he went off by himself somewhere, he never would tell me where. But then he came back all concerned like he used to get and asked me if it weren't dangerous— to *me*, I mean. He was afraid the wolves might do me harm. Isn't that sweet?

"I had to tell him that, yes, it was a bit dangerous. I hadn't been brought up to be a wolf. I think I just blunder my way through. That's what's kept me out of trouble, I think—I act so stupid the other wolves don't know what to make of me." She reached back and adjusted her hair in a way that reminded him of Alice.

"Your Debra must be remarkable to believe what she saw. Most wouldn't, you know. I've been seen changing three times, and on each occasion the person didn't do a thing other than take to bed or see the doctor or get drunk. I used to say to Howard that I should hire out to a psychiatrist to drum up business. Hallucinations can act any damn way they please, because no one takes them seriously."

"I want to take Alice seriously," Erik said quietly. "Can you tell me about being a werewolf, about what it's like?"

"I don't suppose that would do any harm."

"When she is a wolf, will she have any knowledge of me?"

"Knowledge doesn't carry back and forth very precisely. It's difficult to hold things together, remember things, I guess you could say, until you know what you are, so there's some thread to string together this thing and then that. But yes, I would say she would know you. She would know your scent, at least."

"When she told me about being a werewolf, she said she only changed at the full moon."

Ann laughed. "Oh, yes. It happens that way at first. That's when it's strongest, but it's always there. You can always do it. The ocean is still the ocean at low tide. Of course she didn't know that, and it was so difficult for her to accept it. I had it easier, with Howard to watch out for me, especially after we moved here. She grew up with those awful movies, too. That's about all she had to go on. She thought the full moon was the only time she *could* change. That silly psychiatrist taught her hypnosis, and she found the way. Her intention was to learn how to keep from changing." She looked into Erik's eyes. "For you."

Erik shook his head. "I don't want that."

"Why not?"

Erik was silent a moment. "I think it's because I know it's a part of her, that she wouldn't be the same, even as a woman, without it." He thought he might cry and looked down at the floor. "Can you tell me how she's doing? Is she all right?"

"I think so. She doesn't come often. She's asked me to stay away, to let her find her own way as a wolf for a while. She hopes to join a pack. It's hard. It took me years. But when she was here last, she said she was ready, and that I should come back."

"Back?"

"Into the woods, to be a wolf." She smiled, cocked her head. "I'm not quite so ancient there. I can still run. And Howard's gone, you see. I'm hoping it won't be so lonely there."

Erik felt a tingling at the back of his neck.

She rose to her feet but motioned he should stay seated. "You can stay here if you like, for as long as you like. I'm not coming back. I've only been waiting to put things in order now that Howard's gone, and to see if you were coming to look for Alice. I wanted to meet you. Now you've come, so I can leave."

"Please tell me where she is, where this pack is she hopes to join."

"I can't do that." She shrugged her shoulders. "If she and I meet as humans again, I can talk to her. I can tell her how you feel. That's all." She took his hand. "It's been a pleasure to meet you. I wish you good luck." She paused at the door to the kitchen and turned to him. "Please don't follow me," she said. "It might be dangerous."

Erik could hear her walk through the kitchen, hear the creak of the back door. He sat waiting for the sound of its closing. Why, he wasn't sure. She had asked him to stay seated, to let her be. His nerves hummed with caffeine and sleeplessness. He had reached his destination. He must wait.

After half an hour, he rose and went into the

kitchen. The back door was open. The path to the woods sloped down the hill. The sky was a deep, clean blue, and the gold, clear light revealed a perfect emptiness, except for Ann's cane propped against a tree at the edge of the wood and her clothes folded neatly on the ground. He shut the door, opened the refrigerator, and drank milk from the carton.

Ann Rawson's bed was covered with white lace. As Erik pulled off his boots, he felt like a twist on "The Three Bears"—Papa Bear come calling at Goldilocks' house—or, changing stories, the Woodsman waiting in Grandma's bed for Red Riding Hood, who had been the wolf all along.

He woke up in the dark, fumbled for the light, and checked his watch. Was there daylight saving time in Canada? He couldn't remember. It was one-thirty or two-thirty. He lit a cigarette and walked through the house with an ashtray, turning on all the lights except in the darkroom, finding out where each door led. The only searches he made were of the pantry, which held lots of beans and potatoes and of the freezer, which bulged with fish and ice cream.

He went out onto the porch, tried to sense if he were being watched but could feel nothing. He got his flashlight from the car and followed the path into the woods for about a half mile until it became boggy. He turned off the flashlight, put his hands to his mouth, and howled. He knew it sometimes worked, that the park even conducted "public wolf howls" where as many as a thousand people might howl their heads off, hoping to get an answer from the wolves. From the darkness, starry but deep, a single howl rose to join his, then a chorus. The sound reverberated in the air like the tolling of a huge bell. He shuddered, dropping the flashlight in the soft earth, and fell to his knees. The howling continued for perhaps a minute or two longer. His heart pounded, and tears welled in his eyes. He stood up shakily, made his way back to the house, and fell back to sleep.

When he awoke again it was midmorning. He called the park headquarters and arranged to see one of the staff naturalists. He was a teacher from the States, he said, and he had a few questions from his students. Over coffee with a tall, enthusiastic blonde named Barbara, he tried to discover if there were any new wolves that had shown up in the park recently.

"You mean pups?"

"No, adult wolves who migrated in."

"No, nothing like that that I know of, not down here, anyway. The perimeter of the park is fairly civilized around here, at least for wolves."

"How would you go about finding a lone wolf who strayed into the park?"

She looked at him quizzically. "Do you have a particular interest in loners?"

He touched his pack of cigarettes but did not remove one. She'd already told him she'd rather he didn't smoke. "One of my students wanted to know," he said. "He was interested in just how you keep track of a population of wild animals."

"The packs are easier than the loners," she said. "The packs have a clearly defined territory, and the loners don't."

"But a loner might join a pack?"

"Not very often. The pack structure is very precise in many ways. A loner would disrupt things. There wouldn't be a place for him, so to speak. Of course, we spot them eventually. It just takes longer."

"What are my chances of seeing a wolf?"

"Slim to nonexistent, I'd say, especially along the Highway Sixty corridor. The wolves generally shy away from the campgrounds and trails."

"Well, thank you," he said, rising to his feet. "I think you've answered all my questions.

"You're very welcome," she said, rising. "How long will you be staying in the park?"

"I'm staying at a friend's nearby, indefinitely."

"Well, you'll have the park pretty much to yourself for a while—the flies, you know." She smiled. "Let me know if I can help."

"I will," he said, and left, his hands full of maps and booklets she had given him. She took his phone number in case anything happened that might interest him.

Back at the house he spread out a map of the park on the dining room table. It was huge, thousands of square miles. He knew a wolf could travel fifty miles in a day. She could be anywhere.

But she wasn't just a wolf. She was a human who could also spread a map out on a table and plan where she wanted to go. Deep in the interior of the park she would be cut off if she decided to be a human again—naked in the middle of the wilderness. This house was her refuge. She wouldn't stray too far from it, not yet, not until she was sure just where and what she wanted to be.

And she would be leery of areas where she would be surrounded by well-established packs. It might be easier for her to find a niche here, in the border areas between human and wolf territories. At least it gave him a place to look. He'd start hiking the trails. If she wanted to be found, he might find her there.

The man walks below, looking for her, looking for the woman. He is slow and smells nothing, walking and looking, always looking. The woman is angry and hides from him. The woman comes seldom now, like the wolf when the woman gave way to her, and she spent the night in stone.

She moves down the hillside in the low brush, moving closer to the man. She can hear his breathing.

She can see him sitting by the beaver pond on a fallen tree. He is eating. Peanut butter. She lies still and quiet. She smells his sadness, and her sadness smells the same. She calls to the woman to come to her. He is the friend she wants, but she does not come. The wolf smells the smoke and watches it rise from him and drift away. He stands and walks up the hill. She does not follow.

She rises and shakes the dirt from her belly and steps into the open. She goes to the tree where the man had been, sniffs, and marks it.

Her friend is with the pack now. She has heard her calling but is afraid to enter their place. She moves down to the stream and waits for fish. She catches two, swallowing them whole. She stands on a rock and calls to her friend. When the answer comes she moves toward the sound into their place, trotting down the path to the den where the pack waits. Her fear is now too weary to stop her. This place is too vast to range alone.

At the edge of their clearing, the pack stands and looks at her. Her friend scrambles to her feet and comes forward, licking her face and barking. The pack circles them, and her friend slips away and crouches outside the circle, whimpering soft and low.

The wolf lowers her head and vomits up the fish and backs away from it. She is taller than these wolves. She keeps her head down and holds her tail low. The mother circles close, until she is beside her, her legs straight, her shoulder pressed against hers, her snout above hers, a low growl rumbling deep inside. The wolf whimpers and licks the mother's face. The mother clamps her snout in her jaws and pushes her shoulder against her. She rolls to the ground, the mother's paw pushing against her throat. She stays still, all is stopped, she feels nothing. The mother moves away and stands by the fish, her head high. The pups rush in and gobble up the kill.

The wolf rises slowly and shambles to her friend, who rubs her muzzle and lifts her head to begin the howl. The wolf moves in tight prancing circles as she joins in. The pack leaves the clearing, moving in a line along the trail where the scent of deer is strong. The wolf and her friend follow close behind.

Chapter

19

Erik sat at Ann's kitchen table and sipped his coffee, waiting for the morning. The dawn came slowly here, and the rosy glow of the sun appeared early. He had been at Ann's for two weeks.

He spent his days in the park, his evenings studying maps or reading the books he'd brought. There wasn't much on loners, just enough to convince him that Howard's fears for Ann's safety hadn't been foolish. A pack might kill Alice if she invaded their territory, if she failed to show the proper etiquette. Wolves are social animals. The lone wolf is not a romantic recluse, but an outcast.

Algonquin wolves were smaller than most. Alice, as she had said, was a large wolf. This would give her some advantage, but wolves didn't operate on a simple system of might makes right. Wolf pups raised with grown dogs still showed them submissive behavior even after they themselves were adults and towered above their much smaller companions. He'd seen a photograph of an Airedale, her head held high, a timber wolf crouched, licking her face. What was called submission wasn't a matter of master and ruler. It seemed to Erik to be reverence.

He'd been hiking the park every day. He had no notion of what he was looking for. One wolf in a thousand was much harder to locate than a needle in a haystack. At least the needle stayed put and didn't try to avoid its pursuer. He wondered what the wolf knew or thought about him. Did she have Alice's knowledge or emotions? He was sure that somehow she must know he was here. It was too absurd otherwise. He had to accept *something* on faith.

Some nights he heard the wolves howl, though never quite as close as that first night. He found that if he joined them, he could cajole them into howling just a little longer. He fancied he could pick out the one voice that was Alice's. That day in his kitchen, he'd known the wolf was Alice. For a time Adams had persuaded him that he only *thought* he knew because that was what he *wanted* to think. But he hadn't wanted to think Alice could be a wolf. He'd been willing to think her crazy so as not to believe it. But it was Alice. He'd known that before Debra told him. He'd done nothing—distracting himself with old conflicts and old desires—but he had known. Now, when he heard the wolves howling and a certain tone and timbre felt to him like Alice's he believed his senses without having a shred of evidence.

He stayed mostly in two rooms of Ann's house, the guest bedroom and the kitchen. Last week he'd set up a card table on the porch and spent several hours there each evening until the chill drove him indoors. He thought of looking through Ann's things but didn't. She'd all but given him her house, recently stocked with food and fuel. He didn't want to make her into a case study, a specimen yielding clues.

Now, finally, he had a clue. Barbara, the park naturalist, had called him yesterday to say that, oddly enough, she'd heard a report that apparently a pair of loners had attached themselves to the Gordon Lake pack. Would he like to talk more about it over dinner? He thanked her and said no.

He had hiked the Gordon Lake area a few days before and heard the howls of what sounded like a hunting party. He was now sure Alice and Ann were there. It was the only place he'd felt as if he were getting close.

Last night he went into town to get cigarettes and stopped at a bar for a few beers to help him sleep. He didn't want to talk to anyone, but he wanted to be around other people, to nod and smile and exchange the few words it took to buy cigarettes or order a drink and to watch others carry on conversations. He drew designs with the puddles of condensation on the table—stairways, triangles, and circles—as he watched a man and a woman in their fifties on the far side of the room.

The man was small and square with a plaid shirt like a pressed tablecloth. The woman laughed and put her head on his shoulder beside her and had to wipe the tears away when the waitress came to take their order. The man allowed himself a playful grin and kissed the woman's cheek when the waitress went away. Erik couldn't hear what they were saying over the song on the juke box—a country singer who sounded as if he had spent his adolescence locked up with old Dylan records. He liked the song. He thought Alice would, too. And the couple—she would like them even more.

Erik left soon after the couple left. He turned up the street away from his car and walked through the alleys to the edge of town and looked at the stars. He hadn't let anyone know he was staying here. Each day it occurred to him to call Bob and Ruth or his father or Debra or Rupert, but by the end of the day he hadn't called, and it was too late. For now he would rather be alone, looking for Alice. When he found her, or if he didn't, then he would call and tell someone where he was.

Now, looking through the window beside the kitchen table, he could make out the line of shadows where the woods began. By the time he drove to the trailhead, it should be light enough to get started. The air was damp and chilly. If it was like yesterday, fog would hang in the lowlands until midmorning.

He drove to the trailhead slowly, passing moose grazing along the highway and, on the dirt-and-gravel road to the trailhead, a white-tailed doe and her fawn. He shut off the motor and got out. The sound of the wheels crunching on the road seemed to hang in the air. He sat on the hood and lit a cigarette. It was still too dark to hike. The light was blue gray, and fog lay over the trail as it disappeared into a stand of hemlocks.

He drank half a cup of coffee, then walked a little ways into the fog. He could see well enough. He looked down and saw a paw print the size of his hand, like the one he'd seen in Alice's basement, what seemed a long time ago. Should he be quiet, or should he announce his presence?

His howl was not the best. Too many cigarettes or too much restraint. But he wasn't going to kid himself that he could sneak up on a pack of wolves in the middle of their own territory. It would be easier to drop in unexpectedly on the president. He bent his knees with his palms on his thighs and tilted back his head. He howled from the pit of his stomach, with plenty of diaphragm, as his high school choir teacher used to tell him. It still seemed to him a pitiful effort, more like a whine than a howl. But it broke the silence of the woods and echoed in the fog. He listened, his neck still stretched out, but heard no response.

He straightened up and walked on. As he emerged from the hemlocks, he came upon a small lake, a line of black spruce along the shore. Wild orchids grew near the water's edge. The smooth, fog-shrouded water broke into ripples as a loon landed on the surface and glided out of sight in the deeper fog on the far shore. Erik felt as if something were watching him and turned back toward the woods. He thought he saw a shadow move and then another, but as he continued to stare, nothing moved, and there was no sound except the call of a loon. He turned and went on but felt as if whatever had been watching him moved with him.

The clearing beyond, according to the trail guide, was the site of an old farm, but there was no sign of that now. Wolf scat lay beside the trail, and the tracks were numerous here. The path divided, with the main trail cutting back to ascend the hill and a side trail going down to the lake. The tracks followed the main trail. Erik howled again and heard a low moaning cry from the hillside, so brief he could not be sure it hadn't been a trick of the wind through the trees.

The trail was steep and dark as it left the clearing, the woods denser and close to the winding trail. From the corners of his eyes he saw shifting black-and-brown shapes in the forest that vanished when he turned to look. The sound of his boots on the trail seemed thunderous. When he paused, his heavy breathing and laboring heart were all he could hear. Through breaks in the cover he could see the sky brightening into blue as he moved into deeper woods and darkness. The clearing down below would now be glistening with sunlight on dew.

He sat on a fallen tree at a bend in the path, poured a few swallows of coffee from his Thermos, and drank it. Nearby here was a snare site where park rangers used to trap wolves and exterminate them in their desire to eliminate all predators but man from the wilderness. He looked down at his feet and felt as if the forest leaned in closer around him, watching him, waiting. He knew if he looked up, no matter how quickly, he would see nothing. But he knew something was there.

He rose abruptly and continued up the steep incline. The trail emerged at the top of a cliff, then sloped down to a sheer drop. The fog was now almost burned away. The wilderness stretched out below to the horizon. A small pine grew close to the cliff's edge, and he made his way to it, a handhold to quiet his fear of heights. The wind came up from below and filled his nostrils as he clung to the side of the cliff. He felt dizzy with pleasure. I could be happy here, he thought, if I were not so lonely. When he turned back to the path and the woods, he saw, in a semicircle around him, eight wolves watching him with quiet, intelligent eyes. One was larger than the rest. She stepped inside the circle and looked away from him, off into the distance at his back.

This was Alice. He had no doubt. She was off the trail, uphill from him, over loose, rocky soil. He let go of the pine slowly and tried not to think of the long fall at his back. He leaned forward and placed his boots carefully one after another up the hill toward her as gravel rattled from his footsteps and over the edge behind him.

She did not move. The other wolves watched him intently. The ground leveled off a couple of yards from where she stood. He paused, then took the last few steps, knelt, plunged his hands into her ruff, and laid his face against hers. As he held her, she changed. It was like lying in the rapids, clinging to a river. He clamped his eyes shut, felt her body fill his arms.

He held her without speaking. When he opened his eyes, the other wolves had gone, though he hadn't heard a sound. Alice shivered, and he wrapped her in his jacket.

"Thank you," she said.

"I was afraid I would never see you again," he said.

She looked up at him, her eyes puffy, her brow creased with pain. "I couldn't just let you wander around here forever, for nothing." She rose to one knee. "Help me up, would you?"

They made their way back into the woods. She told him to wait and left him sitting by the trail on a log for almost ten minutes. When she returned she was dressed in jeans and a flannel shirt. She handed him his jacket. "Can I have some of your coffee?" she said. She watched him pour. Her hands shook as she took it from him. She sat on the ground in front of him. "It'll take me a few minutes to get my bearings," she said.

He watched her drink the coffee. He wanted to hold her. He wanted to tell her everything that had been running through his mind ceaselessly for weeks.

She looked up at him. "I've come to tell you that you can leave. There's no point in your staying here."

"There certainly is a point. I want to be with you."

"Which one?"

"Both of you."

"Don't be ridiculous."

"Howard and Ann did it for years, didn't they? Why not?"

"You'll be happier with Debra."

"I left Debra to come here. Doesn't that mean anything?"

She looked away. "It could mean a lot of things."

"I love you, Alice."

"Is that why you told Debra all about me, Erik? Is that why you fucked her?"

"That was wrong."

"Which one, Erik? Betraying me or fucking Debra?"

"Both. All of it. I was stupid. I was scared. I couldn't believe you."

"But you believed Debra needed you. What are you doing here? Isn't she waiting for you somewhere? Or does she just reel you back in whenever she wants you?"

"I can't defend what I did. After she saw you . . . change, she was in a pretty bad way. I guess I was, too. She begged me to stay, and I did. But all I could think about was you."

"It's too late, Erik. Just please go, and try not to tell anybody else about me, if you think you can help it."

"I'm not telling anyone, and I'm not going."

"Well, I am," she said, and started to rise. He took her shoulders and stopped her. "Let me go," she said. He pulled her to him and held her. "Let me go," she said again. He clung to her, kissing her face and neck, pushing her to the ground. "Let me go, or I will kill you," she said, glaring up at him.

"I don't believe you," he said, suspended above her. "And if it's true, I don't care. If you want to kill me, then kill me." He turned his throat to her.

She struggled in his arms, pounding him with her fists. "I hate you! I hate you!" she screamed.

He clung to her. She began to cry. Her body shook in his arms. "I love you," he said softly over and over again. After a time she became still. They lay in the middle of the path for several minutes, neither moving. He drew back and tried to catch her eye. She looked past him into the sky, closed her eyes, and sighed.

"Shit," she said. "What are we supposed to do?"

He turned her face toward him and kissed her mouth. She put her arms around him. He unbuttoned her shirt and kissed her breasts. "Damn you," she said.

"I love you," he said.

She took his face in her hands and studied him. "Do you? Do you really?"

"Yes."

"Do you plan to make love to me out here in the middle of the trail?"

"If you want me."

She smiled, looking as if she might cry again. "Yes, I

want you all right." She held his beard in her hands. "But only if you plan to stay."

"Just try to get rid of me."

"No," she said, "I won't."

The line of cars wound through the August night for ten kilometers at a quiet, slow pace like a funeral procession. Rangers in orange vests directed traffic with flashlights. Each car was packed with park visitors hoping to hear wolves howl to them from the wilderness beneath the slender crescent of a new moon.

Erik was giving a ride to a family from Dallas. The father, Stan, sat in the front. The mother, Lydia, and two daughters—Angie, four, and Stephanie, eight— were crowded in the back and spoke in hushed tones as if in a library or a church so that Erik couldn't quite make out what they were saying. He could tell the children were full of questions, and their mother murmured soothing answers. Lydia's face in the rearview mirror was bright and smiling, her eyes wide. She put her finger to her lips, and the girls fell silent.

Stan, who had been looking out the window scowling at the countryside, turned to Erik. "You from around here?" he asked.

"No, I just moved here," Erik said.

The backseat erupted into squirming children, and Erik felt someone kicking the back of his seat. "Get off me," Stephanie hissed. "Mom, Angie won't leave me alone."

"Liar," Angie wailed.

Lydia's voice was still low, and the precise words indistinguishable, but he recognized the tone of a mother laying down the law. Angie cried and Stephanie started to mount her defense, but Lydia silenced both.

Stan, who had cocked his head toward the backseat, announced, "One more sound out of either one of you and you're walking back to the campground with me, got it?"

"Yes, Daddy," two small voices said in unison. Stan smiled. "What kind of work do you do?" he asked Erik.

"I teach biology."

Stan wrinkled up his face as if he'd smelled something foul. "Biology. Jesus, what a nightmare. What was that thing? The Krebs cycle. A fraternity brother drew the damn thing on my palm for the test, but I sweated so bad I couldn't make heads or tails out of it."

Lydia leaned forward from the backseat. "I loved biology. I still know all the bones. I love the names: clavicle, femur, phalanges."

Erik nodded and smiled. The traffic had stopped completely now as the cars began parking one by one.

"Jesus, this is just like Dallas," said Stan. "Ever been to Dallas?"

"No, I never have," said Erik.

"Central Expressway—just like this—any time of day or night. Hurry up and wait. I tried riding the bus for a while." He glanced back toward his wife, then leaned toward Erik. "But I felt out of place, if you know what I mean."

Erik gave him a blank look.

"'Course you don't get many black people here in Canada, I wouldn't imagine. Too cold for them."

"Stan, not everyone shares your views on such matters." In the rearview mirror, Erik saw Lydia's eyes narrowed into hard, angry lines.

Stan rolled his eyes and slumped onto his seat. After the traffic began to move again he said, "Ever been on one of these wolf deals before?"

"This is my third time," said Erik.

"This was my wife's idea. Me, I don't get it. If I want to hear howling, I can just listen to the dogs in my neighborhood whenever a siren goes by. Stupidest

306

damn thing you ever heard in your life. Every dog in town thinks he's a fucking ambulance."

"Stan."

He turned around on his seat. The two girls were grinning. "You didn't hear Daddy say that, okay? You're never supposed to talk like that—you're girls, and girls don't talk that way."

"Stan."

"Okay, okay. *Nobody's* supposed to talk that way. It's real bad, so don't do it, okay?" He turned back around. "You got any kids?"

"No, but I hope to."

"Well, it's no picnic, I can tell you that." He shrugged his shoulders. "But I like it. It's okay being a dad. Don't have to try too hard to be better than mine."

"When are we going to get there?" Angie said.

Stan cocked his head toward the backseat and spoke loudly. "That's what I'd like to know, pumpkin. Think we'll make it there by next week?"

Angie giggled. "You're being silly, Daddy."

Stan laughed. " 'You're being silly, Daddy.' "

"We'll be there soon, darling," Lydia said.

"That's what I told you," Stephanie said to her sister in a voice laden with condescension.

"You keep out of this," Lydia said.

Up ahead Erik could see the cluster of parked cars, the growing crowd of people standing and waiting. Unlike most of the people here, he knew what to expect, but he was still excited, just as he'd been the first time. He pulled onto the shoulder and shut off the engine. Turning to Angie, he smiled. "We're here," he said.

He stepped out of the car onto the damp, spongy grass. The stars were thick and bright in a clear sky. The smell of the wind across the bog was like a spade of earth. He shivered and zipped up his jacket.

Stan waited with arms folded as Lydia guided the

children out of the backseat and set them in place beneath the stars, where they stared straight up and did not move.

Erik looked around at the crowd, incredibly silent, waiting for the last car to stop and unload. He recognized some faces from other nights. Last week he'd met a couple from Ottawa who had been to every wolf howl in Algonquin for eight years. Erik liked them and invited them to visit Alice and him before returning home. He and Alice had moved into Ann's.

The rangers signaled the crowd of at least a thousand people lining the highway that the howling was to begin. The rangers stood near the center stripe, placed their flashlights on the ground, and tilted back their heads, their hands cupped round their mouths. Some of the crowd joined in as the rangers began to howl. Stan glanced around, startled at the howlers.

For a moment there was silence. The wolves didn't always answer. Some nights the crowd was left to imagine the wolves in the darkness, listening but not responding.

But tonight a barking yelp rose to a high note and held. Then another voice and another, until the night vibrated with the clamor of wolf howls sounding like one huge voice echoing in a great bowl of stars, though if you listened closely, you could hear each wolf like a strand in a tapestry.

Erik knew Alice's voice and Ann's, knew some of the other voices as well from what Alice had told him. More and more she could remember her times as a wolf. They would sit on the porch with coffee, and she would tell him about them like fragments from dreams. Tomorrow morning early, she would meet him on the ridge. He would give her coffee, then walk her down the hill and take her home. She spent a day or two each week with the pack, sometimes more. He had arranged for a sabbatical in the fall. He was going to write a book on wolves.

Stan and Lydia were beside him, the two girls

standing in front of them. He'd forgotten about them for the moment. Stan looked as if he might cry and whispered urgently, "Lydia, do you hear that?"

She nodded, and he took her hand.

When the howling stopped, the rangers howled again, but this time there was no answer. The silence held for a moment, then the crowd began to talk. Like the previous times, Erik noticed, many were laughing or crying.

Stan continued to stare at the horizon without moving. "What's wrong with Daddy?" Angie asked her mother. Lydia put her finger to her lips and led the family back to the car. Lydia held Angie in her lap, and Stephanie slumped against her shoulder. Both children were asleep before Erik started the car and joined the slow procession back to their campground.

Stan sat quietly, looking through the window. Erik could see his face reflected in the glass, staring intently as if there were something out there he was trying to see. When Stan spoke his voice was barely audible. Erik would not have been able to make out the words if he hadn't seen his lips moving in the glass.

"It was just incredible," he said, staring into the darkness. "It was fucking incredible."

From the author of
BOY'S LIFE

A new novel of relenting suspense from
the master storyteller of our time.

ROBERT R. McCAMMON

GONE SOUTH

**THE STORY OF A MAN, HUNTED INTO THE
SULTRY SWAMPS OF LOUISIANA, ON THE
RUN FROM A TRAGIC MISTAKE.**

**POCKET
BOOKS**

**Available in hardcover from Pocket Books
Mid-September 1992**